# THE GHOST OF THOMAS PACKARD

## A Three Misfiteers Adventure

DAVE BENNEMAN

*For my good
friend John,*

*David Benneman*

CELTIC
MOON
PRESS

Copyright © 2020 by Dave Benneman
All rights reserved.
The Ghost of Thomas Packard: A Three Misfiteers Adventure
Celtic Moon Press
ISBN: 978-1-948884-39-6 (ebook)
ISBN-13: 978-1-948884-40-2 (paperback)

Cover Art designed by Bailey Brown

Readers are talking...

*"Are you interested in a deft, engaging handling of adolescent friendship and drama, old-time witchcraft-themed horror, and a late 1960s setting? The Three Misfiteers delivers all that and more."* —Virge B., Red Adept, Proofreader

*"Dare you to dive into this eerie tale where a trio of friends play amateur sleuths in a small town haunted by family secrets and a soul-tingling curse, and not get caught in Benneman's sticky, wonderful web."* —Jami Gray celebrated author of the acclaimed Kyn Kronicles, PSY-IV Teams, Fates Vultures, and Arcane Transporter series.

*"Benneman creates a trio of very likeable young protagonists in this eerie mystery set in a small town. Each is struggling with a ghost of his or her own--the future, the past, and a possibly haunted house. And the school bully is dead set on making life more difficult for all of them."* —Stefanie B., Line Editor, Red Adept Editing

*I want to acknowledge all the struggling writers out there who write, not for fame and fortune, but because they must. Those who carve out time from their day jobs, and tip-toe away from their families to defeat the blank page that defies and goads them, because the voices in their head demand attention. If that weren't enough, they proceed to spend the hard-earned money from the aforementioned day job to publish the work. This is not usually about ego or recognition, it's because the characters they create demand a voice. They want to be heard.*
*To you, my fellow warriors (raising a coffee mug) I hope you enjoy.*

*db*

## Acknowledgments

No book worth reading is published without a group of dedicated professionals who slave away in the background. There are those too who are asked to sacrifice much for the artist throughout the creative process. A giant thank you to all of you who helped in this venture.

First and foremost, my wife Charlene, who must endure those times when I am moody, selfish, self-deprecating and an overall ass.

Secondly to the writer's groups and readers who waded through the early drafts of this book. The Seven Evil Dwarves were especially patient. You know who you are. In particular Jami Gray, writer extraordinaire who talked me off the ledge on more than one occasion.

My cover artist, Bailey Brown, whose original work graces the cover of this book.

And finally, my editors, Angie Gallion Lovell, Stefanie Spangler Buswell, and Virge Buck of Red Adept Editing, who made my writing coherent and presentable.

(The band is playing me off but I refuse to give up the stage) For anyone I missed thank you.

## Chapter One

Billy Hashberger stared at the gloomy house from the back seat of Tony's new 1968 Chevy Impala. The new car smell mingled with the stench of sweat.

"End of the line." Tony opened the door, allowing the November wind to whistle through the car. "All passengers must exit the vehicle in an orderly fashion."

Billy climbed out of the back seat. "It looks spooky." He tipped his head back to stare at the moon rising above the craggy silhouette of the old three-story house.

"You're going to love it. You and Suze will have your own rooms." His mother opened the trunk. "Get your sister."

"She's sleeping." He shivered.

"I only asked you to do one thing all day, and the first chance you get, you leave her behind." His mother glared around the trunk, hands on hips.

He ducked into the car and gently stroked his sister's head. "Suze, wake up. We're here."

She whimpered like a tired puppy as she woke. He took her by the hand and helped her out.

"Carry in a bag with you." His mother pushed a paper grocery bag filled with clothes into his free arm then untied the rope that held the mattress to the top of the car.

With the bag clutched in one hand, he steered his little sister with the other, studying the three sagging steps to their new home.

"Come on, Suze." The steps were in need of a coat of paint and they creaked underfoot. The side door led into the kitchen. Once his eyes adjusted to the light, he saw the clutter of boxes and bags containing their meager possessions strewn haphazardly across the cracked linoleum floor. Dead flies congregated in the ceiling light. The living room offered a broad set of stairs twisting toward the second floor. He wrinkled his nose. The house had a sour odor.

"What smells?" he asked.

"Feets smell," Suze answered.

He'd almost forgotten he was holding her hand. "If your feet smell and your nose runs, you're…"

"Upside down." Suze finished their private joke and giggled.

"Let's check out the sleeping arrangements," Billy said.

"No." She nodded.

Billy smiled. This contradiction always got a rise out of his mother, and he guessed that appealed to Suze. Together, they ascended the stairway. One bare bulb lit the hall near the steps, casting shadows ahead of them, only to disappear in the darkness. He sensed a presence he couldn't account for. The house belonged to someone else. He'd lived in numerous apartments, but he'd never had the sense that they belonged to anyone in particular.

Closed doors lined both sides of the upstairs hall. He pushed open the first door on the left. Light spilled out from a spacious, if rustic, bathroom. The claw-foot tub crouched under the harsh glare, rust stains spreading beneath its dripping faucet.

On the other side of the hallway, the next door revealed a metal bedspring leaning against a wall. Moonlight filtered through the window, casting shadows like a giant spiderweb across the blanket covering his lumpy mattress on the floor.

"This is my room…" Billy yawned. "Let's see if we can find yours, okay?"

"I not sleeping with you?" she asked.

For most of Suze's three years, she'd shared a room with him in a variety of dumpy apartments. His mother had managed to keep a roof over their heads by accepting what the state offered in welfare and the kindness of friends. When she was between boyfriends, finances were at their worst. Tony's generosity far exceeded his predecessors', and now they were moving into an actual house.

"You're going to have your own room. Won't that be fun?"

She didn't answer. Instead, she walked into his room, plopped onto the mattress, laid her head down, and curled up in a fetal position. With her thumb in her mouth, she closed her eyes. He backed out of the room and walked down the dim hall. His eyes adjusted to the darkness, and he peered into the next room.

"Mom's room," he muttered, seeing the assembled bed and a bedspread neatly tucked in around the pillows. Across the hall, he found Suze's bed, also made up. A fourth room contained unclaimed bags of their toys and clothes. The ears of a stuffed rabbit poked out of a grocery bag. He lifted it out and found a well-worn baby blanket underneath. He took both back to his sister.

"Suze, look, here's Bunny Rabbit." He placed the

rabbit under her arm and spread the blanket over her sleeping form.

"Billy!" his mother yelled from below.

Walking to the head of the stairs, he stage-whispered, "Up here, Mom."

She appeared at the bottom of the steps. "What're you doing? Where's Susan?"

"She's up here, sleeping." A mattress came around the corner behind his mother.

"Hey, babe, can I get by?" Tony gave a heavy grunt. Sweat ran down his face and into the collar of his shirt, where a tuft of thick hair sprouted around a gold crucifix. He stomped up the stairs, swaying from side to side and rebounding off the wall.

"Shh!" Billy hissed. "Suze is sleeping,"

When Tony reached the top of the stairs, he yelled, "Which room?"

"The one across from ours." Her voice fell flat, and her shoulders drooped as she slowly climbed the stairs.

"Billy? Where are you?" Susan whimpered, winding up for a good cry.

"I *told* you." Billy glared at Tony. "I'm right here, Suze." He walked into the room, bent over, and pushed a lock of curly blond hair out of her face. "I found Bunny Rabbit for you."

"Bunny Rabbit." She sniffled, and her eyelids fluttered closed. His mother's silhouette in the doorway blocked the light from the hall.

"You come and apologize to your uncle Tony right now, mister."

Tony wasn't his uncle, but his mother insisted the title demonstrated a certain degree of respect. He preferred not to call him anything, but when pressed, he resorted to just "Tony."

Billy straightened up and squared his shoulders. "What'd *I* do? *You* two woke her up."

"Watch your tone." His mother shook a finger at him. "Or I'll wash your mouth out with soap."

"If you can find it," he muttered.

"What?" She took a step toward him.

"Babe, the kid's tired." Tony stepped between Billy and his mother. "We're *all* tired, for heaven's sake. Let it be. I've got work tomorrow."

Tony and his mother moved into the hallway, where she lectured him on the finer points of child rearing. Billy took the opportunity to escape from the bedroom. He continued to move down the hall. Behind another door, he found a spiral staircase curving into the darkness.

His mother continued from her pulpit, preaching her brand of parenting. Billy wondered why Tony stayed when his predecessors had always been long gone by now. He closed the door behind him, reducing her tirade to an incoherent murmur, then felt his way up the dark stairs. At the top, a shaft of blue-white moonlight illuminated a rectangle of bare floor. The walls sloped toward the center of the small room, and the ceiling was low. He ducked slightly, even though he need not have bothered.

"Cool."

As he turned, his gaze fell on another door. He reached for the knob.

His mother's shrill voice pierced the quiet. "Billy! Where are you?"

Suze's muffled cries squeezed through the floorboards.

Silently, he moved down the stairs and stepped back into the hall. "I'm right here, Mom. I'm looking for my stuff."

A loud rush of water drowned out her response when Tony opened the bathroom door. "Did I hear someone say 'bed'? Because I'm ready." He released a loud fart. "Did you hear that? Sounds like an infestation of barking frogs. Better call the exterminator, babe."

Billy laughed. "Yeah, they must be giant barking frogs."

"That's quite enough potty talk." His mother pressed her lips into a thin line and wrinkled her nose. "Go find your pajamas while I put your sister to bed. Your stuff should be in there." His mother motioned down the hallway.

"Mom, I think there's an attic."

"You can check it out when you get home from school tomorrow." She went into his bedroom. "Come on, Suze. Let's get you ready for bed."

"School! I can't go to school tomorrow. I can't even find my clothes. It's too late. I don't even know where the bus stop is." His words tumbled out in a rush.

"You'll just have to walk to school naked then, because you *are* going." She reappeared in the hallway, with Suze on her hip. "Don't you want to make new friends?"

"I don't want a new school or new friends."

"I would think you'd be happy to be out of Masonville and that crummy apartment. You have your own room and everything."

He knew Tony was behind the move. Tony hated Masonville. It was too far from his work and too close to his childhood home and his mother. "What makes you think this is nicer than Masonville?"

"Tony looked into it before we moved." She turned to look at Tony for confirmation. "It's better here, isn't it?"

He nodded. "The schools have a good reputation, and there's less crime. On top of that, the rent on this great house is affordable."

Billy rolled his eyes and went to search for his clothes.

"Don't make a mess in there," his mother said.

"Like I could make it any worse."

Billy sensed the rising tide of his mother's anger. He stopped long enough to think it through. Did he want to face the tsunami of his mother's rage tonight, or should he tuck in his tail and ride this one out?

"What did you say?" His mother stepped into the room, stroking Suze's head.

"Nothing!" Billy straightened up, nudging the grocery bag at his feet.

"It didn't sound like nothing to me. It sounded like you smart-mouthing me again. Why is it when boys become teenagers, ninety percent of their body turns into mouth?"

Suze started to cry on her mother's shoulder.

Tired couldn't describe how he felt; the weight of his flesh hanging from his bones pulled him down. "I can't find anything in here."

"Wait until I get Susan changed, and I'll help."

In the other room, Suze's sniffles slowly subsided. He tore open a bag and examined the contents. He went through three bags before he found his clothes. Turning his back on the mess, he walked into the bathroom to brush his teeth. The feeling of being in somebody else's house returned. He finished quickly. Relief washed over him when he stretched out on his mattress and pulled the scratchy wool blanket over his head to fend off the cold.

His body warmed under the blanket, and drowsiness overcame him, but sleep stayed just out of reach. The quiet unnerved him. The apartments had always buzzed with sound. As sleep pulled him under, something tugged him back from the edge. A scratching sound brushed against his ears.

The sound filtered down from the attic. *There it is again.*

He strained to listen. Something dragged across the floor upstairs. *It's just this old house. Houses make noise, right?*

Now fully awake, he slipped out from under the covers. The cold crept up his legs, back, and arms. He tiptoed to the window and used his sleeve to clean years of grime from the pane in order to peer outside. The outline of a giant loomed in the backyard, arms stretching for him. He stumbled backward before he realized he was looking at a tree.

*I'm spooked.* The leafless tree swayed in the cold moonlight, and some of the limbs reached toward the window. The soft hooting of an owl floated across the night air as he turned away.

In the bathroom, he flipped on the switch and covered his eyes as the yellow light flooded the room and spilled out into the hallway. He cupped his hands under the faucet and took a drink before splashing the icy water onto his face.

He stared at the rust stain in the tub. It seemed to ooze down the side toward the drain. A sudden, uncontrollable shiver racked his body, breaking the trance. He went back into the hall, leaving the door ajar and the bathroom light on.

Tony's thunderous snore roared through the house. Billy slid back into his warm bed. The light from the bathroom gave him the courage to close his eyes. Tony's rhythmic snoring lulled him to sleep.

The moon shown though Billy's window, lighting his face like a spotlight. He walked into the bathroom, but stopped short when he saw the blood-splattered walls. A young woman sprawled in the tub, her white dress stained scarlet. He tried to scream, but his voice failed him. He clawed at his chest and tried to drag air into his lungs. Blood flowed from a slash across her throat and trickled down the drain. He tried to back out of the room. No matter how many steps he took, the girl in the tub stayed right in front of him. Her eyelids fluttered open. He sat up in his bed. This time, he did scream. He screamed and screamed.

## Chapter Two

Molly Houlahan crossed the street to the blue mailbox on the corner and double-checked the address on the envelope.

Patrick Houlahan
c/o Adirondack Correctional Facility
196 Ray Brook Road
Ray Brook, New York 12977

She pulled the door down and placed her letter on the surface before closing and opening the door again to make sure it slid down the chute. Satisfied, she slammed it closed. The metallic clang echoed through the cold morning air, relieving some of her frustration. Her brother had never written her back, but she had promised not to give up on him. *Unlike everyone else. If Mom were here, it would be another story. If Mom were alive, we'd still be a family. If...*

The cold bit through her mittens, nipping at her finger-tips as her thoughts drifted to a home once crowded with four boisterous older brothers. They had fought over everything from the keys to their dad's truck to the last donut. It had never been dull, and no matter what, her brothers had always treated her like a princess.

She pushed those thoughts from her mind, shifting her notebook to her left hand and slipping the right into her pocket for warmth. The railroad tracks dividing Lower Willowton from Upper Willowton separating the haves from the have-nots passed underfoot without notice.

An image of Mamo edged its way into her mind, despite her best efforts. Her dad's mother had moved in after Mom died to help keep the house running smoothly. Mamo had bustled around the kitchen, smacking her brothers' hands when they peeked under the lid of whatever simmered on the stove. That was before the accident. The accident had changed everything. With her brothers gone, the house had become a dead place, where Dad drank himself to sleep most nights and Mamo wasted away in her bedroom, lost in a fog of Alzheimer's.

Molly blinked back tears. *Get a grip. Feeling sorry for yourself isn't going to help.* To distract herself, she hummed a melody from the new Dylan album. *I'm not sitting around waiting for this town to eat my soul. I'm getting out of here.* College would be her dogsled out of this frozen wasteland. She'd decided long ago to apply only to schools in the South.

Art provided the only light in her otherwise-dark existence. Last night, she'd stayed up late drawing an album cover with charcoal on paper. She couldn't wait to show her art teacher, Miss Swanson. She scooted through the door into the warmth of the school behind a group of tittering girls.

"Hey, Houlahan, you want some of this?" Derrick O'Riley stepped in front of her and did a pirouette.

"Sorry, O'Riley, but I put the garbage out already.

Maybe next time." She pushed past him, but he grabbed her arm and spun her around.

"Next time, you can kiss this." He pointed to his butt.

"I wouldn't want to put Sal and Ernie out of a job." She yanked her arm free and waved at the two boys who flanked O'Riley. "And if you put your hand on me again, I'll deck you."

"Oooh, I'm so scared of the girl with the big red hair."

"I won't warn you again, Neanderthal."

"Wow, such a big word too. Help me, Sal. I'm shaking."

She walked away. The corridor bustled with the activity of arriving students. Molly pushed through knots of posturing girls and wisecracking boys, on the way to her locker. After twisting the combination, she wrenched open her locker door. She steadied the calendar swaying on the door and reviewed the coming week. *Nothing due.* She stuffed her bulky coat into the locker and closed the door. *Maybe I can get some serious time in on my art.*

At the door to homeroom, she paused and thought about what to say. She walked to the front of Miss Albright's desk and waited to be acknowledged.

"Yes, Molly. How can I help you?" Miss Albright smiled tightly.

"I wanted to know if you think…" She hesitated. "Is it too soon to start looking into colleges with scholarships?"

Miss Albright's sharp gaze seemed to penetrate Molly's thoughts. "Let's make an appointment to talk in private. Ninth grade is a little early, but it's never too soon to look into what options are available. Bear in mind a lot of things can change between now and graduation." She consulted her planner. "I'll put some information together. Can you stay after class tomorrow for a few minutes?"

"Sure, no problem." Molly felt a sharp pain in her

back. She turned in time to see O'Riley's thumb pointed at her as his sidekicks yucked it up.

"Molly?" Miss Albright's voice brought her back around.

"Yes, sorry." Molly tossed her head, which sent her long hair cascading over her shoulders. "Thanks, Miss Albright."

Miss Albright glanced at the clock above the door. "Take your seat. We'll talk about college tomorrow."

As she made her way to her desk, Molly saw O'Riley twisted around in his seat, talking with Sal. His foot stuck out into the aisle. Making a small detour to pass his desk, she stomped on O'Riley's instep, making sure to grind her heel.

"Ouch. Son of a b—"

"Oh, so sorry, I should watch where I'm going." She smiled sweetly and quickly took her seat as the morning bell sounded. *I'd better watch my back today.*

Miss Albright stood at the front of the room, giving her "The Look." Not much escaped the teacher's radar. Molly opened her notebook and busied herself by reading notes for Science. After the morning announcements and Miss Albright's pep talk, the bell rang again.

"Hey, Hooligan. I see you." O'Riley's voice boomed through the noisy corridor.

Molly looked back, checking the distance. "Is that a new skill?"

"Paybacks, Hooligan. I owe you."

"Just scratch your mark on an IOU, and I'll fill it out for you. Okay, caveman?"

"O'Riley's pissed," a blond girl said, walking up to her.

"Really? Thanks for the news flash."

"I mean he's really mad."

"Yeah. I bet he's hopping mad." She laughed at her

joke and strutted into Science class before O'Riley hobbled in. O'Riley had a short attention span when it came to her. She didn't know why. He'd scuffed her up a few times and ridiculed her plenty, but she'd never been beaten or extorted, unlike some of the boys he'd victimized for the past two years. It angered her to see him get away with his constant bullying. *One of these days, he'll get what's coming to him. And I hope I'm the one doing the giving.*

Molly took her seat at the table she shared with Barb and Debbie. The two of them were arguing about how to assemble the components of the catapult spread out before them. Between them, they'd built a catapult that only worked once, before it fell apart.

Molly turned when she heard knocking on the classroom door. "What's Miss Albright doing here?"

"Don't look now, but I think that loser just joined our class." Debbie giggled.

Molly looked the new kid over. Everything about him screamed secondhand, from the badly cut, longish hair to his beat-up shoes. He must be living in lower Willowton, but she hadn't heard anything about a new family moving in. Her neighbors were nosy gossips, and any time somebody moved in or out, the news always spread like poison ivy.

## Chapter Three

Frank Bordeaux checked his appearance in the bathroom mirror. His mother always straightened or adjusted something when he got to the kitchen. One day, he would walk out of the house without her fussing over something. *Father endures the same treatment. I think he deliberately leaves his trademark bow tie crooked, so Mother could fix it.*

His teeth, hair, shirt collar, fingernails, and shoes were all perfect. With his shoulders back and spine straight, he took the stairs two at a time. The smell of bacon wafted through the air.

His mother turned from the stove with a plate weighed down with breakfast. "Good morning, Francis. Let's have a look at you."

"I'm fine, Mother." He gave her a full turn anyway, while his mouth salivated.

"What a handsome young man." She smiled. "You may want to pull up your zipper before you go."

He turned away, his face burning.

"Sit down, dear, and hand me your glasses. I'll clean them while you eat."

"Thanks, Mother." He sighed, handing over his glasses as his shoulders slumped. *How could I have missed something so obvious? I may as well have had a booger hanging from my nose.* The bacon and fresh biscuits soon helped him forget his embarrassment.

"Nice and clean." She held out his glasses.

He paused just long enough to slide them on before devouring the rest of his breakfast. "Did you ask Father about the new frames yet?"

"I did, and he thinks those wire frames are just a fad." She sat down across from him.

"How would he know? He wears a bow tie everywhere." He sopped up the last of his eggs and stuffed the dripping biscuit into his mouth.

"Wire frames are for those hippie types."

"But they aren't, Mother. Everyone's wearing them. Just look around."

She reached across the table and wiped Frank's face with a napkin. "Wait until your next appointment, and we'll talk about it then."

"Fine." He stretched the word out with a sigh of resignation.

"Make sure you dress warm." She pushed up from her seat. "Your father said it's colder than usual."

He groaned and shuffled out of the kitchen, with his mother right behind him. She took his coat from the hanger and held it for him.

"I can do it." He pushed his arms into the waiting coat. "I'm not six, you know."

"It's only six months, Francis. I promise I'll talk to your father then." She fastened the top button under his chin and handed him his hat. "Have fun."

"Sure." He stepped outside and let out a soft whistle. *Cold doesn't cover it. Try freezing, frigid, arctic, bone-chilling, numb-*

*ing, icy, or glacial.* He racked his brain for other words as he walked.

When he arrived at school, he waited for his glasses to defog, as usual. He liked arriving early and was probably the first person there on most days, besides Shorty. *Shorty probably lives in the basement next to the boiler or something.*

After stopping at his locker, he went to the gymnasium. He sat in the bleachers and opened his notebook to the catapult diagram Mr. Hunter had given the class yesterday. Frank had built it last night to test its distance and accuracy. The simple construction used a balled-up sheet of notebook paper as a projectile. He had hit his target eight times in ten attempts. He would have to do better. Eighty percent wouldn't cut it at NASA.

He flipped through his notebook to the list of facts he'd collected on the Apollo Space Program. *Apollo 7* weighed over thirty-six thousand pounds, and the scientists and engineers had just sent it into orbit around Earth. When it launched next month, *Apollo 8* would weigh almost twice as much, and it would orbit Earth and the moon. *How many sheets of paper would it take to reach a weight of seventy thousand pounds?*

Frank stared at the cobwebs on the gym ceiling while imagining the infinite reach of space beyond. "Space: the final frontier." He packed up his stuff and headed to homeroom, while the words of Captain Kirk's weekly lead-in to *Star Trek* echoed around the empty gymnasium. His shoes scuffed along the empty corridors as he trailed a finger along the rows of lockers.

"Good morning, Miss Albright." Frank waved at her as he took his seat in the front row, to the left of her desk.

"Good morning, Frank." She didn't look up from her book.

"What are you reading?"

"*True Grit*, by Charles Portis. It's a western." She closed the book and looked him in the eye. "More importantly, what are you reading? Have you decided what you're doing your report on?"

"Not yet."

"I know you're interested in science. Have you thought of Jules Verne or H. G. Wells? They are considered the fathers of science fiction."

"I like science. It's the fiction I don't get." He held her gaze, chewing on his pen.

"You don't have to choose from my list, but I have to approve whatever you pick."

He scrunched up his face.

"What about this?" She dug around in the canvas bag, which always occupied a spot next to her desk. She stretched her arm over the desk to pass him a book. "Take a look."

"*2001: A Space Odyssey*." The cover depicted a space station revealing only a slice of an unknown planet in the background. It captured his imagination.

"Let me know."

"Can I take it home?"

She smiled. "Of course. Take good care of it. I haven't read it yet."

"Thanks." He opened the book to the first page and read until Sal Delgado banged into his desk, snorting with laughter. He kept his head down. No point getting on O'Riley's list this early in the day. Once O'Riley picked someone out of the herd, that person's day would take a turn for the worse. Sometimes, Frank got off easy with a punch in the shoulder and fifty cents. On other occasions, nothing could save him from a beating.

## Chapter Four

Billy dreaded the first day at a new school. This one was followed the normal routine of being passed from person to person until he was delivered to his class.

Mr. Hunter, his science teacher, stood him in front of the room. "Class, this is William Hashberger. He's joining our class. Take a seat with Frank. He'll show you around today." Mr. Hunter gestured toward a boy with sandy hair and black-framed glasses. Balls of paper littered his table. A catapult built from newspapers, rubber bands, and a plastic spoon stood ready to fire. Frank aimed at a trashcan in the front of the room.

"Watch this. I'm five for five." Frank let go of the spoon.

"Nice shot," Billy said. Just then, a ball bounced off Frank's glasses before landing on the table in front of him. A roar went up across the room. Billy cleared his throat. "Hey, I think those kids are shooting at you."

"Yeah, it's great." Frank shrugged. "I don't have to make my own projectiles."

"Yeah, great." Billy smirked.

"You want to take a shot, Billy?" He slid the catapult over.

"My name is William."

"My name is Francis, but only my mother uses it."

A wad of paper sailed past Billy's face and caused another whoop across the room. A redheaded boy flashed a cold smile.

"Okay, let me take a shot." Billy loaded the catapult, turned it quickly, and fired at the group of three boys who appeared to be targeting Frank. The wad of paper hit one of them in the face.

"Hey." Frank grabbed at the catapult. "You can't…"

"Just did."

"O'Riley's going to kill us," he hissed.

Billy's laugh caught in his throat when O'Riley's eyes narrowed into a predatory stare.

"All right, class. Let's start cleaning up, please. Leave your catapults on my desk," Mr. Hunter announced from the front of the room.

The students uttered a collective groan.

"Why can't we take them home, Mr. Hunter?" a voice yelled out.

"Because you will use them to launch food in the cafeteria. And then *I'll* get an earful from Mrs. Buchanan."

Frank gathered up his notebook and trash. "Can you set this on Mr. Hunter's desk for me?"

Billy set Frank's catapult down next to several others and marveled at its sturdiness compared with the rest. A boy banged into Billy, pushing him into someone else. He looked up and saw the kid he'd shot—a redhead with a cold smile.

"You better watch where you're going," the redhead snarled.

"Yeah, sorry." Billy backed up and moved around him

to the stool next to Frank. He caught a girl with bushy red hair giving him a strange look.

"When the bell rings, run for the door," Frank whispered into Billy's ear.

"What for?"

"Because O'Riley and his pals will want to talk."

"So?"

Frank shrugged and pushed his glasses up with his index finger. "Conversing with them is not usually a pleasant experience, if you catch my meaning. It's your funeral. I'm making a run for it. You never should have shot O'Riley."

## Chapter Five

Molly knew she was no longer the target *du jour*. O'Riley preferred fresh meat every time. When the bell sounded, she expected the new kid to run for the door with Frank, but he took his own sweet time.

*He's new, ignorant and stupid. That's a bad combination.* She casually followed him out. When O'Riley and his thugs, Ernie and Sal, formed a semicircle around the new kid, she moved quickly.

"Excuse me! Pardon me!" She grabbed him by the arm and dragged him along. *What am I doing?* Before she had a chance to dwell on it, she turned to Billy. "Nice shot in there."

"Yeah. Thanks?" He stumbled while trying to keep up with her.

"You better keep moving. I'm Molly Houlahan."

"B—William Hashberger."

"And I thought my name was a mouthful." Molly smiled and motioned toward a door.

He stepped aside and let her go into the classroom first. He followed her, and she pointed to a seat behind Frank.

"Sit." She stayed on her feet until O'Riley made his way to the back of the room, then she took her seat only after Mrs. Atkins entered the room.

"Books open, mouths closed. William Hashberger?"

"Yes, here."

"Come up front, please." The whole class listened to Mrs. Atkins's standard speech.

"I'm Mrs. Atkins." Her grating voice carried to the far corners of the room. "This is your mathematics textbook. You are responsible for the care and feeding of this book. It should never be left in your locker. Take it home every day, read it, put it under your pillow when you sleep at night, and most importantly, turn it back in at the end of the year in the same condition in which you received it. Understood?"

He nodded.

"Sign this." She slid a log across her desk.

Fumbling for a pen, he leaned over her desk and scratched his name.

"Take your seat."

"Yes, ma'am, thank you."

Mrs. Atkins started writing math problems on the board, and Molly's attention began to drift. With a critical eye, she studied the sketch she'd done the night before, catching things she'd missed last night. The too-large mouth and wild curly hair both needed refinements. She compared the eyes next. Those, she captured. The serious gaze of Bob Dylan appeared to stare straight into her soul from the paper. His eyes reflected the very essence of him. The real Bob Dylan, not the singer who made money selling records, but the prophet, the poet. The man.

Molly watched Frank pull the new kid out of his seat and head for the door when class ended. Gathering her books together, she thought, *If he sticks with Frank, maybe he'll survive his first day.* She sensed their presence before she heard them.

"Hey, Hooligan. You're really pissing me off today." O'Riley loomed over her, preventing her from leaving her seat.

"That's just one of the many services we offer here at Molly's Emporium." She bared her teeth in a smile. "Why don't you leave the newbie alone for one day?"

"Maybe you're right." He picked up Molly's drawing. "This is pretty good." He let it float to the floor.

Molly grabbed for it and missed.

"Mr. O'Riley, do you enjoy math so much you will be staying for the next class?" Mrs. Atkins peered in through the doorway.

He looked up with a broad grin. "No, Mrs. Atkins. Would you look at the time? See you later, Houlahan. Mrs. Atkins is giving us the bum's-rush." He sauntered off with Sal and Ernie in his wake.

Molly bent down to gather her sketch, which now had a footprint across it, but Bob's eyes remained unscathed. She'd known that intervening for the newbie would end badly for her. *Where is my head today? My brothers would say I caught a case of the stupids. When will I learn to leave well enough alone?*

The last of the locker doors banged closed, and feet pounded to class as the bell rang. Late for art class, with a ruined drawing, she kicked at a stray pen and missed. Furious, she stomped it into small pieces and ground them into dust underfoot.

When Molly arrived in Art, Miss Swanson looked up and motioned her to her seat. Without missing a beat, the teacher continued her explanation of depth and perception, utilizing a bust as her model. Molly's heart raced at the sight of O'Riley's grinning face. She took a deep breath when Miss Swanson approached her.

"Sorry I'm late." She handed over her sketch, footprint and all.

"This is marvelous. Bob Dylan's album cover from *Blonde on Blonde*, right?"

"You recognize it?" Molly relaxed her grip.

"Of course. You young people may think you discovered Bob, but I saw him in concert at college. I'll bring in the album cover, and we can hang them next to each other for comparison."

"I have it." She pulled the album out of the messy pile in her arms.

Miss Swanson held them at arm's length side by side. "You've got a very good eye for detail. This is quite good. I'll show you how to clean this up." She pointed at the footprint.

"That's sort of why I'm late."

"Don't worry about it. Give me a minute." She turned back to the class. "Remember, you're drawing a three-dimensional object. Everyone will create a different drawing, depending on his or her point of view. There is no right or wrong in art; there is only interpretation."

Molly stared into the depths of Bob Dylan's eyes.

## Chapter Six

Frank tapped Billy on the shoulder and leaned over. "Art's a real snooze fest. Good thing we only have to take it for one quarter. Miss Swanson is nice, though."

"You mean you won't be answering every question, like you did in math?" Billy asked.

"Math is important. My father says mathematics is the international language."

"Lunch is important too. When do we eat?"

Frank grimaced. "Lunch is next."

Billy jerked a thumb at Molly. "Look at her drawing. She's good."

"No kidding. Half the stuff on the wall is hers." Frank swung one arm around, indicating the sketches plastered all over the walls.

"Which one is yours?" Billy asked.

"Miss Swanson doesn't see the beauty in stick figures. Perception, my butt."

Billy laughed. "I guess I don't have to worry about getting on the wall, then."

Frank smiled, shoving Billy's shoulder. "A fellow stick figure guy! I knew I liked you."

As the clock closed in on the hour, Frank gathered his books and nudged Billy. "Get ready, it's lunchtime. I'm going to my locker. I bring my lunch. Are you buying?"

Billy nodded and pushed his hair out of his eyes.

"Just follow the crowd. I'll save you a seat at our table."

"We have our own table?" Billy cocked his head to one side.

"Not just us. The whole class sits together."

"What, are we in kindergarten?"

Frank shrugged as the bell rang. In the corridor, he watched Billy walk away and hoped he would avoid O'Riley. When Frank arrived in the cafeteria, he saw Billy paying for his lunch. He stood next to the table until Billy gave him an almost-imperceptible nod. Sliding his tray onto the table next to Frank, Billy took a seat and poked at his food with a fork.

"It's mystery meat day. Not the best day to buy lunch," Frank said, with a mouthful of sandwich.

"Hey, newbie, nice shot in there," O'Riley said. "So where are you from?"

"Masonville."

"Where do you live?" Ernie asked from O'Rileys left.

"A big house on State Street."

Frank gagged and struggled to swallow his lunch. "Not the three-story house with the big porch."

"Sounds right." Billy tasted the meat.

"For real? You're living in the old Packard house?" Molly asked.

"So?"

"Did you see any ghosts yet?" O'Riley asked. "You *do* know your house is haunted, right? I mean, everyone knows that."

"Haunted?" Billy gave the meat a pass and poked a cube of green Jell-O with unidentifiable pieces suspended in it.

"Yeah, haunted. You know. Dead people running around in white sheets saying 'boo.' Like that."

The whole table exploded into laughter.

"No one has ever lived there," Ernie added in a low voice.

"Not since that guy chopped up his whole family and stuffed them in the furnace."

All heads swiveled to look at O'Riley.

"They say you can still hear their screams at night."

Frank saw Sal sneaking up behind Billy, too late to warn him. Sal pushed Billy's face into his tray. Frank jumped up from his seat as mashed potatoes and gravy flew into the air. The table erupted into laughter again. Frank reached for a napkin and pressed it into Billy's hand as gravy slid from his chin and plopped onto his shirt.

"Quiet," someone hissed. "Here comes Barracuda."

"Sit down, Bordeaux, before you get us all in trouble," O'Riley threatened.

Frank took his seat, careful not to sit in the messy over-flow of Billy's lunch.

"What is going on at this table? It looks like I may have my cleanup committee for today."

"We weren't doing anything, Mrs. Buchanan," someone sang out.

She gave them all a sharp look. "Then how do you explain this young man who appears to be wearing his lunch on his face?"

This produced stifled snickers from the table.

"And you are?" Mrs. Buchanan asked, motioning Billy to stand.

"Billy—I mean, William Hashberger."

"Please excuse yourself and get cleaned up in the restroom."

"Yes, ma'am. Where is the boys' room?"

Mrs. Buchanan let out a long sigh and rolled her eyes.

"I'll show him, Mrs. Buchanan. He's new," Frank offered as an explanation.

"Fine, Mr. Bordeaux."

Frank led Billy out of the cafeteria and down the hall to the restroom. "I'm really sorry. O'Riley's a jerk, and his stooges, Ernie and Sal, will do anything he says."

The smell of urine and bleach comingled as Billy pulled his head out of the sink and blinked through dripping water. Frank returned his gaze in the mirror.

"So, which one shoved my face into my lunch?"

"Sal, black curly hair. He might've done you a favor —I mean, if you were planning to eat the mystery meat."

Frank grinned and pushed his glasses up the bridge of his nose with his index finger. Billy pulled a long section of brown paper towel from the roll to dry his face. When he emerged from behind a handful of crumpled paper, Frank pointed at a brown clump clinging to the front of Billy's white shirt like a giant leech. It seemed to be sucking the white out of the fabric.

"Oh man. My mother's gonna kill me." Billy returned to the sink.

"Take your time. Barracuda will have our table cleaning the whole cafeteria until the bell rings. We might as well let O'Riley and his goons pick up our share." Frank grinned again.

Billy scrubbed at the spot with another yard of paper towel. "My mother never understands how this crap always happens to me."

"I know what you mean."

Billy shot him a sharp look. "Oh, really? Are you the new kid all the time?"

"No, but you don't have to be the new kid to have O'Riley on you."

"Yeah, well, I'm always the new kid," he muttered to his wet shirt.

Frank sensed a familiar sadness emanating from Billy. "You'd better dry off. The bell's about to ring."

The shrill sound of the bell echoed in the tiled cavern of the bathroom.

Billy studied the discolored, damp spot. "Good enough."

As they walked down the abandoned hallway, Frank broke the silence. "Do you really live in the old Packard house?"

"I guess so. We moved in last night." He absently wiped his shirt with the back of his hand.

"Did you see anything—you know, weird-like?" Frank paused with his hand on the doorknob.

"No," Billy lied.

Frank looked him in the eye. "It really is haunted, you know." He walked into Social Studies without waiting for Billy's reply.

The rest of the afternoon, Frank's intense concentration faltered. The stories he had heard about the Packard murders ran laps in his mind. *How could Billy be living in that house? The son murdered the rest of his family there. No one has lived there since, as far as I know.* Social Studies, PE, and English flew by in a blur.

Miss Albright reviewed the reading list and reminded them of their pending book reports as the afternoon drew to a close. "Tonight's assignment is on the board."

She summoned Billy to her desk with one finger. Frank

felt every eye in the room boring into Billy's back. Frank bit his lips while his stomach did somersaults.

"Is there anything you'd like to share?" she asked.

"About what?" Billy asked.

"The incident in the cafeteria."

"Oh, that. I can explain."

"Please, enlighten me, William."

Frank winced, sensing the ears strained in Billy's direction, trying to hear every word. Billy said something stupid about his tray flipping up and spilling his lunch in the process. Frank watched the incredulous look arrive on Miss Albright's face, like a train coming into the station.

"So, your lunch spontaneously erupted onto your face?" Miss Albright asked. "Is that what you want me to believe?"

"Yes, ma'am, it's the truth. Then Frank showed me to the boys' room," he finished.

Frank nodded rigidly, while inside he was struggling with disbelief.

Miss Albright fixed her legendary stare on him. "Do you have anything to add, Frank?"

He closed his mouth and looked at Billy, suddenly finding resolve. "I didn't see anything. Mrs. Buchanan told me to take him to the boys' room. That's all I know."

"Fine." Miss Albright shook her head in incredulity. "This is your locker assignment and the combination." She handed Billy an index card.

"Thank you."

"Where are all your things, by the way?"

"Frank's locker."

"Of course." She sighed. "Take your seat."

As the clock approached 2:25, Frank turned around. "We leave by rows, so don't go running for the door."

Billy nodded in O'Riley's direction. "What about him?"

"Since you didn't rat Sal out, you're probably in the clear for now."

"Keep it down, people," Miss Albright reminded them. "Civilized conversation, not pool hall trash talk."

The noise level in the room sank to a low murmur.

## Chapter Seven

The bell signaled the end of Billy's first day, and the students filed out row by row. No pushing or shoving to be the first out the door. That astonished him. Everyone waited their turn and exited the room calmly. When his turn came, he noticed all the desks were cleared. The kids in Masonville would've run these kids over when the first hammer of the bell struck. Papers thrust into the air would hang there until the vacuum created by the students' exodus allowed them to drift to the floor.

He retrieved his things from Frank's locker before they went to locate Billy's locker.

"You want to walk home with me?" Frank pulled his hat on by the straps. "My mom will make hot chocolate for us."

Billy considered the chaos that awaited him at home. "Sure, if it's okay with your mom."

"She won't care if I bring a friend home." Frank pushed through the doors to the outside.

They broke into a run. The chinstrap of Frank's hat bounced off the frozen features of his smiling face as the wind tore at their coats. The smell of burning leaves drifted through the streets of Willowton. Frank stopped in front of a house with a tidy yard and empty flower boxes hanging from the front porch rail.

He shooed Billy though the door, shouting, "Mom, I'm home."

"Are you all right?" a melodic voice asked. "You're late."

"I had to wait for my friend, Billy."

A tall woman with wavy, shoulder-length brown hair came through the doorway. A smile lit up her face. She dried her hands on a frilly apron and extended one to Billy.

"I'm Mrs. Bordeaux. Pleased to meet you."

"Billy—uh, William Hashberger. Nice to meet you."

"You two must be freezing. Francis, hang up the coats and show your guest to the kitchen. I'll be right there," Mrs. Bordeaux said in a soft voice.

Billy followed Frank past the dining room table set with matching plates and glasses for three people. Cloth napkins and a lacy tablecloth made the whole room feel ethereal. The heavenly aroma wafting through the house made Billy's stomach grumble, and he began to salivate. "Something smells good."

"It's just dinner." Frank shrugged and proceeded to ransack the pantry.

*Just dinner? Even Christmas dinner doesn't smell this good at home.*

"What are you looking for?"

"These." Frank triumphantly set a plate on the table. The sweet smell of the cookies, which were stacked in a circular pyramid, assaulted Billy's senses.

"Sorry, it looks like oatmeal raisin today," Frank said.

Billy stared.

"You okay?" Frank asked.

"Yeah. Oatmeal raisin, huh? Homemade?"

"Of course they're homemade." Frank stuffed a whole one into his mouth. "Still warm." He spoke around a mouthful of cookie. "Go ahead."

"Are you sure it's okay?"

"Why else would she bake them?"

Billy reached for a cookie as Mrs. Bordeaux drifted into the kitchen like a warm breeze. He pulled his hand away from the plate as though he'd touched a hot stove.

"I see you found the cookies, Francis. Now, don't spoil your appetite for dinner. I'll get the hot chocolate on right away. Dig in, William." She pulled a saucepan out of a cupboard with one hand and a bottle of milk from the refrigerator with the other. In no time at all, Mrs. Bordeaux had stirred in the cocoa powder and poured the steaming brew into two matching mugs with snowmen on the sides.

"Are we still out of Marshmallow Fluff?" Frank asked.

"I picked some up today. Look in the pantry." She did a double take when she saw the few orphan cookies. "How were the cookies?"

"I wish you'd made the Tollhouse ones instead," Frank whined from the pantry.

"Delicious," Billy blurted out. "Oatmeal raisin is my favorite."

"I like chocolate chip best," Frank countered.

"You would eat nothing but chocolate chip cookies if I let you." She tousled Frank's hair.

Frank pushed her hand away. "What's wrong with that?"

"It's boring, for one, and it's not good for you, either," Mrs. Bordeaux scolded.

"They feel good for me when I'm eating them. Can Billy stay for dinner?"

"What a wonderful idea. Can you join us for dinner? Is it Billy or William?"

"I guess my friends call me Billy." His stomach growled at the thought of staying for dinner. "I'd better head home. My mom is going to wonder where I am."

"Call her on the telephone," Frank suggested.

"We don't have a telephone—yet." *And probably never will,* he thought grimly.

"Maybe next time?" Mrs. Bordeaux said.

"Yeah, I'll ask my mom." Billy stood in place awkwardly. He didn't know what to do or how to leave. "Thanks for the hot chocolate and cookies, Mrs. Bordeaux."

"You're welcome. Come back anytime. Get his coat, Francis."

At the front door, Billy shrugged into his coat. "See you tomorrow."

"Yeah, I'll see you." Frank waved from the door.

---

Billy leaned into the wind and made his way home, his belly full of homemade cookies and hot chocolate topped with Marshmallow Fluff.

*I wish Mom could cook.* He imagined his mother in a frilly white apron, sliding a dish onto the kitchen table covered with a spread resembling a horn of plenty. The images shattered when he walked into the kitchen. It looked worse than it had when he'd left for school.

"Hi, Mom, what's for dinner?"

His mother spun around and gave him a haggard look.

"You'll be a man someday for sure." The sneer on her face would have made Elvis Presley jealous.

He didn't know why growing up to be a man should be a bad thing. "Sorry, it's just, ah… I'm late, and I thought you might have started dinner."

"Take Susan in the other room and watch her for me. Tony will be home soon, and I have to get this mess straightened up."

"Come on, Suze." Billy took his little sister by the hand and led her into the living room.

"How was your first day at school?" Billy mimicked his mother. "Oh, just fine. I ate mashed potatoes through my nose. The other kids think I'm weird because I live in a haunted house. I made a friend whose mom actually cooks. I know. Weird, huh?" He continued under his breath while he sat on the floor with Suze. His mind drifted back to the comments about the house being haunted, and he recalled what he'd heard and seen the night before. He had a sudden urge to go up to the attic to check it out.

"Let's go upstairs, Suze." Standing, he lifted her onto his shoulders and carried her up the steps.

"No."

When he opened the door to the attic, Susan squirmed and kicked to get down.

"No!" she shrieked.

"That's your answer for everything. Come on." He took her hand.

"No. Bad man." She sat down, folding her arms.

He paused. *Does she know the house is haunted? Nah, that's ridiculous.* "I'll get you a cookie later if you come up with me."

"No. No cookie." She pointed at the steps. "Bad man."

"There's no one up there." He sighed. "I'm going up there without you, then."

"Don't go, Billy. I'm scared," she whimpered.

He tugged her arm gently then changed tactics, offering her lavish bribes such as piggyback rides and playing airplane. Her refusal caused him to rethink his plan. *She's really afraid of something up there. Did she dream something last night, too? How could I find out?* He pushed his hair out of his eyes and considered these things until Suze went into the spare room and pulled out a stuffed bear. *Besides, this could work in my favor. She'll never come up the stairs and mess with my stuff if she's afraid.*

He rooted around in the bags he'd ripped open the night before, until he found his cache of comic books. He gave Suze a jack-in-the-box, which set her into a fit of giggles every time the jack popped up. He settled in with an issue of *Daredevil* he'd read a dozen times already. His mother yelled upstairs as he closed the comic book.

"Billy, Susan, come down for dinner!"

There were two flat boxes on the kitchen table. *Pizza!* His mom seemed a little less frazzled as they pulled triangles of thin crust attached by long strings of cheese from the boxes. *Pizza was obviously invented by a genius. It required no cooking, no pots or pans, no dishes, and no cleanup.* He eyed the last slice greedily.

"Go ahead, Billy, finish it off. You're a growing boy." Tony pointed at the almost-empty box.

"Thanks." He devoured the last slice. "May I be excused? I've got some homework to do."

"After you thank Tony for the treat," his mother said.

"Thanks for the pizza. I could eat pizza every night for dinner," he said, remembering Frank's remark about chocolate chip cookies.

He grabbed his schoolbooks and headed straight for the attic. At the top, a silver rectangle of light poured in through the window, creating dark, shifting shadows. He stood very still, listening as his breathing slowed. Something brushed lightly against his ear and caused him to jump. He reached out, found a string, and gave it a tug. The ceiling bulb set the room ablaze with light and pushed the shadows back into the corners.

In the harsh light, the room lost its ominous feel. Crazy angles created by the dormer windows and the uneven roofline made it feel out of kilter. The walls and ceiling were covered with stained and faded wallpaper. *At least nobody is running around in old sheets, saying, "Boo."* The full moon shone through cobwebs across the window.

"This is great. No little sisters. Maybe even Mom will leave me alone up here." His words died in the still air.

He turned to the closed door opposite the window. He walked over and pulled the handle. The door scraped the floor, and the blood ran cold through his veins. *The noise from last night.*

Listening closely, he moved it again, generating the same scraping sound. Screwing up his courage, he peered into the room beyond the doorframe. A single bed stood against one wall with a small desk pushed up under the slanted roofline. A chair lay on its side in front of a dresser.

He bounced on the bed. Good as his own, maybe better. Silver threads shimmered in the space between the wall and the mattress. He waved his arms through the cobwebs and bounced a few more times, which caused dust to rise into the air. He righted the chair and sat down at the desk.

"My own desk. How neat is this?" He opened his textbook and read the assigned chapter.

"Billy? Where are you?" his mother yelled.

"I'm up here, Mom. Come see. I've got my own desk and everything."

"Billy?" His mother's voice echoed up the stairs.

"Yeah, Mom, come see!"

"I am *not* climbing one more flight of steps tonight. It's time to get ready for bed. Come on down here."

"Can't I stay up here?"

"Not tonight. We'll discuss it tomorrow. Right now, I want you down here, brushing your teeth and getting some sleep so you're not so hard to wake up in the morning."

He pulled the string and felt his way down with one hand on the wall. "You should go see, Mom. It's great. There's a desk and a bed—"

"Not tonight." His mother gave him her I'm-sick-and-tired face. "Get ready for bed."

"Yes, Mom. Will you look at it with me tomorrow?"

"Sure, tomorrow."

He put on his warmest pajamas and kept his socks on. His mother checked on Suze and headed for the stairs.

"Good night, Bill," she said.

"G'night, Mom." He listened as she made her way down to the living room. As soon as she settled in with Tony, he crept out of bed and headed up the stairs. At the top, he felt a pocket of cold air and shivered. A rectangular object wrapped in a smooth cloth on the desk immediately drew his attention.

"Where did this come from?" He scratched his head and unwrapped a leather-bound book tied closed with a leather thong. The first page simply read "My Journal" in ornate red-and-gold letters with intricate swirls. Underneath, written in elegant script, was the name Thomas Zachariah Packard. His skin rippled with goose flesh as he flipped the page.

*November the Tenth, Nineteen Hundred Twenty-four*

*My father has locked me in the attic. One of the yard hands installed bars on the windows and a large hasp on the door to keep me inside.*

Billy stopped reading and approached the window slowly. The bars were there, just as described in the journal. *Why didn't I see them before?* They had sharp points on the top and decorative swirls at the bottom. There could be no mistake about their purpose: to keep something out, or in this case, to keep someone in. He shuddered, chilled to the marrow by the cold and the words he had just read.

"Forty-four years ago," he muttered to himself. "This is creepy." He picked up the journal, flopped onto the bed, and continued reading where he had left off.

*Mother hid this journal under a napkin when my meal was delivered. She would have to keep it from Father. He would never approve. My only visitor today was Reverend Pane. He waved his Bible in the air and prayed for me. He thinks I'm possessed. Mother believes I am ill. She begged my father to call the surgeon. She wants him to cut something out of me to heal me. Dear Mother. Poor Mother, if she only knew! I'm healthier than all of them.*

*Nevertheless, this is an improvement over the fruit cellar where I spent yesterday. At least I have windows and can watch the moon. Bars on the windows shall not keep me imprisoned for long. They do not understand. Father believes I'm completely mad. I'm an embarrassment to him—an obscenity tarnishing his precious family name. If his Bible-thumping friends would allow it, he would take me out back and shoot me as though I were a lame horse. Then he could*

*bury me in an unmarked grave to save him the embarrass-
ment of a son like me.*

*I will show him! I will show them all. I am not afraid of
Father. He cannot hurt me. He is but a silly mortal and has
no inkling of the power I possess. Tonight, I will cast the
spell I learned from Tearneach. If I succeed, I will never be
locked in a cage again.*

*TZP*

Billy's eyelids began to droop as he read, and he struggled to stay awake. He lay back on the bare mattress. *I'm
just gonna rest my eyes for a minute*, he thought drowsily.

He dreamed of the cold. A dark figure stood in the
shadows, one hand extended, palm-up. Something black
dripped from the outstretched hand. He tried to turn and
run, but couldn't move. A scream tore from his throat as
the figure reached for him.

Billy woke, gasping for breath. He shivered when his
mother's voice penetrated his consciousness. Quickly, he
fled down the twisting stairs and up the hall to the second-
floor landing.

"Billy! What are you doing?" his mother yelled from
downstairs.

"Nothing, Mom," Billy answered between gasps for air,
hoping he sounded calmer than he felt.

"What's the matter? I heard you howling or
something."

"I had a bad dream. Sorry."

"Did you wake Susan?"

Relieved she no longer concerned herself with him,
Billy checked on his sister. "She's still asleep."

"What a relief. She kept me hopping all day. Get some sleep. It'll be morning before you know it."

"Okay, Mom. Good night." In his room, his pulse beat rapidly in his temples. He lay down and pulled the blankets close to ward off the cold, which again penetrated his bones. A clammy sweat trickled down his face.

# Chapter Eight

Molly wiped her feet before stepping into the kitchen. "Mrs. O'Brien, I'm home." She hung her coat on a hook behind the door and lifted the lid off the pot on the stove. "Mmm, stew." She stepped into the dining room and flipped on the overhead light. "Mrs. O'Brien?"

"I'm coming, child. I'm slow, not deaf." *Deaf* rhymed with *leaf*.

"How's Mamo?"

"Her color is better today." Mrs. O'Brien clenched the railing with both hands as she negotiated the stairs one at a time. "She took a bit of stew."

"I'll make her some tea." Molly returned to the kitchen and put the kettle on. Then she put the casserole dish Mrs. O'Brien had left for their dinner the day before into a shopping bag.

"Thanks for taking care of her."

"Shush." She slid into her tattered coat. "Mary Margaret and I have been friends our whole lives. I wouldn't know what to do with me self if I didn't have her."

Molly wondered what it was like to have a life-long friend. "Here's your dish. You make the best hunter's pie."

"Aye, t'was, fine, if I say so myself. There's some soda bread in the oven. Warm it a bit to dip in the stew." She opened the door and walked outside. "Get the tea to Mary before she goes off to sleep, child."

"I will." Molly tuned the radio on the cluttered kitchen counter to the underground rock station from State University in Albany while the tea steeped. When the kitchen timer dinged, she carried the tray up to Mamo's bedroom. Balancing the tray on one hand, she opened the door. Her grandmother sat in an overstuffed chair next to the bed, chin resting on her chest, eyes closed. A crucified Jesus stared at Molly from above the bed. The dried palm fronds draped behind the cross would be replaced with fresh ones when Palm Sunday rolled around. She slid the tray onto a nightstand and touched Mamo's frail hand. Her blue veins stood out against the dry, papery skin.

"Mamo? I brought you some tea."

"Who's there?" Mamo lifted her head. "Is that you, Shannon?"

"It's Molly." The distant, unfocused gaze told her all she needed to know. Aunt Shannon had been gone a long time. Her grandmother seemed to live in a past Molly had never been a part of, yet she would spend the next few hours answering to the dead woman's name.

She poured the tea and placed the cup in Mamo's hand, carefully wrapping her fingers around the porcelain cup. She guided the teacup to Mamo's lips and waited for her to take a sip.

"Ahh, the tea." The cup became steadier in Mamo's hand, and Molly released it.

She pulled over a straight back chair, fixed a cup for herself, and studied Mamo's face. Every crease told a story.

"I'll be right back." Molly hurried to her room and returned with a sketchpad and charcoal pencils. Balancing the pad on her lap, she scratched away. She'd never drawn a live model before. Mamo's head drooped. Molly sighed and took the empty cup from her slack hand. She would have to finish another time. The challenge of sketching Mamo had absorbed her. When she glanced at the little clock on the nightstand, she realized her father wouldn't be home for dinner. A knot formed in her chest.

*He's at Moe's Dew Drop Inn again.* She put her things away and cleared the tea. In the kitchen, she heated the stew and soda bread and ate alone at a table that used to be crowded with noisy conversation. With each passing minute, her jaw clenched more tightly, until her teeth ached. Water slopped from the sink as she banged the dishes around.

*I'm done waiting for him.* She stomped up the steps passing family photographs.

"Mamo, let's get you into bed now." She pulled back the blankets and bent to help her grandmother stand.

Her grandmother brightened. "Thank you, child. I can do it." She slowly straightened up and shuffled over to the side of the bed. "Where's your father?"

"He's not home yet."

"More than likely, he's hoisting a few pints down at Moe's."

Molly blinked, unsure of what to say. "Maybe he had to work late."

"You're a good daughter, but as me mum used to say, 'When the wine is inside, the sense is outside.' My Noel hasn't worked a day in years." She patted Molly on the head. "Off to bed with you."

Realizing Mamo still thought she was Shannon, she stopped holding her breath and exhaled before helping her grandmother into bed. "All set?" She pulled the blankets up and tucked them in.

"Grand altogether."

She smiled at the lilt in Mamo's voice. *Why didn't I pick up her accent?* She brought a glass of water from the bathroom, selected a medicine bottle from the nightstand, and shook out two pills.

"Take your pills." She held them in her open palm, with the glass in the other hand. Patiently, she waited for the shaking hand to find the pills. *I don't understand Alzheimer's. She remembers the past in perfect detail, but she doesn't know who's putting her to bed. She thinks she's putting Shannon to bed.*

"Can I get you anything?"

"I only have need of three things: health, freedom, and honor."

"You have all those."

"Then I am thrice blessed."

"Is it all right if I sketch in here for a little while?"

Mamo waved her hand as though she were brushing crumbs off her lap. "Of course, dear."

Before she had settled in with her sketchpad, Mamo snored softly. Molly's shoulders sagged. Her longing gaze fell on the image of Jesus. She felt the weight of his scrutiny. She gathered her things before retreating to her room. As she changed for bed, she heard her father's truck rumble, cough, sputter, then die in front of the house. She slipped between the sheets and turned off the lamp.

## Chapter Nine

Frank breezed through his homework. His gaze lingered on *2001: A Space Odyssey*. He smelled the pipe tobacco before he heard his father's voice.

"What have we here?" His father picked up the novel and started reading.

"I'm doing a book report on it for English."

His father sat down slowly in his usual chair and read a few pages. "This is very interesting." The words came out slowly as he turned another page.

"Miss Albright loaned it to me."

"Is everyone in your class reading this?"

"No, this is for my individual book report. You can pick any book you want as long as it's not *The Cat in the Hat*." Frank slid his glasses up his nose and pursed his lips. "That's a joke."

His father finally looked up and forced a smile. "Yes, I got it."

"Is something wrong?"

"No, not at all. Have you read any of it yet?"

"Just the first few pages." He closed his notebook and stacked his other books on top.

"I'm not sure you'll like it." His father stood up and leaned toward the kitchen. "Blanche, is there any more coffee?"

"It will keep you a-wa-ke," came his mother's sing-songy answer.

"Your mother is too good to me sometimes," his father whispered. "I'll ri-isk it," he sang back in reply.

"Why don't you think I'll like it?"

"You shouldn't judge a book by its cover." His father held up the book up. "It starts out with ancient apes, or hominids, if you prefer. A lot of ground to cover before you get to space travel."

His mother set a cup and saucer down with a soft clink.

"I haven't decided yet. I thought I'd read some tonight."

"Are your other assignments completed?"

"Yes."

"Then you get started on this book, and we'll talk about it tomorrow." He slid the book over to Frank.

The dining room chairs were hard, and Frank read until he could no longer feel his rear end. He heard the television being turned off in the other room.

"Francis, you need to get to bed." His mother whisked into the room and kissed the top of his head. "Are you feeling all right? You've been awfully quiet tonight."

"I've been thinking about Billy. He seems nice, doesn't he?"

She sat next to him and touched his hand. "Yes, a very nice young man."

"I hope he comes for dinner tomorrow."

"I do too. I'd like to get to know some of your friends."

He looked at his mother's sad countenance. *Me too.*

"School tomorrow. I'll put your books by the door." She stood up, gathered his books, and gave him one of her looks.

"I'm going." He stiffly rose to his feet. "Can you make chocolate chip cookies tomorrow?"

"Chocolate chip it is." She smiled. "Now off with you."

"Good night." He stuffed *2001* under his arm.

In his room, Frank rolled a towel up and laid it along the bottom of his door. Then he draped a shirt over one side of his lamp so his mother wouldn't see the light. The book had captured his imagination in the first few pages. His father would be surprised. He read late into the night, taking notes. The book confused him at times, but he got the gist and believed the next page would explain everything. When he finally fell asleep, he dreamed of monoliths.

Relief washed over Frank as Billy rush into homeroom just before the late bell. "I thought you might not come back after yesterday."

"Yeah. If only I had somewhere else to go."

"You could stay home. You know, play sick."

"One's as bad as the other."

Frank digested that. For him, home provided a safe haven. "School is okay, except for O'Riley. It'll be easier once you get used to him." He patted Billy's shoulder. "You'll see."

He tried to look out for his new friend throughout the uneventful morning. It seemed O'Riley had dropped it. Just in case, he tugged Billy aside in the cafeteria. "Just ignore them if they start on you today."

"Sure, I'll just ignore them when I'm wearing my lunch home again."

"Don't look at them. It's because you're new."

"I'll be fine." Billy waved him off.

At the table, Frank peered into his brown bag and kept an eye on O'Riley and friends while Billy paid for his lunch. He couldn't tell if they were plotting anything.

Billy sat down and twirled his fork in his spaghetti. O'Riley and Billy stared at each other from opposite ends of the table like a couple of gunfighters.

"Take a picture; it lasts longer," Billy finally said.

*Oh, crap. Here we go again.* "There's an oldie but a goodie, right?" Frank forced a laugh.

"Hey, Hamburger, relax. I was impressed with the way you handled yourself yesterday."

"I didn't do it for you."

"I thought maybe I would ask you sit on this end of the table, instead of down there in Loserville."

"I'm fine right here."

"I didn't *ask* you yet, loser."

This brought on a big guffaw from Ernie and Sal. O'Riley beamed at his brilliance.

"Way to go, O'Riley," Molly said. "Here comes Barracuda. If she expects me to pick up the trash again, I'm telling her the truth, you jerk."

"I wonder if the other table would mind giving up the trash detail today? What do you think, Mr. O'Riley? Do you want to make it two days in a row?" Mrs. Buchanan asked.

"Mrs. Buchanan, Houlahan is causing all the trouble, *as usual.* I don't think the whole table should be punished because of her." O'Riley's voice oozed syrupy sweetness.

"Thank you so much for your insight. I must admit it doesn't seem fair to punish the entire table for the actions of one student, but then life isn't always fair, is it, Mr. O'Riley? Consider this your last warning."

Mrs. Buchanan walked away slowly, keeping her gaze in their direction until another noisy table drew her attention.

"You're an ass, O'Riley," Molly said under her breath.

"Keep up that foul mouth of yours, Hooligan, and I'll call the Barracuda back over here. She'll have you wiping down these tables for a week," he threatened.

"Go ahead. Call her, big shot. Let's see it," Molly challenged.

Frank kept his head down. *This is out of control. Glad it's not me this time.*

He sighed with relief when Mrs. Buchanan strolled over and stood near their table for the rest of lunch, keeping a close watch until the bell sounded.

Frank walked next to Billy until someone shoved him from behind. Stumbling a few steps, he turned to see Sal and Ernie flanking Billy.

"Hey, watch it, Hashberger." Sal pushed Billy into Ernie.

"Watch where you're going, Hamburger." Ernie shoved Billy back.

"Are you some kind of a klutz, Hamburger?" Sal pushed him again.

"Why don't you two jerks leave him alone?" Molly yelled from behind.

"Stay out of this, Hooligan, or you'll be next." O'Riley one-armed her to the side.

"I told you to keep your hands off me. I won't warn you again."

"Real brave, picking on a girl. What's next, O'Riley? Stealing candy from babies? Kicking puppies?" Frank yelled as he ran for Mr. Overby's classroom.

Mr. Overby stepped into the corridor with his arms folded and Frank at his side. "Is everything all right, William?"

"Oh, yeah, everything's peachy." Billy ducked under his gaze into the room.

"What about you, Derrick? Do you have anything to add?"

"Not me, Mr. Overby." O'Riley flashed an angelic smile as he entered the room on Molly's heels.

Frank managed to keep Billy out of O'Riley's way for the rest of the day. In Miss Albright's class, he sensed trouble as she glared at the students filing past her at the door. Miss Albright pulled the door closed behind her with more force than necessary. The slam instantly quieted the room.

"Let me be the first to congratulate you. It seems my homeroom has distinguished itself in the eyes of our Mrs. Buchanan. Not once, but twice, in two days, your behavior in the cafeteria has been brought to my attention. It appears my presence is required tomorrow to assist Mrs. Buchanan. To help me better understand why my lunch must be interrupted, each of you will write an essay of one hundred words on proper conduct in the cafeteria. This will be completed as homework, and it will be on my desk tomorrow morning during homeroom. Your essay will be graded as a quiz. No extensions. No excuses. Failure to turn in your essay on time will result in a zero."

The students' murmurs swept across the room. She cleared her throat.

"Are there any questions?" She gave them The Look, which signaled there should be no questions. She turned to the blackboard. "Good. Let's pick up where we left off yesterday."

The tension in the room eased a little at the end of the

day, when she gave them a nod, which indicated they were free to talk for the last three minutes before the final bell. The room erupted in muted conversation.

"Are you coming for dinner tonight?" Frank asked, turning around in his seat.

Billy shook his head. "I have an essay to write now."

Frank looked disappointed. "Chocolate chip cookies today. We could do our homework together."

"Not tonight. I want my mom to check out this really neat room in the attic so I can make it my bedroom."

"You're not serious!"

"Why not?" he asked.

"You can't sleep up there." Frank's voice squeaked up an octave.

"Quiet conversation," Miss Albright said from her desk.

"After class," Frank whispered.

The class became perfectly still as the final bell sounded.

"Good afternoon, class. I will see you all tomorrow. Don't forget, one hundred words on behavior in the cafeteria on my desk before the morning bell."

In the hallway, Frank waited for Billy. "I'll meet you out front." They went in separate directions to their lockers.

Frank stepped outside. He slowly backed up into the school again and bumped into someone.

"Sorry." He turned and saw Billy approaching. "Let's go to the library." He pulled Billy in the opposite direction.

"I can't. I've too much homework to do."

"You can't go out there. O'Riley and his thugs are waiting."

"What do they want? I didn't do nothing to them." Billy pulled out of Frank's grip.

"That's the thing with O'Riley. You don't have to do anything for them to beat you up. It's what they do."

"We'll see."

"It's your funeral. I'll be in the library, writing my essay." Frank went to the window to watch him go.

Billy cautiously pushed open the door and peered out. He pulled his collar up against the cold as he started down the steps. Three shadows swiftly fell in behind him.

## Chapter Ten

Molly stepped out of the school just in time to see Billy running from O'Riley, Sal, and Ernie.

*I wonder if he'll make it home. He has a good lead.* Billy had grown on her. He was either brave or crazy. Either way, he'd stood up to O'Riley more than once in two days. That had to be a record of some kind. Frank had latched on to him too, which showed promise. She hoped Frank didn't get hurt. He had a way of attracting train wrecks. The door opened behind her, and she turned.

"Speak of the devil."

Frank gave her a bewildered look. "Who were you speaking to?"

"Myself. A girl's got to keep up her reputation, you know." Molly twirled a finger on one side of her head. "I think your boy had company on his walk home."

"Yeah, I know. I told him they were out here, but he went anyway."

*So maybe crazy then.* "Let's walk." She turned around and Frank caught up snugging his hat on. "No offense, but that is the ugliest hat I've ever seen."

"Maybe, but it's warm. We can't all have hair like you."

She arched one eyebrow. "Count your blessings. Red frizz is not in fashion, not that *you'd* notice."

"Are you cutting on my glasses?" Frank pointed to his face. "I tried to get new ones, really, but my dad thinks wire frames are just a fad."

"I'm not talking about your glasses. I'm talking about the Kamikaze hat, doofus." She cuffed him on the side of his head. "And you shouldn't take fashion advice from a guy who wears a bow tie to the hardware store." She watched a wave of embarrassment pass over his face like a dark cloud. "Hey, I'm kidding around. Lighten up."

"What did Miss Albright say about college?"

Molly noted Frank's abrupt subject change. She'd known him since the first grade, but she didn't *really* know him at all. She understood, though. She didn't talk about her family, either. "Not much."

"I'm going to MIT," he said without hesitation. "That's where my father went."

"Are you going to start wearing bow ties too?"

"No, but I'm keeping my hat. It's cold in Boston."

She laughed. *There goes any chance he'll meet a girl in college.* "Where are your books? No homework?"

"I did most of it in Art."

She flashed back to her unfinished sketch of Mamo. She had no eyes yet, making it creepy looking. Molly had tried several times, but she couldn't capture Mamo's eyes. She'd nailed the muddy, confused look, but had erased it. She wanted to remember the old Mamo.

"Hello? Is anybody home?" Frank waved a hand in front her face.

"Sorry, just thinking. What did you say?"

"I'm worried about Billy."

"He had a good lead when he cleared the gate. He's

pretty fast. Maybe he'll make it. You know the quote, 'He who fights and runs away, may turn to fight another day'?"

"It's from the Roman historian Tacitus. Do you know the rest of it?"

"Does anyone? Hold these a minute, will you?" She handed him her books and adjusted her scarf to keep the steadily increasing wind from blowing her hair into her face.

"The rest goes, 'But he who is in battle slain, will never rise to fight again.'"

She took her books back. "What *are* you? The dark cloud in every silver lining?"

"He who spends his days with books never learns to fight the crooks."

"Cute, Frank. Do you want to try a limerick now? I know the one about the man from Nantucket."

"Molly Houlahan, you do not."

"Hah. You'd be surprised what's written in the girls' room."

"All we get is, 'Here I sit broken-hearted.'"

"It's a proven scientific fact girls are smarter than boys, which explains why we have a higher caliber of graffiti." She shifted her books from one arm to the other with a grunt.

"Is not. Boys and girls mature at different rates, and that's a fact. I'm not sure I'd consider your example a higher grade of graffiti anyway."

"You're too serious. If you're going to hang with the new kid, try to pick up a few things."

"You should talk about serious." He gestured wildly.

"Calm down. Everyone knows you're going to be an astronaut."

"I'm going to put the astronauts in space. I'm not going with them." Frank straightened his back and lifted his chin.

"Pardon my ignorance. I thought you were going to fly rockets."

"I am. They are flown from the ground. A dog rode in the first rocket into space. He didn't fly it."

"Perfect." She laughed so hard, she dropped her books. "Perfect."

"What is so funny?" he asked, helping her gather her books.

"You're such a doofus. I'm going this way. I'll see you tomorrow."

"Yeah, I'll see you."

She stepped off the curb, stopped, and turned around to find Frank watching her. "I hope your friend made it home okay."

"Thanks." He gave her his lopsided grin. "Me too."

She crossed the street. *That boy is wired too tight. At the rate he's going, he'll die from a heart attack at eighteen.* She found herself smiling as she thought about their conversation, the longest one she could remember. *He's a good kid. A little nerdy, maybe, but good.* Crossing back to her side of the railroad tracks, she hunched her shoulders.

Six older boys stood on a corner, harmonizing to what sounded like some old song from the fifties. They weren't bad, but as the night wore on and empty wine bottles mounted, they would get louder and off-key. A shiver passed over her. It felt colder in her neighborhood. She couldn't put it into words, but she knew it, as sure as she knew she would be getting out of this dump at the first opportunity. Her pace quickened.

## Chapter Eleven

The sound of footsteps passing through the school gate echoed behind Billy. He had several blocks to go, but he could run. He rounded the corner onto State Street. *All downhill from here.*

His heart raced, and his lungs burned, but he could really fly downhill. It felt good to be running hard. He had a comfortable lead closing in on home. He put his head down and pushed.

A shadow fell across the sidewalk in front of him, and he recognized O'Riley too late to stop. His attempt to jump over the outstretched leg caused him to get tangled up. Before he knew it, he was airborne. Good hang time, but the sidewalk grew larger as he hurtled toward it. He tried to break his fall with his arms and managed to turn his head just before making contact with the concrete.

"You're kind of clumsy, Hamburger. You shouldn't run if you're clumsy," O'Riley sneered, glaring down at him.

Sal and Ernie arrived, panting and smiling broadly.

"Good one, Derrick," Ernie said.

"Yeah, good one," repeated Sal.

"You want to get up and take your beating like a man? Or should I finish you down there?" O'Riley asked.

"What'd I ever do to you?" Warm blood ran down the right side of Billy's face.

"We don't like homework. Miss Notsobright is trying to fail us already and… You're. Helping. Her." The last three words were each punctuated with a hard kick.

Searing pain radiated from Billy's ribs through the rest of his body. He balled himself up as tight as he could, to make as small a target as possible, and to protect his face and stomach. Multiple feet stomped on him as he lay on the sidewalk and absorbed the beating. His mind reached out for something to focus on besides the pain. He thought of the journal. Being locked in the attic by your father would suck. He heard a loud, fluttering sound.

"What the hell is that?" one of them hollered.

"I think it's an owl."

Someone screamed. The kicking stopped, and Billy heard his attackers' fading footsteps as they ran. He lay there, adrift in his thoughts, almost dreaming, until the pain in his ribs urgently reminded him to get up. Slowly, he sat up and felt his bruised body. Everything hurt. He tried to spit, but no saliva formed in his mouth. Getting to his feet, he steadied himself against a wrought-iron fence along the sidewalk. His textbook lay ten feet away, apparently no worse for wear. His head pounded as he hobbled home in the fading light. An owl hooted in the distance.

Peering through the window into the kitchen, he saw his mother at the sink. A newly hung clock over her head revealed the time as four thirty. *At least I'm not late.*

He walked around the porch to the front door. *I'll make a run for the bathroom, get cleaned up, and work out a believable story.* The door creaked open, and he tiptoed across the living room. One painful step at a time, he made it halfway up the staircase. After taking a shallow breath, he yelled, "Mom, I'm home. I've gotta go. I'll be down in a minute."

He ducked into the bathroom and heard his mother's greeting through the closed door. Stepping up to the mirror, Billy got the first look at his face. He'd scraped the right side of his face from temple to chin. Blood oozed from the shallow cuts. His coat had another hole in it, but it blended in nicely with the rest of them. The tear in his pant leg created a problem he would have to delay indefinitely. His mind revved to full speed as he gently dabbed at his face.

He changed and went downstairs. In the kitchen, his mother stood at the stove, cooking, unless his eyes deceived him. To Billy's surprise, it smelled good.

"Hi, Mom."

"Hi yourself." She didn't look up from the pot she stirred. "Homework?"

"Yeah, I should get started on it."

"Uh huh." She stared into that space she escaped to. Billy knew she wasn't really there.

"I got beat up by three kids, and the teacher is a witch. She wears a pointy hat and everything," he muttered.

"That's nice, honey. Check on Susan for me, will you? Thanks."

"Sure, as soon as I feed the dragon."

"Feed what?" She blew on the spoon she held above the pot.

"Nothing, I'll check on Suze." Billy backed out of the kitchen.

Susan slept in her playpen, so he prepared for another ascent up the stairs. The wrapped journal sat on the desk. Billy stared at it. *I left it on the bed last night.*

Using willpower and his fear of Miss Albright, he pushed the journal aside, opened his notebook, and started to write the essay. His left hand absently rubbed his ribs as he tore another false start out of his notebook, balled it up, and threw it into the corner with several others. Finally giving up on the essay, he moved on to his Social Studies text. He scribbled down answers to the chapter before his mother's shrill voice carried up the circular staircase from the kitchen.

"Billy, dinner."

He closed his book. *Here goes nothing.* He slowly walked downstairs.

When Billy entered the kitchen, he locked eyes with Tony. "What the hell happened to your face?"

"I hit myself with my Social Studies book to see if any of the stuff would sink in," Billy replied with a forced smile.

"I hope the book looks worse than you do, but I'm not sure that's possible." Tony pulled the cork from a bottle of red wine with a soft pop.

His mother finally looked up from pouring the sauce over the pasta.

"Oh, honey, what on earth happened?" She held Billy's head in her hands for a closer look, twisting it right then left, as she examined the damage.

"I tripped horsing around with some kids from school. It only hurts when I laugh." He forced a laugh then grimaced.

"A little ice will keep it from blowing up like a beach ball." Tony reached into the freezer.

"There's no ice. Yes, just one more thing I haven't gotten around to yet." His mother banged a pot onto the stove for emphasis.

"A cold washcloth," Tony pressed. He pulled a dish-cloth out of a drawer, wet it, and laid it in the freezer. "Let it chill a few minutes."

"We're about to eat." His mom set a handful of silver-ware on the table. "Sit."

Tony took his seat.

"Billy has an owie," Suze said from her high chair.

The spaghetti sauce and meatballs were courtesy of Tony's mother. Tony served everyone dinner and talked about the men he worked with at the 3M plant. Billy liked this part of dinner. Tony always made him laugh. Just the nick names of the men Tony worked with conjured up funny images. "No Neck" was Tony's partner on the loading dock. His boss was "The Weasel." Tonight's story featured "Stuttering Louie," the forklift operator.

"Stuttering Louie has a plate in his head so... he... well, you know, he stutters." Tony gestured with the fork he held in one hand and the spoon in the other. "So, this driver comes in and Louie said, 'Wh-wh-what y-y-ya g-got?' And the driver goes, 'What's wrong with you? You a retard?' Louie looked at the driver and said, 'I c-can sh-sh-show you a re-ta-tard.' Then he drove the forks right through the side of the guy's truck."

Billy had an image of one of his mother's dinner plates riding on top of Louie's head with his hair stretched over it. "How did Stuttering Louie get a plate in his head?"

"That's another story. He worked the big top in Barnum and Bailey's Greatest Show on Earth." Tony twirled his forkful of spaghetti on the spoon and lifted it to his mouth. Pausing, he took a bite and washed it down with a sip of wine. "One day, he fell from the high wire and landed on his head. They patched him up with the plate, but he hasn't been right since."

"Stop telling him stories," Billy's mother spat out, frowning at Tony. "You know he believes every word you say."

"He should believe me. It's all true. They used to call

him Louie the Great. Now we call him Louie the Plate."
Tony burst out laughing at his own joke.

Milk shot from Billy's nose and swamped his empty
plate. His nose burned, and he coughed, which sent a
sharp pain across his ribs.

His mother shook her head. "You are excused, young
man. Get the dishcloth out of the freezer and finish your
homework."

The cold cloth felt good when he pressed it against his
face. Still laughing, he started up the steps to the third
floor. He passed through a pocket of cold air, which caused
him to check the windows in the attic. Standing still, he
looked around the room slowly. The weight of someone
watching him rested on his shoulders. The hair on the back
of his neck stood at attention.

He sat down and tried his hand at the essay again.
Another false start from his notebook, he crumpled it up,
and tossed it into the corner, where its predecessors all
danced around the wastebasket. Giving in to his real
desire, he unwrapped Thomas's journal.

*November the Twelfth, Nineteen Hundred Twenty-four*

*It's been two days since my last entry. I do not remember
them at all. Full trays of food lay on the steps. My bones are
weary, and although I can see I have not eaten, my belly feels
full. My sister, Mabel, came up and asked where I hid
yesterday. She said Father is in a lather because he could not
find me when he came looking for me. He has, of course,
blamed my mother for my absence. I told Mabel not to worry
about me. I would probably be gone by tomorrow for good.
She does not understand, of course. Like my mother, Mabel
thinks I am sick and with enough rest, I will get better. I tell
her I am tired, and she hurries off, wishing me sweet dreams.*

*I do need some rest before I attempt the spell again. It is a drain on my energy.*

*TZP*

*November the Thirteenth, Nineteen Hundred Twenty-four*

*I slept the entire day. I am sure my need for rest is a side effect of commanding the powers of nature to do my bidding. I am well rested now. Tonight, I will recite the spell again. Mother just came up to see me, relieved to find me home, but frightened also. I can see the fear in her eyes. I am not sure if she is frightened by me, or for me. I told her I would be leaving soon. She cried and asked me to try to get well. She has no understanding of what I can do or how powerful I am.*

*Sitting in the deep window niche, waiting for darkness to descend, I watched Father and Mister O'Riley engage in a heated discussion. I could not hear his voice, but Father's face turned as red as a beet. He waved his arms about like the wings of a headless chicken. It was comical to watch from a distance. A different experience, to be sure, when he is waving those arms in your face. Mister Houlahan tried to calm Father. I could have told him he engaged in a fruitless cause. Once Father gets angry, it must run its course. He is like a river flooding over its banks. The water must be allowed to recede; it cannot be forced.*

*I am writing the spell down, so as not to forget it. Tearneach taught me everything in witchcraft must be done with precision to avoid unintended and horrific consequences.*

### *The Spell*

*Draw a large invoking pentagram. While standing in the center, face east and recite the spell.*

*I cast a circle round about*
*A world within a world without*
*Mother Earth and Father Sky*
*Through the air I wish to fly*
*By the light of yon snow moon*
*Feather and talon be mine soon*
*In the darkness of the night*
*Protection grant by magick's might*
*By might of moon and of sea*
*As I do will so mote it be*
*Owl flies in silence death on wing*
*Until the morning bell doth ring*

*Turn and face west and repeat, then south and finally north.*

*TZP*

Billy's eyelids closed against his will, and the journal fell from his hand and thumped to the floor.

Later, an insistent shake woke Billy. "I've been calling you," his mother said.

"Sorry, I must've fallen asleep."

"Downstairs, get ready for bed now. What're you doing up here anyway?"

"My homework."

His mother marched him downstairs and waited until he crawled under the covers. "Good night, Mom."

"Sweet dreams." His mother stomped down the stairs, muttering something Billy couldn't hear.

## Chapter Twelve

He sat, poised on the edge of the deep windowsill, and stared into the darkness. Involuntarily, he leapt, as though someone else controlled him. The earth raced up to meet him. Air roared in his ears as he fell toward certain death. He squeezed his eyes shut and prayed it wouldn't hurt too much when he hit the frozen ground. The cold air bit at his skin, and the fresh scent of fall filled his nose as he waited for the sudden, painful stop.

Intense pain engulfed him. He felt squeezed from all sides, as though his body were passing through a funnel. The squeezing became tighter and tighter until he couldn't breathe. He should have hit the ground by now. He opened his eyes, surprised to see the ground gliding beneath him as he soared through the air. The scent of a field mouse drifted up from below. He fanned out his wings, dropped to the earth, and extended his talons. In one smooth motion, he seized the mouse, flapped his wings, and regained altitude. He perched on the limb of a large oak tree while his razor-like beak shredded the mouse before he gulped it down.

As he turned his head, Billy realized he could see clearly in the dark. He saw things he'd never observed in daylight. Alighting from his perch, he effortlessly glided above the ground with a feeling of exhilaration, while his sharp eyes picked out the most, minute details in the terrain. The soft sound of cold air passing over his wings filled the night. He detected a large rat sniffing the air near a barn and swiftly turned on the wind currents. The rat squealed loudly as he carried it aloft, talons piercing the warm, squirming flesh.

Billy suddenly sat up in bed as sweat ran down his face in spite of the cool air embracing him. His ragged breathing raced in and out of his lungs. His bedroom looked unchanged, and he waited to catch his breath. The memory of bloody talons tearing at the rat and gulping down the pieces caused a tremor to pass through him. The musky taste lingered at the back of his throat. He gagged and jumped from his bed, soaked with sweat. His bare feet hit the cold floor and sent a shiver up his spine. He retched.

With a blanket over his shoulders, he tiptoed to the kitchen. *I'll stay awake until morning if I have to.* His body trembled, but not from the cold. The visions from his dreams haunted him. He tried to shake them. *Think happy thoughts.* He pulled two chairs together and tried to find a comfortable position before nodding off into an uneasy sleep.

"Hey, kid. What're you doing down here?" Tony asked from the doorway, scratching the stubble on his chin. "Are you okay?"

Billy jerked awake. "Huh? Yeah, I'm good."

"Why are you sleeping in the kitchen?"

"I had a bad dream."

Tony sat down and examined Billy's swollen face.

"You don't look so good in purple and yellow, kid. Go get cleaned up. I'll freeze another dishcloth to help with the swelling. After I get the fire going, we'll have us some breakfast." Billy rose stiffly from the chair. As he left the room, he heard Tony say, "Keep it down so your mom doesn't wake up."

"Okay." Dragging the blanket behind him, he made his way to his bedroom.

He couldn't remember ever being ready for school so early. Normally, when Billy woke up, Tony was gone without a trace. He kept the frozen cloth pressed against his face as he watched Tony move around the kitchen efficiently. Coffee perked, the toaster hummed, and a pan on the stove sizzled when Tony flicked in a chunk of butter.

"How do you like your eggs, kid?"

"I don't care. Mom always scrambles them."

"Over easy it is. You'll like this, trust me." Tony flashed his smile.

"Do you do this every morning?"

"What? Make breakfast? Sure. No offense, but your mom can't cook."

Billy rolled his eyes. "Yeah, I think I figured that out."

"I'm sure you have," Tony said softly. "Well, belly up to the table, my friend. Breakfast is almost ready."

Tony sent a plate sliding across the table with two eggs, a pile of fried potatoes, and two slices of buttered toast on it. The plate stopped right in front of him. He looked at Tony, who smiled broadly.

"Dig in." Tony set a plate on the table for himself.

The clinking of forks on plates punctuated the quiet. When they finished, Tony cleared the plates, poured himself a second cup of coffee, and sat down next to Billy.

"You want to talk about it?" Tony asked.

"About what?"

"Start with the dream so bad you were afraid to go back to sleep. Or maybe you need to tell someone how you got those bruises on your face."

"I don't remember much of the dream now," Billy lied. "Except how real it felt. I sorta—flew." He shuddered involuntarily.

"What else do you remember?" Tony asked.

Billy didn't really want to talk about catching and eating a rat. His thoughts went back to the moment when he realized he was soaring through the air instead of falling to his death. He shrugged.

"If you die in your dream, will you die for real?" A lump formed in his throat, choking off his voice.

Tony sipped his coffee as a smirk formed on his face. "I don't know where you come up with some of these things. I'm pretty sure that won't happen. If you were scared, why didn't you come in and wake us up?"

"I'm not a baby! A bad dream is no big deal."

"Right, it's no big deal, but you spent the night on two kitchen chairs." Tony winked. "What about those bruises? You want to tell me how you got them?"

"Just like I said. Fooling around with some kids from school. No big deal," Billy repeated.

"There's that phrase again. Why is it when you say 'no big deal,' I'm not convinced? Look kid, it's okay to tell me. I won't tell your mom. I wouldn't want her running down to the school and embarrassing you. I just thought it might help to talk about it."

"I'll be all right," Billy said in a tone he hoped sounded convincing. "I'll have to deal with them sooner or later."

"I know I'm not your dad or anything, but if you want to talk…" Tony's voice trailed off as steps thumped overhead. He put his finger to his lips and pointed at the kitchen ceiling with the other hand. Then he ruffled Billy's hair.

"I've got to get out of here before I'm late for work. Sorry I woke you up so early, kid." Tony spoke in a voice loud enough to be heard upstairs. He winked at Billy.

"Thanks for breakfast."

"Good morning, sunshine. It looks like I woke up the whole neighborhood."

Billy's mom scuffed into the kitchen, wearing a white chenille bathrobe pulled tightly around her waist. Her fuzzy slippers peeked out from underneath with every step. She stopped in her tracks when she saw Billy. "I don't even want to know what managed to get you up at this hour."

Billy smiled. "The barking frogs woke me."

Tony let out a belly laugh and kissed her on the top of her head. "I've really got to go. I'll see you tonight." He patted her on the butt as he turned to leave.

Billy walked Tony to the door. "Thanks again, for breakfast and—and everything."

A frigid blast of winter rushed into the house as Tony left. Billy watched as Tony backed his car out of the driveway and onto the street. The headlights played across the blacktop, illuminating brown oak leaves chasing each other around in a game of tag. He found himself wondering again why Tony hung around.

His mother shook her head. "I don't believe it."

"What?" Billy asked in his most innocent voice,

knowing full well how hard he was to get out of bed in the mornings.

"Never mind." She tightened her robe and put the teakettle on.

"I've got to finish up my homework." Billy left her with her disbelief.

When he got to the attic, he saw several of his ill-fated attempts at the essay smoothed out and lying on the desktop. He scratched his head and pushed them around. His notebook lay open, and a completed essay stared up at his incredulous face. He read it through and decided he could work with it. *But who had wrote it?*

The writing looked familiar, but it clearly wasn't his mother's. The script was a little like the one in the journal, but that was, of course, impossible. It had to be Tony. *I wonder why he didn't mention it this morning?*

Billy's opinion of Tony improved by the second. Billy set about rewriting the essay in his own handwriting, changing some words and rearranging a couple of the sentences. When he finished, he looked for the journal. He checked everywhere, but had no luck. Had Tony taken it? *No, it must have been Mom. She came up here last night.*

The room suddenly felt crowded. A chill enveloped him. Billy grabbed his notebook and limped down the stairs, wincing and holding a hand against his ribs. He decided to ask his mother if she'd seen it.

"Mom, I'm going," Billy hollered from the living room.

His mother appeared in the doorway. "Isn't it early?"

"Yeah, but I'm meeting Frank at the library to go over some homework. He asked me to come for dinner, okay?"

"Who is Frank? A new friend?" she asked in her "I told you so!" tone.

"Yeah, he's in my class," Billy answered, ignoring the smug expression on his mother's face.

"You should definitely accept the invitation to dinner." She looked Billy over and leaned forward to straighten his collar. "Mind your manners when you're at the table. And don't be too late. It's a school night."

"Yes, Mom, thanks." Billy pulled on his coat. "Mom, did you see an old book in my room last night?"

"No. Do you need it?"

"No, Frank loaned it to me to read, I'll look for it when I get home."

He headed to school a full half hour early. The cold air felt good on his bruised face. As he walked, he thought it might be a good idea to get there early to avoid O'Riley and his thugs. His ribs were killing him. He wouldn't be out-running anyone for at least a few days. He would have to be careful.

---

"Good morning," Billy called to the black man polishing the brass door handles at the entrance to the school.

"Good morning, son. You're in a mite early," he replied.

"I guess I am. Can I go in?"

"Oh yes! My lands, I would never discourage anyone from getting to school early." He smiled brightly. "You're new here. The name is Lionel Shorts. My friends just call me Shorty."

Billy extended his hand.

"Pleased to meet you, Mr. Shorts. William Hashberger, my friends call me Billy."

"The pleasure is all mine, Billy," Shorty said as he pulled the door open with a flourish. "You can call me Shorty, but the principal thinks it's disrespectful, so watch your p's and q's around Mr. Brady."

Billy nodded as they walked down the empty hall.

"Your shiner looks mighty fresh. You want to tell me who you gone and run up against already?" Shorty asked.

"I fell down fooling around with some guys."

"I see." Shorty winked. "I reckon I saw the start of that 'fooling around' heading out the main gate yesterday afternoon. Yup, I reckon that's what I saw, all right."

"Yeah, I… ahh…" Billy looked down at his shoes for the answer. "It's no big deal." The words no sooner left his lips when he thought of Tony's comment earlier.

Shorty locked eyes with Billy. "I'm going to give you a piece of advice. Derrick O'Riley is bad news. A regular chip off the old block, I might add. His old man's a hard case too. Least when he went to school here. You would do well to steer clear of him."

"Thanks, Mr. Shorts. I think I learned that already."

"Yes, I'd say your lesson came with some lumps. Thing is, Derrick's not a boy who will let up. You get my meaning?"

"Yes, sir, I think so."

"Follow me."

Shorty led Billy through the cafeteria and the kitchen, stopping at a door with Janitor stenciled on it in black letters.

"This here is my office. Back there is the loading dock." Shorty pushed through the door.

Billy wrinkled his nose at the stench of garbage and the greasy surface of the concrete underfoot. Mops and buckets stood in a neat line along one wall. An army of steel trashcans stood at attention along another. The soles of his shoes pulled away from the floor with a sticky sound, like packing tape being pulled from a carton.

Shorty pointed down a small flight of steps. "If you follow the driveway up, it brings you to Locust Street. You can find your way home from there, I reckon, just in case you find yourself facing another encounter with our budding mobster. Understand?"

"Okay, but—"

"You don't want to go around looking like a piñata all year, do you now?"

"No… What's a piñata?"

Shorty laughed, "A piñata is something Mexican kids beat with a stick until candy falls out."

Billy scratched his head. "Ookaaay. I'm not sure what…"

"Let's just say, you don't want to go around looking like *that* all year." Shorty gestured at Billy's face.

He nodded in agreement.

"We'll leave it there. I've got to get back to work now. You mind what I said about young O'Riley." Shorty shook Billy's hand. "Now git."

Billy walked to his homeroom. The door stood open, and Miss Albright sat at her desk. Her attention was focused on whatever she was working on until Billy stopped in front of her.

She looked up with a start. "Good morning, William." She quickly regained her composure. "You're in early today."

"Yes, ma'am. Where do you want this?" Billy asked, flourishing his essay.

She pointed to the corner of her desk. "There is fine. Sit down and tell me what happened to your face, please."

"I had an accident. It's nothing."

"It looks like something. Would you like to go see the nurse?" She furrowed her brow.

"No. Tony, my… ahh… my mom's boyfriend looked at it. He put a cold washcloth on it for the swelling."

"William, look at me." Miss Albright held Billy's gaze. "You tell me the truth. Did Tony do this to you?"

The accusation stunned him. "No! He wouldn't dare touch me. My mom would kill him. An accident, like I said, no big deal." *There I go again.*

"William, you can talk to me."

"Thanks. Can I go now?"

"Yes, you *may*."

## Chapter Thirteen

Frank stopped in the doorway. His eyes teared up at the damage to Billy's face. *O'Riley caught him all right, and he got him good.* Frank shuffled from foot to foot. *Should I interrupt?* He peeked around the edge of the door and saw Billy rise from the chair and head toward him.

"Oh, man, look at you." Frank pointed. "Did O'Riley do—"

"Shut up." Billy pushed Frank down the corridor away from the door. "Where can we talk, like, in private?"

"This way."

Frank hurried Billy around the corner and turned down a dark corridor that led back to the gymnasium.

"No one uses the gym first thing in the morning." Frank pushed through the door. "Tell me what happened."

"O'Riley tripped me going top speed. I took a face-plant on the sidewalk."

"That looks bad." Frank winced. "Does it hurt?"

"Not as much as my ribs." Billy pulled up his shirt.

Frank's stomach and groin tightened when he saw the

78

bruises all over Billy's left side and back. "What did they do?"

Billy tucked in his shirt and told Frank about the ambush and the way they had kicked him.

"Then what happened?"

"I don't know who, but someone yelled something about an owl. The next thing I knew, they were running away."

"An owl?" Frank pulled open the door. "We should get to class; the bell's going to ring any second. You must be hurting."

The bell rang just as they reentered the classroom. Frank put his essay on top of the pile.

The morning moved by at a glacial pace as Frank did his best to keep Billy out of O'Riley's path. When the bell finally signaled lunch period, Frank's stomach felt like a bowling ball was rolling around in there. There was no way to hide in the cafeteria. When Frank and Billy walked out of Art, Derrick O'Riley cornered them in the corridor, with Ernie and Sal on either side.

"Hey, Hamburger, you don't look so good. Did you learn anything last night?"

Molly stepped in front of O'Riley and jerked Frank forward a step with her. "I didn't know you were allowed to bring trained monkeys to school, Derrick. You'd better get to the cafeteria before all the bananas are gone."

"Oh, Hooligan, you're a scream. Good work, Hamburger, let a girl fight your battles for you." O'Riley leaned to the left to make eye contact with Billy, who stood behind Frank and Molly. Then he lunged toward Frank and stomped his foot. "Boo!"

Frank jumped back and stepped on Billy's foot. "Sorry." His face heated up, and his hands shook.

"Come on, guys, let's get out of Loserville." O'Riley

led Ernie and Sal toward the cafeteria, roaring with laughter.

"Don't you need a leash when you bring a pet to school?" Molly hollered after them.

Ernie turned around and sneered, "You're gonna be next, Hooligan."

Billy and Frank both grabbed Molly and started to move her in the other direction. She struggled against them.

"It can speak and drool at the same time—wow! Do you know any two-syllable words?" she yelled over Billy's shoulder as Frank and Billy continued to push her around the corner.

"Just cool it, will you? You want to get us killed? Look at what they did to Billy." Frank adjusted his glasses. "Show her your ribs."

"No." Billy frowned. "This isn't your fight. You two should stay out of it."

"Boys are such jerks. Present company included." Molly shook off Frank's grip on her elbow. "I don't know about you, but I'm not letting O'Riley and his trained monkeys push me around. I thought *maybe* we could watch each other's backs. If you're too macho to accept my help, forget it. I'm not the one with a punching bag for a face." Molly stomped off.

"Wait, I'm sorry. I didn't mean to sound like a jerk. Thanks for sticking up for me and all. It's just—those guys are mean. I don't want them to hurt you too." Billy looked down.

Molly came back and gave them a hard look. "Let's see if we can get into the library." She moved away while talking over her shoulder. "We can talk there."

"We don't have a pass," Frank said.

"Follow me." Molly sighed.

Frank shrugged. "Let's go. I've lost my appetite after looking at your face all morning."

When they caught up with her, Molly wove a long story for Mrs. Esposito, the librarian, about why they were there during lunch period. Molly looked over her shoulder and gestured to the boys as though their presence proved her point. Turning back to Mrs. Esposito, she said, "See?" She walked over to a study table.

Frank followed, sneaking a glance at Mrs. Esposito in order to gauge her reaction. "Now what?"

"I'd like to know what happened to him, for starters." Molly tossed her mane of hair over one shoulder with a flick of her head as she pointed at Billy.

Billy retold the story about yesterday's run-in with O'Riley. Frank noticed a few embellishments to the version he had gotten in the gym earlier. Reluctantly, Billy eventually agreed to go into the stacks to show her the bruises on his ribs.

Frank waited at the table, chewing on the cap of his pen. He noticed Mrs. Esposito watching him, so he pretended to write. He wondered what he had gotten himself into. *I'm going to get my butt kicked—I just know it. On the bright side, if they break my glasses, I can get the wire frames I want.*

Molly and Billy joined Frank back at the table. "I know this sounds hokey, but we should stick together. Safety in numbers and all that."

"I know a back way out of the school." Billy leaned his chair back onto two legs.

"I say we go to my house after school today?" Frank suggested.

Molly raised one eyebrow. "What for?"

"That's just not right." Billy pointed at Molly.

"What?" she asked.

"The eyebrow thing you do. How do you do it?" Billy contorted his face in an attempt to copy her. "I can't." Finally, he pushed one eyebrow up with a finger.

"She's always had that talent." Frank waved his hand dismissively.

"What's the matter? Don't people in Masonville have eyebrows?" Molly did it again.

"Yeah, but they move together like normal people's." Billy's eyebrows moved up and down.

"If your face is normal for Masonville, I feel sorry for the whole town."

"Are you guys going to talk eyebrows all day, or what?" Frank threw his hands in the air.

"What kind of cookies are we having today?" Billy pushed one eyebrow up.

"Cookies?" Molly asked.

"Homemade cookies," Billy said.

"If there's cookies, count me in. My dad promised to be home on time today." Molly stood and pointed at the clock. "We should go."

They traveled through the halls together for the rest of the day. Frank found himself between Molly and Billy more often than not. He decided he liked it.

At the sound of the last bell the trio utilized the escape route Shorty had shown Billy. They made their way along Locust Street and remained side by side until they reached Frank's house undetected. Frank lowered his mug, and Billy and Molly burst into laughter. "What are *you* laughing at?"

"Frank, wipe off your nose. You look ridiculous," Molly finally said.

Frank wiped his face with a napkin. "How long do you think O'Riley and company will wait at the front of the school for us?"

They laughed at the image of O'Riley, Ernie, and Sal freezing while Molly, Billy, and Frank ate homemade Tollhouse cookies and drank hot chocolate.

"If the rest of the school ever finds out your mother makes you hot chocolate and cookies every day, you'll never live it down." Molly reached for another warm cookie.

They resolved to walk home together from now on and, of course, to stop at Frank's to check out the cookie special of the day.

"We can do homework while we're here, too," Molly suggested.

"Speaking of homework, I should probably hit the books," Billy groaned.

Frank reached for another cookie.

"You might want to take it easy on those cookies. No offense, but they're starting to show." She puffed out her cheeks.

"Real nice, he shares his cookies with you, and you tell him he's getting fat," Billy said.

"I didn't say anything about fat. Not yet." Molly pointed at Frank's stomach. "Maybe he's big boned."

Frank's face warmed. "Can we talk about Billy's homework?"

Molly shifted in her chair. "Do you have more than the rest of us?"

"They're afraid I won't keep up. Maybe it's because in Masonville, they treated us like high school students not kindergarteners."

"What's that supposed to mean?" Molly raised one eyebrow.

"Again, with the creepy eyebrow." Billy turned his head. "I'm gonna have nightmares."

"You'd better get used to it," Frank said.

"Answer the question newbie."

"What's with staying in a group all day and sitting at the same table in the cafeteria? That's kid's stuff."

"Brady." Molly said in disgust. "He thinks it promotes teamwork or some crap he learned at some military school."

"Yeah, some team we have." Frank scrunched up his face. "I guess O'Riley is our captain."

Molly snorted. "Stupid rules aside, we can help with your extra homework. Right, Frank?"

"Before we do, I want to know about your house." Frank leaned forward.

Billy leaned his chair back and tugged on his ear.

"Tell him it's haunted. He doesn't believe me." Frank gesticulated wildly.

"Of course, it's haunted. Everyone knows that," Molly said.

"How do you know?" Billy drained his mug and set it down with a solid thunk. "Have you seen these supposed ghosts?"

"I tried to tell you yesterday." Frank leaned over the table. "You can't go to the third-floor room. That's where they locked the crazy guy up before he slaughtered the family. We've all seen him standing in the window, watching the street. He can't get out of there—ever."

Billy rolled his eyes. "You're telling me you've actually *seen* Thomas looking out the window of the attic?"

"Yeeaah, right," Molly said sarcastically.

"Hold on." Frank frowned. "How do you know his name?"

Billy said nothing.

"How *do* you know?" Molly narrowed her intense green eyes and looked at Billy.

"I must've heard it somewhere."

"Billy Hashberger, you shouldn't lie to your friends." Molly pointed a finger in his face. "You're not very good at it."

"You've seen him, I bet. Maybe you even talked to him! Did you? Huh?" Frank pushed.

"Spill your guts, Hashberger, or you'll find yourself walking home alone," Molly threatened.

"Yeah, and no more cookies for you." Frank pulled the plate away.

Billy remained quiet.

Frank's mother bustled into the kitchen. "Did you invite your guests to stay?" Her fathomless energy filled the room. "How many for dinner?"

No one answered her. Molly and Frank continued to stare at Billy, who stared at the plate in front of Frank.

Mrs. Bordeaux slipped her apron over her head and tied it behind her back with practiced ease. "Francis?"

"I don't know yet. I'm waiting for Billy to snap out of his trance and tell me."

"Go into the parlor and decide. I have work to do. You're both welcome to stay. There's plenty of food." She pulled two woven potholders off the hook above the stove and opened the oven in one fluid motion.

Frank led the way into the other room. "Do you want to stay for dinner?" he asked Molly. "You can have Billy's seat."

"I'll have to call home to make sure my dad's there. What about him?" She lifted her chin toward Billy.

"Only if he comes clean about the ghost," Frank said with finality.

In the front room, Billy sat on the couch, stalling. "Okay, I'll tell you what I know, but it's not much."

"Hold that thought." Molly motioned to the end table. "Can I use your phone, Frank?"

"Of course."

When Molly hung up, she smiled. "I can stay."

"Hold on! Don't start without me." Frank jumped to his feet and ran to the kitchen. "Two extra for dinner, Mom," he shouted too loudly. He ran breathlessly back to the front room and performed a home-plate slide on a throw rug, landing right on Billy's feet. Crossing his legs, he looked up at Billy expectantly.

Billy and Molly moved to the floor, and they sat in a circle.

## Chapter Fourteen

Molly leaned in and looked into Billy's dark eyes as he started to whisper. *The eyes are the windows of the soul. I'll know if he lies.*

"Two nights ago, I went up to the third floor to look around. Someone left a desk, a bed, and a dresser there. My mother called me down for dinner, and when I went back later, a book wrapped in an old cloth sat on the desk. I'm *positive* it wasn't there before."

Frank sucked in a breath.

Molly scrutinized Billy's face. "Are you sure you just didn't see it the first time?"

"Right in the middle of the desk. I couldn't have missed it."

"Go on," Frank said.

"The first page said, 'My Journal. Thomas Zachariah Packard.' The writing had all these curlicues. He wrote out the date and spelled out the numbers instead of just writing them. I don't remember much else, except," he paused, "he wrote out some kind of spell or something."

"A spell?" Molly asked.

"Yeah, you know, like: 'eye of newt and leg of lizard, mix it all up and shove it down your gizzard.'"

"That's not what it said." Molly poked a finger into Billy's chest. "You're holding out on us, Hashberger."

"I didn't memorize it. Something about the moon and sea and dark of night."

"*Did* you see him or not?" Molly demanded.

"I'm getting to that. The next day, from the street, I saw something in the attic window. It might have just been a shadow or something." Billy shrugged.

"That's what everyone says." Molly leaned in closer. "Someone stands in the attic window, looking through the bars."

"I think I saw it once." Frank's voice cracked. "Where is this journal?"

"I don't know. I mean, I read it again last night. It's kind of spooky. Anyway, when I went up there this morning, I couldn't find it."

"Show your guests where they can wash up for dinner," Mrs. Bordeaux said.

Molly was engrossed in Billy's story and started at Mrs. Bordeaux's voice.

"Be a dear, Francis, and put up two more place settings. Your father will be home any second now."

"Yes, Mother." He rolled his eyes and sighed as if that were too much to ask. "This way, guys." He stood up and pointed them toward the guest bathroom.

"Be a dear, Francis." Billy mimicked Frank's mother.

"Shush your mouth, Hashberger. She'll hear you," Molly said. Unable to resist adding her own barb, she looked at Frank. "Now, dear, where is the powder room?" She batted her eyelashes at Frank for good measure. Then she turned to Billy. "We're not done with you, Hashberger. Don't forget where you left off."

Frank's father came in just as they were helping put the food on the table.

"This meatloaf smells so good, Mrs. Bordeaux," Billy said.

They sat down, and Molly silently said grace and crossed herself discreetly. The dishes were passed around, and they began to eat.

"My mom never makes salad. This so good."

Mrs. Bordeaux blushed slightly. "Thank you, Billy."

"These mashed potatoes are amazing. What is that?" Billy pointed to a flake of something.

"I use garlic rosemary and thyme in the potatoes. Doesn't your mother use fresh spices?"

"My mother doesn't even use stale spices."

This prompted a round of laughter around the table. This time, Billy blushed.

"And this gravy is..."

"You're going to give her a big head if you keep telling her how delicious everything is, young man," Frank's father finally said.

After dinner, Mr. Bordeaux excused himself and moved to the front room with his newspaper and pipe.

"Help me to clear the table, Francis, and you can do your homework at the table."

They all helped clear the dishes. Then Mrs. Bordeaux shooed them out of the kitchen.

Molly looked at Billy expectantly. "Well?"

"Well, what?"

"Finish telling us about the journal?" Molly rolled her eyes.

"Yeah, and when can we read it?" Frank added.

"I told you, not much to tell. I haven't read it all yet." Billy flipped open his Social Studies book.

"Fine," Molly said. "What do you have to do?"

"In Social Studies, I have to answer the questions at the end of each unit until I catch up to where you guys are now," Billy said dully.

"Holy shit," Molly blurted out. "Oh, sorry, Jesus." Molly quickly made the sign of the cross and murmured a prayer with her hands pressed together.

Frank watched in awe, glancing from her to Billy and back to Molly again.

Molly opened her eyes. "What?"

"What are you doing?" Frank asked.

"Praying. Don't you ask for forgiveness when you curse?"

"I never pray, but you only said *shit*," Billy said.

"It's not as if S-H-I-T is the worst word you can use," Frank added.

"Just because you were raised as heathens, there's no reason for me to go to hell with you. I mean, we're friends and all, but a person has to draw the line somewhere, so I'm drawing it at burning in hell for all eternity. You got a problem with that?" Molly glared.

"No, no problem." Billy raised his hands in surrender. "I'm cool."

"Me too. I'm cool," Frank agreed.

They quickly completed ten chapters. Molly closed the book with finality.

"Ten chapters? Thanks, you guys."

Molly cleared her throat. "You should probably change a couple answers. It won't look good if you get them all correct."

Mrs. Bordeaux served them each a dish of ice cream.

Frank tapped his bowl with the spoon. "No harsh words over dessert. It's a house rule."

"I'm sure." Molly leaned over to Frank. "Is your father always so quiet?"

"Pretty much."

"What's he do?"

"He works over at the Naval Air Development Center. He can't tell anyone what he's working on. It's all secret government stuff."

"Secret like spy stuff?" Billy asked.

"Nah, he's an electrical engineer. He designs stuff."

"Speaking of fathers, I've got to get going. My old man is going to have a fit." Molly stood up.

"I should get going, too," Billy added.

"I'll get your coats," Frank said.

Frank helped Molly with her coat.

"Good night, Mr. and Mrs. Bordeaux," Molly said.

"Yeah, and thanks for dinner," Billy added.

Frank's father rustled the pages of his newspaper and grumbled something sounding like "good night."

"You're welcome, children," said Mrs. Bordeaux. "Come back anytime."

The cold air rushed past Molly as she walked out the door.

"I'll see you in the library with the candlestick," Frank said.

"You are such a nerd, Professor Plum," Molly yelled over her shoulder.

"See you tomorrow." Billy waved.

## Chapter Fifteen

Billy watched Molly's hair swirl around her face in the cold night air. "I can walk you home."

"No, you can't. I live in the other direction." She turned and started on her way.

"I don't mind, really."

"Just do as you're told, Hashberger. I'll see you in the library—early!" she yelled over her shoulder.

Billy backed down the street, keeping his eyes on Molly until she turned the corner. He ran home, oblivious to the freezing cold, as dry leaves flitted around his feet. Tony's red-and-white Impala turned in to the driveway just as Billy got home.

"You're getting home late." Billy blew warm air into his cupped hands.

"Yeah, the Weasel authorized overtime to finish loading a truck. How's the face?" Tony held the kitchen door open for Billy.

"It looks worse than it feels."

Tony's laugh stopped short when they saw what awaited them in the kitchen. On the table sat a plate with something masquerading as a meal. Congealed gravy covered the meat, which bore a strange resemblance to a sheet covering a corpse. Peas and mashed potatoes rounded out the ensemble. He pointed to the plate. "Is that for you or me?"

"I ate at my friend's house, so I'd say yours."

"Lucky me."

"Maybe you ate at a friend's house too?" Billy offered.

"Hey, Maude, sorry I'm late. I had to work overtime," Tony yelled from the kitchen.

Billy sensed Tony testing the waters.

"I'll go first." Billy walked into the living room. "Mom, I'm home."

Asleep in an overstuffed chair, wrapped in a comforter, an Erle Stanley Gardner book about to slip from her hand, she looked peaceful.

Billy took the book, being careful to keep her page. He set *The Case of the Horrified Heirs* on the end table then gently touched her hand. "Mom, I'm home."

She opened her eyes. "Oh, it's you."

"Yeah, Tony's in the kitchen. Eating his dinner," Billy lied. "He had to work late tonight."

"Oh, good." Her voice was weighted with sleep. "What time is it?"

"Almost eight."

"Do you have homework to do?"

"I did most of it at Frank's house. I've got a little reading to finish. I'll see you in the morning."

"Okay." She covered her mouth and yawned.

Billy went back to the kitchen and found Tony washing his plate. He suspected the bottom of the trashcan had eaten the dinner.

"It's safe," Billy said.

"I heard. Thanks, kid." Tony ruffled Billy's hair. "I owe you."

"That reminds me, thanks for writing my essay last night," Billy said.

Tony looked at him quizzically. "What essay?"

Billy froze for a moment, but recovered quickly. "I guess Mom did it then," he said nonchalantly. "See you tomorrow."

"Yeah, sleep tight, kid."

In the attic, Billy pulled the string for the overhead light and found the journal sitting in the center of the desk again. *I know it wasn't there this morning.* He slowly looked around the room for anything else out of place. He felt a presence in the room. *I'm not alone.* He opened the journal.

*November the Fourteenth, Nineteen Hundred Twenty-four*

*It sounds mad, but I flew again this night, gliding over fields and above rooftops. Free of this prison cell and free of the bonds of human form. I saw things as though for the first time. I perceived the most exquisite details. Every vein of a leaf still clinging to a branch stood out; the cold air passing through my feathers played a symphony.*

Billy continued reading even as his hands shook with the cold that encompassed him, recounting his own experience of flying in his dream last night. Bile rose in his throat, and he retched when Thomas talked of eating the creatures he caught during his flight. He recalled too well the sensation of tearing apart the rodent and swallowing the pieces. Thomas had closed the entry with the need to reach out to Tearneach to get advice on how to control his animal form. Cold proceeded to seep through Billy's skin, and he hunched forward against the chill. He continued reading through another entry, relieved to find no more details about flying. Thomas's father had come, angry about the pentagram he had drawn on the floor, and made plans with the pastor to send Thomas away. Billy felt ill. *What a terrible life! How long was he locked in this attic room? How long was he an outcast from his family?*

The room seemed to close in around Billy. He looked at the window, hoping to find the source of the cold. Instead, he found the letters *TZP* scratched into the frost that formed inside the glass.

"Who's there?" he croaked. His teeth chattered as the cold intensified. Barely able to control his urge to run from the room. He shouted, "What do you want?"

The letters appeared one at a time in the frost: R-E-S-T.

Billy's hands shook. The icy cold spread up both arms and into the rest of his body. He slowly backed out of the room and down the steps. His eyes were focused in front of him; he hoped he would be spared any additional apparitions. His hands trembled in time with his racing heart long after he sat down on his own bed.

*What just happened? Am I losing my mind?* Billy's thoughts raced around in his brain. The longer he sat, the harder it became to believe what had happened upstairs. *Another dream, maybe…* He absently rubbed at his bruised ribs, lost in thought, then his bedroom door slowly swung open. Billy jumped to his feet and backed against the window.

"Hey, kid, you left this in the kitchen." Tony held up Billy's notebook. He squinted at Billy. "Are you all right? You look like you've seen a ghost."

"Yeah, a ghost. Funny." He reached for his notebook.

Tony stepped into the room and put one hand on Billy's shoulder. "Should I send your mom up to check on you? You look kind of gray around the gills."

"Nah, I'm all right. Just tired, you know? Those kitchen chairs aren't all that comfortable."

"Did you tell your mom about the nightmare you had?" Tony absently touched the crucifix at his neck.

Billy shook his head. "She's kind of... ahh, busy, you know?"

"I don't want to get in the middle of whatever you two have got going on, but if you need to talk..." Tony patted him on the shoulder.

"Yeah, thanks, Tony. It's cool."

"See you tomorrow, then." Tony's smile returned to its usual place, a thousand gleaming watts strong.

"Yeah, see you tomorrow."

Tony pulled the door closed, leaving Billy alone with his thoughts.

---

Billy quietly walked into the kitchen, where Tony faced the stove, humming softly. When Billy's books thumped onto the table, Tony jumped and raised the spatula in a defensive position as he turned.

"Never sneak up on an Italian," Tony said, grinning.

"Why? Do they attack with kitchen utensils?"

"No, we usually faint. It's a survival instinct. We play dead until the shooting is over."

Billy laughed. "I'll remember to be noisier next time."

"Over easy?" Tony turned back to the stove.

"Sure, can I help?"

"Put the toast in." Tony cracked an egg into the pan with one hand. "No nightmares?"

"Do that again." Billy ignored the question while motioning at the eggs.

"Nothing up my sleeve, and presto." Tony added another egg to the pan. "So yes?"

"I flew, like an owl." Billy lifted out two slices of toast and put in two more. "Hunting for mice and stuff."

"You didn't come downstairs." Tony deftly flicked the pan in the air and flipped the eggs over in one smooth motion.

"Too tired." Billy buttered the toast. "You know, flying really takes it out of you. I just fell back asleep."

"You okay?"

"Yeah. I mean, I don't like the dreams, but I figure maybe it's the new house and all."

"You could be right." He turned the eggs out onto a plate. "Batter up," he said, sliding the plate onto the table.

Billy set out two forks and the toast before he sat down and poked at a round patty on his plate. "What's this?"

"It's a potato cake, from the leftover mashed potatoes. I doctored them up a little. Try it!"

"Mmm, that's good. Where did you learn to cook, anyway?"

"In the army. I served my time in Korea cooking for a MASH unit near the front."

"As in *mash* potatoes?" Billy chuckled at his own joke.

"No, wise guy, as in the Mobile Army Surgical Hospital. The 8076."

"I didn't know you were in the army."

"It's not something I talk about outside." Tony's smile wavered. "I mean, with civilians."

"Oh, I'm sorry I brought it up." He cleared the table and poured coffee for Tony, who stared into the distance.

"It wasn't all bad. We had our moments. We patched up too many kids who weren't much older than you. A lot of them made it home because we were there."

Billy started washing the dishes. "What about the others?"

"Let's not go there."

"What do you think about Vietnam?"

"Let's not go there, either. Tell me about how you made out at school yesterday with the remodeled face."

"I made a couple of friends."

"A treaty with the guys who did that?" Tony lifted his mug and gestured at Billy's face.

"Hardly. Two other kids who don't seem to get along with them, either. We're like the class misfits."

Tony laughed, spilling his coffee. "Shit, I've got to get outta here," he said as he looked up at the clock. "I'll see you tonight, kid. Keep your head down."

"Yeah, I'll try."

## Chapter Sixteen

Molly tucked her chin in against the wind as she approached the school. She moved through the door swiftly and pulled off her mittens before unwrapping her scarf.

"Good morning, Miss Molly."

She jumped and turned. "Good morning, Shorty. How are things?"

"Any better, I'd be twins." He leaned on a large dust mop.

"Wow, double your pleasure." She stuffed her mittens and scarf into her coat pockets.

"When you get to be my age, you just' glad the Lord give you another day."

"I hope he keeps giving you days."

"Not too many now, jus' enough." Shorty pulled a scraper out of his back pocket and bent to the floor.

Molly mulled that over. How many days were enough? Had her mother or her brothers gotten enough days? She shook her head grimly. "Have you seen Frank this morning?"

"Surely did. He's in the library."

"Figures. He's an overachiever."

"He's a smart one." Shorty examined something stuck to the scraper. "Isn't he?"

"He's smart, all right. I'd better catch up to him before he gets too smart. See you later."

"Good day, Miss Molly." Shorty swirled the mop around and started down the corridor.

She stopped at her locker first then headed to the library. Frank already had his nose in a book.

"Hey, Frank."

"Good morning." His face erupted in a smile.

"No sign of Billy yet?"

Frank shook his head. "Not yet."

Molly pulled out a chair. "I hope he shows."

"He will be here." Frank paused. "What do you think of him?"

"He's not the brightest bulb in the chandelier, but he's seems okay." In truth, Molly was still trying to get a read on the new kid. "He's guarded. That makes him hard to trust."

The library door was flung open before she could ask Frank how he felt about Billy.

"Billy, over here," Frank shouted.

Molly punched Frank in the shoulder.

"You're in a library, for Pete's sake." She flipped her hair over her shoulder.

Billy grinned. "You're going to get us thrown out of here if you don't knock it off." He pulled out a chair and dropped into it with a groan.

"What's wrong with you now?" she asked.

"My ribs still hurt like hell."

"Get over it, already. That's yesterday's news." Molly dismissed Billy's complaint with a wave of her hand.

Frank pulled his chair in close to the table and looked at Billy intently.

"What?" Billy scooted his chair in.

Molly reached across the table with her hand open.

"Let's have it, Hashberger, or I'll turn you over to O'Riley and his thugs."

"Have what?"

"The journal, you twit. Unless you made it up."

"I forgot it." He shrugged.

Frank reached over and scattered Billy's books across the table. "It's not here."

"How could you forget it?" Molly asked. "Maybe you *are* as dumb as you look."

"Let me explain," Billy whined. "This may sound a little crazy…"

"We're all ears." Molly crossed her arms and leaned back.

"I haven't told you guys everything." Billy moved closer and lowered his voice. "First of all, the other day when we had the extra assignment, I fell asleep working on it. I never finished it. But the next morning, there it sat, as pretty as you please. The first time I found the journal, it lay in the middle of the desk. No matter where I leave it, when I come back, it's always in the middle of the desk."

"If you're making this up, I'm going to beat the crap of out you myself." The sound of her knuckles popping broke the quiet.

"Last night, when I went upstairs, the journal sat in the middle of the desk again. While I read, the room got cold. I looked at the window to make sure it was closed all the way and saw the initials TZP scratched into the frost."

"No way." Frank gnawed vigorously at his nails.

Molly leaned across the table. "That's it, I'm going to beat the crap out of you right now."

"I thought you believed in all this ghost stuff?"

"Seeing a shadow from across the street is one thing, but when you start telling me a ghost is scratching his initials into the frost on your window… You're pushing your luck, Hashberger."

"Listen to me," he pleaded. "It's true. I didn't believe it myself until last night."

"Continue your story. You saw his initials in the frost. Then what?" Frank tilted his chin down and peered over his glasses, attempting to look stern.

"I freaked out. So, I said, 'What do you want?' Then, right before my eyes, I saw four letters form in the frost as I watched. R-E-S-T."

"Why does he want you to rest?" Frank asked.

"I don't know. And I didn't stick around to find out."

Molly whispered, "Were you scared?"

"Well, a little, I guess."

"Oh bull! If you're telling the truth, you were crapping your pants, and you know it!" She tried to make ghost noises. "Ooo, ooo, ooo."

"Ahem, excuse me," the librarian sniffed. "Even though you are the only three students in here, I still expect you to respect the library regulations. This is *not* the playground." The librarian glared at them, then she turned and left as quickly as she had appeared.

"Sorry, Mrs. Esposito," Frank said softly.

Molly pointed at the clock mounted above the door. "We should get to class anyway."

The three of them filed out of the library and walked shoulder to shoulder along the corridors, which were now bustling with students. Suddenly, O'Riley cut in front of them, Sal and Ernie on his heels. Molly stopped and extended an arm, forcing Billy and Frank to come to a halt.

"Oh look, boys. The bus from Loserville just pulled in," O'Riley sneered.

"At least we don't ride the short bus to school," Frank said.

"Watch it, Lardo, or your face will match Hamburger's," O'Riley threatened, faking a punch.

Frank flinched, eliciting a laugh and a snort from Sal and Ernie.

"Go ahead, take a swing." Molly thrust her notebook at Frank hard enough to knock him back a step.

"You keep it up, Hooligan, and you'll end up in jail with the drunk who killed my brother." O'Riley poked a finger into her shoulder. "So back off."

"You don't talk about my brother."

"Watch me."

Molly's muscles tensed, and her heart rate throbbed at her temples. She stepped forward, turning slightly to her right. Without thinking, she threw a quick left that connected solidly with O'Riley's nose. His head snapped back, and he sprawled on the floor. Molly moved forward and stood over him. "I warned you about laying your filthy hands on me before."

A chant immediately started around them in the corridor. "Fight! Fight! Fight!"

"I've had enough of your shit. Everybody knows my brother wasn't driving that car. I don't know what strings your daddy pulled, but if you say anything else about my family, I will rip your arm off and beat you over the head with the bloody end. So you want to try again, O'Riley? Get up! Come on. Not so tough when you're bleeding on the floor."

Molly watched his eyes the way her brothers had taught her. She saw his surprise transform into rage. He scrambled to his feet, glaring. Molly assumed the boxer's stance her brothers had taught her. O'Riley got to his feet and lunged at her, swinging wildly. She slipped his punch, stepped in, and punched him in the stomach with her right before coming around and catching him square in the side of his face with her left. He looked up from the floor again, blood trickling from the corner of his mouth and his nose. The crowd was chanting, "Fight! Fight! Fight!"

Billy and Frank stared at Molly in amazement.

"What are you two looking at?" Molly's voice quivered.

"Enough!" A teacher moved down the hall toward them. The teacher seized Molly by one elbow and stood her against the wall. "Stay." He pointed his long index finger in her face. "Unless the rest of you want to spend the next week with me in detention, you will get to your classrooms *now*."

The crowd quickly dispersed. Billy and Frank went to Molly's side and stood with her while the corridor emptied with lightning speed.

"Salvatore, help Mr. O'Riley to the nurse's office."

"Yes, Mr. Amato." Sal bent to help O'Riley up off the floor.

"Mr. Amato, can I be of assistance?" Miss Albright asked.

"Yes, thank you. You might want to stop Mr. Pasquale before he escapes." Mr. Amato indicated Ernie, who surreptitiously backed away from the scene. "I'm sure he knows something about what happened here."

Ernie assumed his most innocent expression and looked up. "Who, me? I didn't see nothin'."

"Yes, I'm sure you didn't see *anything*. Just the same, come along," Miss Albright said.

"B-but, I didn't," Ernie protested.

"Humor me." Miss Albright grabbed him by the ear and led him down the corridor. She stopped at the door to her classroom and surveyed her flock. "I trust everyone who is talking has read the assignment on the board?"

Mr. Amato looked down at Molly, Frank, and Billy with a bemused expression. "Are you okay, Molly? Do you need to see the nurse?"

"My hand hurts a little, but I'm okay."

Mr. Amato turned his head, unable to stifle his laughter. "Let me have a look." He took Molly's left hand, flexed it, and examined her knuckles. "A little ice is all you need."

"Mr. Amato," Frank started, "Molly was only defending herself. O'Riley started it, and she decked him."

"Save it, Frank." He escorted Billy, Molly, and Frank to the principal's office. "Sit down." Mr. Amato motioned toward a bench in the corridor. He looked at Billy. "I don't know you. What's your name?"

"William Hashberger. I'm new."

"What happened to your face?"

"I fell down on the way home from school a few days ago," Billy said, breaking eye contact.

"I see. Did Mr. O'Riley have anything to do with your fall?"

"I tripped over something. End of story."

"Have it your way. I'll tell Mr. Brady you're waiting for him." Mr. Amato walked into the main office.

"Where did you learn to do that?" Billy asked.

"More importantly, can you teach me how to do it?" Frank shadowboxed on the bench. "Pow! Pow! You were great!"

"I have four bro... had—" Tears interrupted the explanation, and she buried her face in her shaking hands. Adrenaline had flooded her system, and now she was left with no means to expend what remained. "I'm dead. My dad's going to kill me when he finds out."

"Why?" Billy leaned forward on the bench, looking around Frank. "You stood up for yourself. End of story."

"You don't understand. He might *really* kill me."

"What about your mom?" Billy asked.

Molly lost what little control she had left and started sobbing.

"Her mom died," Frank said softly.

"I'm so sorry." Billy reached across Frank and touched her arm.

Molly shook him off. "Shut up, all right? Just shut up." She wiped away her tears with the back of her hands.

Mr. Amato returned with a bag of ice. "Keep that on your knuckles."

She mumbled her thanks and nodded.

## Chapter Seventeen

Billy sat back, feeling more alone than ever since moving to Willowton. He was bewildered by the flashes of information that came at him too fast to understand. *How do these things happen, and why do they always happen to me?*

Mrs. Spencer leaned out the door. "Molly, Mr. Brady will see you now."

When she had gone in, Billy asked, "Why is she so upset?"

"Molly's mom died when she was a baby. Even before I knew her. Then two of her brothers were killed in an accident, and another one was driving. So he got convicted of manslaughter and is in prison. The oldest brother joined the army, and as far as I know, he's probably in Vietnam. Her grandmother has dementia, and her dad…"

"What about her dad?" Billy moved to look Frank in the eyes.

"Never mind. Isn't that enough"

"Yeah, and I thought my life sucked."

"I think it was Ghandi who said, 'I cried because I had no shoes, until I met a man who had no feet.'"

Billy knocked on Frank's head. "How do you fit all this stuff in there?"

Frank shrugged.

"What's gonna happen to her now?"

"It's an automatic five-day suspension for fighting. Which means O'Riley's out of here too."

"He never touched her, unless you count hitting her in the hand with his face," Billy said.

Frank laughed. "I know. Pow! Pow!" He threw two punches in the air and sent his glasses flying.

Billy watched Frank grope for his glasses. But he was thinking about Molly, wondering how she coped. *I can't even imagine.* "I hope she's all right."

They sat in silence. Billy stared up the hall toward the exit. He wanted to run for the door to get as far away as he could from here.

"Frank, Mr. Brady is waiting for you," Mrs. Spencer called out.

Frank disappeared into the office, leaving Billy with his thoughts. O'Riley and Sal made their way up the corridor toward him. He felt sick to his stomach at the thought of them catching him alone in the hall. *Could today get any worse?*

If Molly's story was any indication, the answer was a resounding yes. The nurse came into view, walking purposefully behind them. He let out the breath he'd been holding. The nurse's shoes squeaked in an apparent objection to being pressed into the polished floor by her size. Billy marveled at the strength of the white fabric of her uniform, which contrasted with the dark color of her skin. *It must be as strong as steel to hold back the avalanche of fat roiling under its taut surface.*

The bag of ice that O'Riley held against his face failed to hide the malicious leer he directed at Billy. The nurse opened the door to the office and ushered O'Riley and Sal inside.

---

Ernie, Sal, and Frank had all returned to class. Billy fidgeted awaiting Mrs. Spencer summons.

As if on cue, the office door opened, and Mrs. Spencer stuck her head out. "William."

She escorted him right past Molly and O'Riley and into the principal's office.

Billy stood before the desk while Mr. Brady ignored his presence.

Mr. Brady finally looked up as if unaware Billy had been cooling his jets for a couple minutes. "Well, Mr. Hashberger, I can't say I'm happy about meeting a new student under these circumstances." He had hands the size of baseball mitts. The military crew cut and stern expression indicated a low tolerance for bad behavior. He tapped a pencil on his desk blotter. "What do you have to say for yourself?"

"I don't have anything to say for myself, sir. I didn't do anything."

"Mr. O'Riley disputes that. Why don't you tell me what happened?"

He described what had happened earlier in the corridor, including the insult to Molly's family prompting her to punch O'Riley. When he finished, he desperately tried to hold back the grin spreading across his face.

"Do you find something amusing about this incident?"

"The look on O'Riley's face was pretty funny."

Mr. Brady rose out of his chair, shot his arm across his desk, and caught Billy by the front of his shirt. "This is no laughing matter, son. This is a serious infraction of school policy, and at least two students will be suspended, if not all six of you."

Billy watched as Mr. Brady's ruddy complexion rapidly turned a frightening shade of red. "I'll want to see your parents in this office tomorrow so I can inform them insubordination will not be tolerated in my school."

"Yes, sir," Billy rasped out.

Mr. Brady released his grip and sat down heavily. The chair squeaked in protest. "Let me make one thing clear." He paused, looking down at the file lying on his desk. "William, this is a small school. Not much happens around here I don't know about. The incident in the cafeteria on your first day, for example."

Still shaking from the sudden attack by Mr. Brady, Billy nodded. "But that was an accident."

"How did you get the shiner?"

"I tripped on my way home from school."

"You are either very clumsy or lying. Which is it?" Mr. Brady demanded.

"I guess I'm pretty clumsy." He looked at the floor in front of Mr. Brady's desk.

"I'm keeping an eye on you, young man. Straighten up your act."

"Yes, sir." Billy swallowed the lump forming in his throat.

"You're excused. Mrs. Spencer will give you give a pass to return to class. One more thing, get a haircut."

Billy nodded again. He could detect the anger simmering in Mr. Brady, but it puzzled him. Why was he so mad? That kind of thing had happened at Billy's old school all the time. Kids got suspended every day. Billy had been suspended once. The principal had lectured him about falling in with the wrong crowd, but hadn't blown a gasket.

Mrs. Spencer was at her desk, whispering into the phone, when Billy walked out. Molly sat in one corner of the room while O'Riley nursed his damaged ego in the other. Billy tried to make eye contact with Molly, but she refused to look up at him. Mrs. Spencer did, however, and gave him a signal to stay away from Molly. She finally hung up without saying a word.

"This is your pass to return to class, William." She held out a slip of paper. "What is your phone number?"

"We don't have a phone yet."

"I'll have to give you a letter to take to your mother. Come back at the end of the day. Can I count on you?"

"Yeah."

"Very well. I'll see you then."

He left without another word. Molly finally looked up as he backed out the door. Her eyes were red and puffy, but underneath, a defiant look held its own. He tried to smile as he shut the door. The thought of running from O'Riley and his henchmen for the rest of his life or until his mother moved them again cluttered his head during his walk back to class. He had a good idea which would come first.

## Chapter Eighteen

Frank was still shaken by the threat he and Billy had received from O'Riley's thugs at his locker. Billy didn't look like he was handling it any better. They slowly headed to the office to pick up Billy's letter.

Molly sat where he'd last seen her. Billy opened the door, and they quietly slipped inside. No sign of Mrs. Spencer.

Frank sat next to Molly. "You okay?"

She shrugged, pointed toward Mr. Brady's office, and held a finger to her lips. Frank understood she was trying to listen in. Then Mr. Brady's voice boomed, "He's either at work or wetting his whistle at Moe's. Send her home with a letter."

The door to the inner office opened, and Mrs. Spencer walked out, shaking her head. "William, have you been waiting long?"

"I just walked in."

Mrs. Spencer picked up an envelope from her desk and handed it to Billy. "See that your parents get this. Mr.

Brady wants to see them. Is there something I can do for you, Francis?"

"I'm waiting for Billy."

"Of course you are." She motioned to the door. "Wait outside."

Frank went to the door. "Can Molly leave?"

"She needs to wait for a letter to her father before she can go." She sat down and rolled paper into her typewriter. "If you're waiting for her, do it outside."

"Yes, ma'am." Frank pulled open the door, then he and Billy hurried out.

"Geez, what's with everyone today?" Billy swept a hand through his unruly hair. "Is there a full moon or something?"

Frank had a similar thought. They watched through the plate-glass window as Molly received her letter. Molly walked out of the office, her head held high, and started toward the main entrance.

Frank stumbled then took several quick steps to stand in front of her. "Are you crazy? We can't go out the front."

"Frank's right. Let's go through the cafeteria," Billy said.

"O'Riley won't be waiting for us today." Molly shouldered her way past Frank and continued toward the front door.

"How can you be so sure?" Billy blocked her at the door. "He's going to want revenge."

"I saw his old man drag him out of the office. I don't know if he was pissed because Derrick got suspended or because a girl split his lip open. Either way, I don't think there's any chance he's waiting for me." Molly forced a smile. "And if he is, he'll get another helping of whoop ass. Now get out of my way."

Billy stepped aside.

"Are you coming over?" Frank asked.

"I have to deliver this." Molly waved the sealed envelope in the air.

"Just for a few minutes," Frank pleaded.

"I told you I have to go home to see what my dad has to say about this. The suspense is killing me, and I wouldn't want to take *that* pleasure away from him," she said bitterly.

"Why would your dad be mad at you for standing up to a bully like O'Riley?" Billy asked.

"If you were from around here, you'd know. O'Riley's old man owns this town and everyone in it. Including Mr. Tough Guy Brady and my father. How do you think he'll take the news his only daughter beat up his boss's son?"

"I don't know, but—"

"But nothing!" Molly interrupted. "My old man is going to have a fit, and it won't be pretty. So just go have your cookies and cocoa at Frank's and leave me alone!"

Billy put a hand on Frank's shoulder. "We'll walk you home. Maybe if we explain what happened…"

"*Nobody* is walking me home. I can take care of myself. I think I've made that pretty clear already today."

No one talked until they reached Larch Street, which ran parallel to the railroad tracks. Frank knew they needed each other more than ever now. He also knew Molly well enough to know there was little chance of changing her mind once she had made it up. Molly continued straight across the street.

Frank stopped on the corner. "I guess we'll see you later?"

Molly waved a dismissive hand and yelled back, "Yeah, sure."

Billy tugged on Frank's sleeve. "Let's go." He followed after Molly.

When she reached the curb, she spun on her heel and glared at them as they hurried to catch up with her. "What do you think you're doing?"

"The last time I checked, we still live in a free country." Billy raised his head high. "We can go anywhere we want."

"You're free to get another black eye too."

"But we're the Three Musketeers." Frank waved an inclusive arm. "We have to stick together."

"More like the Three Misfiteers if you ask me," Billy said. "Either way, you're going to have to trust me and Frank."

"Right," Frank chimed in, not sounding completely convinced. Molly smiled. Frank sensed her defenses failing.

"The Misfiteers, I like it. Not bad for a dummy from Masonville. I'll let you walk me as far as the railroad crossing *if* you can name the all three Musketeers." She looked at Billy.

Frank started to speak, but Molly cut him off before he could utter a single sound. "No help from you, Brainiac."

He glanced at Frank.

"Thirty seconds," she said.

"Wait, I just need to think. Aramis, Porthos, and…"

Molly shot out her hand, holding it in front of Frank's face. "Not a word."

"I didn't say anything." Frank was bursting at the seams to blurt the correct answer.

"Just in case," Molly said, threatening Frank.

"Shh, it's…" Billy scratched his head. "Athos! Right?"

Molly stared at him with reluctant approval. "I thought you'd guess d'Artagnan for sure."

"Yeah, I guess I'm smarter than I look."

"Thank God." Frank held up his hands. "Wait! Don't hit me."

"I'd never hit you. That's her job." Billy smiled.

"What are you grinning at?" Molly asked, pointing a finger at Frank.

"I'm grinning at my friends."

They marched off together side by side. "You should've seen Frank imitating you this morning. He knocked off his own glasses—pow, pow." Billy threw two uncoordinated punches to show Molly.

"Is that true?" Molly asked.

"Well, yeah, but you were great. Tell her." Frank flailed his arms wildly. "Pow, pow." Once again, his glasses flew from his face.

Molly retrieved Frank's glasses as her laugh echoed along the deserted street. "If you keep it up, you're going to give *yourself* a black eye."

"What are you going to do now?" Frank asked Molly.

"Sleep late and watch *General Hospital*. Nothing else to do."

"Won't they let you back in school if your dad talks to the principal? That's the way it worked in Masonville," Billy said.

"Sure. He'll just throw himself on the mercy of the court, and all my problems will just go away." Molly snapped her fingers in the air. "This is Willowton. O'Riley's old man will get him out of his suspension, I'm sure. My old man, on the other hand—"

"What?" Billy pushed.

Molly stopped at the railroad crossing and turned to face Billy and Frank. "Someone has to pay, and that someone is me." She paused. "Don't look now, but I think we have company."

Frank turned his head in time to see two shadows move out of view. "Oh, shit."

"Do you kiss your mother with that mouth? I told you not to look."

"Who is it?" Billy asked.

"It's Sal and Ernie. Follow me. We'll lose them in my neighborhood." Molly turned and walked away at a brisk pace. Daylight faded quickly as Molly made a series of left and right turns. She stopped in a trash-strewn alley and pushed the boys up against a tall wooden fence. The fence threatened to give way under their weight.

"Don't talk and stay right here." Molly moved toward the end of the alley.

The alley smelled of rotting garbage and stale urine. A distant streetlight bled a yellow circle of light near the end of the alley where Molly's silhouette crept along. Billy nudged Frank and pointed as Sal and Ernie walked under the light, looking around as though they were lost.

Molly returned. "They'll be wandering around for hours."

"So, will we. I've never been here before," Frank said with a nervous laugh.

"It's easy. Follow this alley to the end. Make a left and the first right. Keep going until you get to the tracks. Follow them to the old mill. That's Spruce Street. You should be able to find your way home from there."

"What about you?" Billy asked.

"I'm going home."

"Meet us at Frank's house tomorrow after school. We'll bring your homework for you."

"You really know how to take a girl's breath away, don't you?" Molly placed both hands over her heart and pretended to swoon.

"How about the journal, then?" Billy asked.

"Now you're talking. If I can get out of the house, I'll meet you at Frank's tomorrow." With a wave, Molly left them standing there.

Frank started walking in the other direction until Billy pulled him back. "Wait here."

When Molly disappeared around the corner, they followed after her, hurrying to catch up. When he reached the end of the alley, he peeked around the corner and saw her turn left again.

"What are you doing?"

"Shh! Come on, before we lose her." Billy ran to the next corner.

"There she is." Frank pointed.

"Yeah, she's going into that house."

They crept along until they stood outside Molly's house. The blue light of a television flickered through a window. Suddenly, the window flared with light, brightening the weed-choked yard.

A male voice shouted inside the house. "What did you do now?"

"Maybe you should read this tomorrow, when you're feeling better," Frank heard Molly say.

"Give it to me now!" The words were harsh.

The house went quiet for a moment. Frank rubbed at the back of his neck. The silence bothered him more than the shouting. The sound of breaking glass shattered the otherwise-quiet night. A heavy glass ashtray came flying through the window and landed in the yard.

"Are you trying to get me fired? Is that what you want?"

"No, Dad. He's a bully. He's always pushing me and my friends around," Molly said.

"Oh well, that's a whole different story altogether then. Nobody should embarrass you in front of your friends. Not if they know what's good for them." The voice had a mean, sarcastic edge.

"He's mean and arrogant, and I'm tired of taking his

shit." Molly's voice came through the broken window defiantly.

"We should go," Frank said, tugging at Billy's sleeve.

"Yes, of course, and you're going to change all that. Meanwhile, your Mamo and I can live in a cardboard box under the bridge because you decided to pop the son of my paycheck."

"Maybe you wouldn't spend so much time at Moe's if you didn't have a job!" Molly yelled back.

Frank heard another loud crash, and he pushed Billy down the street. "Come on, we shouldn't be here."

"Do you think she'll be all right? I mean, she did say he might kill her." Billy turned and faced Frank at the end of the street.

"It's just an expression. Haven't you ever said your parents were going to kill you for something you did?"

Billy nodded as he remembered telling Miss Albright his mother would kill Tony if he ever laid a hand on him. She might beat him within an inch of his life, but she would never really kill him. "I guess you're right."

"There's the mill," Frank pointed to a tall building covered in leafless vines.

Billy looked up at the brick structure looming over them. "What did it mill?"

"It's a textile mill. They make yarn."

"You mean that creepy place is still being used?"

"Yeah, if you work really hard, O'Riley's old man might give you a job someday."

A large shadow passed over them, and Frank looked up and heard the ominous rustle of wings.

## Chapter Nineteen

"I can throw things too," Molly shouted, overturning a chair in front of her father before she ran up the stairs. She collapsed in the overstuffed chair next to her grandmother's bed, crying hard. A frail hand marked by blue veins showing through the dry-papery skin reached out to her.

"What is it, my child?" Mamo stroked Molly's hand.

"Oh, Mamo, Daddy's drunk again, and…" Molly looked into her grandmother's green eyes, surprised to find the usual, vacant stare replaced by an alert and sympathetic look. The door to Mamo's bedroom opened, and Molly's enraged father strode in.

"Get out, Paddy! Molly and me are having women talk here." Mamo gave him a stern look and dismissed him with a wave of her withered hand.

Molly watched her father pull back in surprise before closing the door softly. Molly shook her head at the way this small, frail woman had just ordered a man as large and imposing as her father to leave. She began to wonder what kind of power the woman had held over her son all these years.

"He drinks too much. God knows that's the truth. Do not judge him too harshly. It seems the Lord has seen fit to give him more than his share of troubles. Ever since your mum died, God bless her, he's not been the same."

Molly looked at the portraits of JFK and Pope Paul VI, which hung side by side on the dingy wall across from where she sat. "I'm in trouble, Mamo. I punched the son of Daddy's boss at school."

"That wouldn't be the O'Riley boy, would it, now?" Mamo's hand squeezed Molly's.

Molly sniffled and nodded.

"Aye, if he's cut from the same cloth as his father, he deserved it, of that I'm sure." Moving slowly, Molly's grandmother reached for a box of tissues on the cluttered nightstand and handed it to Molly. Her shaky hand patted Molly's leg. "There, there. Things have a way of working themselves out."

"But Daddy's so mad. He thinks he'll get fired." Molly blew her nose. "Because of me."

"At the heart of every injustice lie three things: greed, lies, and rage. I'm sure he'll pay a price for your short temper, but O'Riley likes lording his position over your father. Don't worry yourself over it."

Molly blew her nose and swiped at her tears with a tissue. "Why are there always three things?" Mamo's emerald green eyes were as bright and clear as Molly could ever remember them.

"It's just the way of things." Mamo sat up straighter in her bed. "I'm feeling a bit peckish. Would you fetch us some tea? Maybe you could find a couple of biscuits for an old woman's sweet tooth, as well."

Molly looked at her doubtfully. Her grandmother ate so little these days, any strength at all surprised Molly. "Sure, but Daddy—"

"He's probably sleeping it off by now. If he gives you any trouble, you tell him I want to see him."

Mamo knew her son very well—his snores resonated from his bedroom. Molly put the kettle on and found a tin of butter cookies in the pantry. After arranging everything on a tray, she headed back to Mamo's room. Molly nudged her grandmother's door open with her foot, and came into the room expecting to find her asleep. Instead, she was sitting up in bed, knitting.

"Tea's ready." It had been far too long since Molly had seen her grandmother this alert. She felt a strange mixture of relief and sadness.

"Set the tray down here, child," Mamo said, patting the edge of her bed. "You're the image of your mother. Quite the beauty in her day, she was. What she saw in my Paddy, I'll never know."

"Tell me about her." Molly fixed her grandmother's tea, carefully filling the delicate china cup.

"Praise the saints, she possessed a rare beauty, just like you. Paddy worshiped the ground she walked on. He would have done anything for her." Her delicate hand shook as it brought the cup to her lips.

"I don't remember much about her."

"You were just a baby when the Lord took her from us. You have the same fire in your eyes. She ruled the roost around here. Your four brothers, and even your daddy, wouldn't so much as lift an eyebrow when she laid down the law."

Molly sniffled, and her eyes filled with tears again. "Why did she die so young?"

"She got very sick after you were born. She had some good days and some bad, but she never recovered. Doctor's said she had lung cancer."

"Lung cancer? Did she smoke cigarettes?"

"Sure, everyone did back then. Your dad had to sell the mill to pay her hospital bills. Your *seanair* must've rolled over in his grave the day your daddy sold his share of the mill to O'Riley." Mamo got a faraway look in her eyes. "No loss in my mind. T'was bought with blood money. That godforsaken mill made your grandfather prideful. Things were never the same after."

"Like what?"

"We moved into the big, drafty house on Congress Street next door to the O'Rileys. My Noel and Miles were as thick as thieves."

Molly sat up straighter. "That would be Derick O'Riley's grandfather."

"Yes, he and your grandfather were…" Her voice grew quiet, and a distant look came over her face. "Run along now; I'm tired. Thank you for the tea, dear."

"But what about the mill? Wait, you can't say something like that and then just go to sleep!" *Too late.*

Mamo's head rolled to the side, and her eyes closed. Thoughts raced around in Molly's head. *What blood money? Whose blood?* She picked up the tray and headed downstairs again. After putting away the teacups, she went outside and picked her way through the dark to recover the ashtray. She did her best to cover the broken window with tape and cardboard, which kept some of the cold from flowing into the house. Loneliness descended on her, and she suddenly felt the absence of Frank and Billy more sharply.

Everything would be different if only her brothers were still home. The tears threatened to return, so she busied herself with cleaning up the rest of the mess in the front room and throwing away her father's empty bottles. The house smelled of stale beer. Her thoughts returned to what Mamo had said about her father's love for her mother and how he had sold the mill to pay for her care. She'd heard the family had fallen on hard times, but she knew very few details.

Why had it been a secret? She knew Brendan was in Vietnam but had no idea how to reach him. Patrick was her only hope. With the doors and the lights out, she walked through the dark house to check on Mamo. Back in her own bedroom, she wrote to Patrick, telling him about her fight with O'Riley, although she left out why she had lost her temper. She included what she had heard from Mamo about the mill, as well as all of her questions. She demanded answers and closed with the hope he would provide them for the sake of their family. After she sealed the envelope, she affixed a six-cent stamp and went to bed. Sleep eluded her for a long time as the day's events reeled through her mind.

Billy and Frank occupied her last thought before she finally fell asleep. She wondered if they had gotten home all right. Images of angry faces and the phrase "blood money" haunted her dreams.

## Chapter Twenty

Frank's mother met them at the door. "You boys are late tonight." She gave Frank a reproachful look. "Your father will be home in a few minutes, and I have to get dinner on the table."

Frank was not familiar with this tone in his mother's voice, but he recognized it for what it was. "I guess that means no hot chocolate."

"Not tonight. Your father will want to talk to you about the call I got from Mr. Brady today, so I'm afraid Billy can't stay."

Frank walked him to the curb.

"Why don't you meet me here?" Frank asked.

"It's two blocks out of my way. I'll see you in the library." Frank walked slowly back into the house. Staring out the front window, he waited for his father to come home. He'd never been in real trouble before and didn't know what to do. He wiped his sweaty palms on his shirt and went to seek his mother's advice.

His mother looked disheveled.

"Can I help with something?" he asked.

"You can tell me where you've been." The dish she pulled out of the oven was accompanied by a puff of dark smoke. "I was worried."

Frank had never seen smoke come from his mother's oven. "We walked Molly home to make sure she was okay."

"What exactly happened at school today?" She set a blackened roast chicken on a serving platter and shook her head in exasperation.

"I didn't do anything. I'm guilty of watching Molly punch Derrick O'Riley. That's it." Frank shoved his hands into his pockets to stop them from waving around in the air.

"That would be the Houlahan girl."

"We're friends, Mother. Derrick O'Riley has been bullying Molly and me for years." His right hand escaped his pocket to emphasize the word *years*. "Just the other night, they beat up Billy."

She looked at him, the large spoon in her hand poised in the air halfway to the bowl of roasted potatoes. "Is that what happened to his face?"

"That's only the half of it. You should see his ribs. He won't tell anyone, but I think they might be broken."

"Why haven't you ever told me about any of this?"

"I'm not the only one. Derrick bullies a lot of kids. He's always gotten away with it too, until today."

His mother set the spoon down and hugged him. "Are you telling me that all those times you said you fell on your way home—"

He hugged her back, feeling a little weird. He heard her sniffle. "I'm not as clumsy as you might think." Frank tilted his head back and grinned.

"Oh, Francis." She pulled his head into her chest. "Why didn't you tell me?"

*Okay, now this is beyond weird.* "Mother! I can't breathe." He extricated himself from his mother's embrace. "Because you would have walked me to school. You'd probably have escorted me to every class, maybe even cut my meat for me at lunch."

"I would have done anything to protect you!" She sobbed.

"Exactly, Mother. But I'm a big boy now. I've got to learn to take care of myself."

She put her hands on her hips. "Just how are you taking care of yourself?" she demanded.

"I haven't been doing too good so far, but I'm learning. I learned that having friends helps keep my head out of the toilet." He laughed at how stupid that sounded.

His mother looked at him with swollen red eyes and smiled. She glanced ruefully at the ruined meal. "I've burned dinner."

"I thought I noticed something weird." This time, they laughed together.

"What's your father going to say?"

"I feel like Chinese. Who's coming with me?"

Frank jumped at the sound of his father's voice behind him.

"Oh, Milton, how long have you been standing there?" She wiped her tears away with her apron.

"Just long enough to get a craving for Chinese food."

"But the kitchen, and-and I'm a mess."

"Yes, I know. I think it's a little bit wonderful." He smiled, pulled his bow tie crooked, and ruffled Frank's hair. "Come on. Hop Sing won't wait all night." He turned around and gestured for them to follow him. "Let's go. The car is still warm."

Frank sat between them in the front seat of the car for the first time in years. It made him feel like he was a baby again. His mother had insisted until he crawled in next to his father. This night certainly kept getting stranger and stranger.

"When was the last time we went out for Chinese food?" his father asked.

"That's easy. Never!" Frank said.

"I was talking to your mother."

"Milton. Please don't bring that up."

"It's time our son knew the truth, Blanche. Are you going to tell him, or shall I?"

"I'm certainly not going to tell him, and neither should you."

Frank chewed his nails, and butterflies fluttered in his stomach. "Did you find me in a basket on the porch steps?"

"Oh, Francis, how can you say such a thing?" His mother nudged him with her elbow.

"You're the ones keeping secrets!" Frank was jostled up against his mother as the car bounced into the parking lot next to a restaurant called The Great Wall.

They piled out of the car, and his father held the door for his mother before greeting the owner in Chinese. Frank looked around for the hidden camera. *This must be some kind of joke.* The owner grinned from ear to ear and offered them a table big enough for ten, then he chattered away with his father. Two waiters came running over to pull chairs out for them.

His mother leaned over. "Your father likes to show off sometimes."

"You speak Chinese? Is that the secret?"

"No, I learned Mandarin in college. It's not as useful as you might think." He laughed. "We're lucky the proprietor speaks Mandarin rather than some other dialect."

"So, are you going to tell me this big secret or not?"

"When I was writing my thesis, your mother and I got married. I worked part-time and went to school. Your mother stayed at home and... How should I say this?"

"I stayed at home and burned things. There, are you happy now?" She folded her arms over her chest.

His father giggled. Frank had never seen his father so giddy.

*Maybe I should have gotten in trouble a long time ago.*

"She's not kidding. She burned everything: breakfast, dinner, my shirts—your mother burned almost everything in our apartment, including herself. We lived in China-town, and literally in order to keep a shirt on my back, I took a job at a laundry. That's where I learned to speak the language. Every night, I'd come home to a smoke-filled apartment. It got so bad that the neighbors started to bring us meals."

"Milton! What has gotten into you? You're exaggerating. It wasn't as bad as all that. The truth is, I had never cooked a thing in my life before we were married. I'll admit that the first year was bad. Whatever I didn't burn, I ruined in some other way. It's not as though I didn't know I was a terrible homemaker. I simply thought that cooking just came naturally to women, like childbirth."

Frank rubbed at the back of his neck. "It doesn't?"

Four waiters came out of the kitchen, carrying trays laden with food. The table was quickly covered with steaming dishes that Frank couldn't identify.

"Milton, did you order all this?" his mother asked.

"My Mandarin may be a bit rusty, or I may have gotten carried away."

"Just a little bit, I'd say."

Frank eagerly followed his father's lead, sampling a little bit from many of the dishes. Next, he took on the chopsticks. His father tried to show him how to hold them correctly, but very little food made it to his mouth. Finally, his father called the owner over.

The little Chinese man pulled up a chair next to Frank and patiently showed him how to use two sticks to eat. It took a while, but Frank improved as the evening wore on. The owner poured tea for everyone when he brought over a bowl of fortune cookies.

"Now, Mr. Frank, you must pass them around, allowing everyone to select their own cookie. In that way, the fortune can seek out the correct person," he explained.

They broke open their cookies. His parents waited.

"Am I supposed to read it out loud?"

The owner nodded. "It is appropriate to share your good fortune."

Frank pushed up his glasses. "It takes a year to make a friend, but you can lose one in an hour."

"That sounds very appropriate," his mother said. "Here is mine. It is better to light a candle than to curse the darkness."

Frank's father cleared his throat and shot the sleeves of his jacket. "The person who says it cannot be done should never interrupt the person doing it."

"Very good fortunes for all, yes?" The little man clapped. "Friendship, wisdom, and accomplisher."

*Of course, they're good fortunes. You put them in there.* Frank washed down the cookie with a sip of tea. "What would happen if I took another cookie?"

"You may have many fortunes." The restaurant owner lifted the bowl over Frank's head. "Select, please."

Frank reached into the bowl. "With true friends, even water drunk together is sweet."

The little man reached for Frank's fortune and read it himself. He shook the bowl. "Select another, please." Frank saw a look pass between his mother and father. Concern or surprise, he couldn't tell.

The cookie cracked open, and Frank read his third fortune of the evening. "To know another is not to know his face, but to know his heart."

The owner forced a smile. "You have powerful friendships. Very powerful indeed." He rattled off something in Chinese to the waiters and took a seat next to Frank again.

Two young men came over and started to box up the leftover food.

"Three fortunes about the same thing. Very curious. You understand? Very curious indeed." He held the bowl, which still contained a half-dozen cookies, on his lap.

Frank nodded slowly. "You put the fortunes into the cookies."

"It is true, but there are many different fortunes. I buy them. Too many." He touched one of the young men who was packing up the food on the arm and said something to him. The waiter hurried off to the kitchen. "My wife make cookie. Fresh every day."

The young man returned with a cardboard box with Chinese characters printed on it. He placed it on the floor at Frank's feet. Frank peered into the box and saw thousands of tiny slips of paper. The old man reached in and pulled out a handful, quickly reading and showing them to Frank. Of the first dozen he read, no two were about the same topic.

The old man took Frank by the wrist with a grip that was so strong, it surprised him. His dark eyes bored into Frank's. "Select one more fortune from box."

*This guy is creeping me out.* He looked across the table at his father for help.

"You're a scientist. What are you afraid of?"

"I'm not afraid." Frank was sure that the intense look

on his father's face was concern, but he couldn't fathom why. *Mathematically, what are the chances?* He reached into the box and pulled out another small strip of paper.

"It is easier to visit a good friend than to live with one." Frank read the fortune, his voice barely audible.

A sharp intake of breath from his mother followed his utterance of the word *friend*.

"That is a very interesting coincidence, don't you think?" his father asked.

Frank nodded without taking his eyes off the little man sitting next to him. *He doesn't think it's a coincidence.*

His father paid the check, and they carried out the boxed-up leftovers. The owner pulled Frank aside just before he made it through the door.

"You are special, young man. Come back any time." He patted Frank on the shoulder and smiled.

"Thank you." *I think.*

Frank rode home in the back seat, the smell of their dinner permeating the car. Only the sound of wind outside the car windows marred the silence as they made their way through Willowton. When they arrived at home, his mother went into the kitchen to clean up. Frank's father signaled him to have a seat in the living room.

"Can you explain to me why you got into a fight today?" His father cleared the bowl of his favorite pipe and packed it with tobacco.

"I didn't get into a fight. My friend Molly hit Derrick O'Riley. Billy and I were there, but it was over in a flash. Molly knocked him down with two punches. That's the truth."

"Molly would be the young lady who joined us for dinner last night?" Smoke drifted above his head.

"Yes." Frank squirmed and sank deeper into the couch.

"That is understandable at least." A cloud of blue

smoke circled the air around father and son. "There has been bad blood between the O'Riley's and Houlahan's as long as we've lived here."

Frank nodded.

"I don't understand why Mr. Brady wants to see your mother and me if what you are telling me is true. Are you leaving anything out?" His father frowned.

"No, sir. That's everything." Frank held out his hands, palms up and shrugged. "I don't understand, either, except maybe because of O'Riley's father."

"Mmm, yes, there is that to consider." Frank's father thoughtfully tugged at his neatly trimmed goatee. "I imagine we'll get to the bottom of it tomorrow."

Frank waited while his father continued to stroke his goatee. "I'll call the school tomorrow morning to confirm our appointment for nine o'clock. You'll be going in late."

"But I told Billy I'd meet him in the library before school. Without Molly there, he'll be alone!"

"Then call to tell him you won't be there." He gestured at the telephone with his pipe.

"He doesn't have a telephone." Frank was embarrassed to hear his own voice hit that pleading note he despised.

"After your recent fortune cookie experience, I understand that you feel you have to be there for your friend, but I'm sure Billy will be fine in school until we arrive at nine."

"I could go over to his house and warn him."

"It's far too late to be barging in unannounced. He will figure it out." His father's voice carried a tone of finality.

"Yes, sir." Frank lowered his head. He couldn't warn Billy, and yet, he felt he should be doing something. He found his mother stacking clean dishes in the drying rack. The earlier mess had been replaced with shine and order. "Good night, Mother."

She turned, dried her hands, and kissed him on top of his head. "Good night. Are you all right?"

"I'm worried about Billy. If I'm not there tomorrow…"

"He will be fine. What did that man at the restaurant say to you before you left?"

Frank was unable to hide his surprise. "He said that I'm special and to come back any time."

Frank's mother went to the kitchen doorway, peered out at his father, then returned. She spoke in a soft voice. "You are special. I love your father. He's the smartest man I've ever met, but he doesn't have much imagination. I don't believe in coincidences."

"What do you think…?" Frank grew silent, not knowing which questions to ask.

"I don't know what to think. I'm keeping an open mind. You should do the same."

Frank nodded.

She tousled his hair. "Don't stay up all night reading."

The events of the night rolled through his head as he prepared for bed. It had been quite a night.

## Chapter Twenty-One

Billy paused at the kitchen door and peered through the glass. A lone plate of cold food sat on the table in his usual spot. A deep breath filled his lungs, and he pushed open the door. "Mom, I'm home!" Billy tossed his coat onto a chair.

"In here, and don't yell. I just put your sister to bed."

In the living room, his mother sat on the sofa. She leaned against Tony with a book in her hand. Tony looked up from the sports section. Those were all good signs. Billy knew their little slice of calm was about to explode into a storm.

"Hey, kid, where you been?" Tony asked.

"My friend Molly got in trouble at school today, so Frank and I walked her home. You should probably read this." His hand shook as he passed the letter to his mother. Glaring at it, she snatched it from his hand and tore it open. He braced for the coming tirade.

"What's this about?"

"I don't know, Mom. My friend Molly punched this

kid, Derrick O'Riley, and Mr. Brady jumped off the deep end." Billy's voice shook.

She sat up straighter and waved the letter in Billy's face. "And you had nothing to do with it, I suppose."

"We were there, but…"

Tony set his paper aside and looked cautiously at Billy.

"Who's we?" His mother demanded.

"My friend Frank, you remember I ate at his house the other day. His parents have to go too."

"I hope you're not falling in with a bad crowd. I thought we put that behind us when we moved."

Billy laughed.

"This isn't funny. Your principal wants me to come to the school tomorrow."

"If you only knew Frank. He's like the class genius, a real nerd. He never gets in trouble."

"You're telling me you and this genius just happen to witness a fight between a girl and someone else, and your principal feels I should drop everything and meet with him?"

"I guess." Billy tried to swallow a lump forming in his throat.

"Does he think I've got nothing better to do than to run at his beck and call? Who the hell does he think he is?"

"Molly and Frank said O'Riley's dad owns this town and everyone in it, including Mr. Brady."

Snapping her book closed with a loud pop, she glared at him. "I've got a news flash for Mr. O'Riley—and Mr. Brady too. Nobody owns me!"

"I'm sure if you just write a note saying you're too busy to come, he'll forget about it." Billy liked the sudden direction the conversation had taken.

"Like hell. If he wants to see me in person, then, by

God, I'll not disappoint him." She handed the letter to Tony.

Tony held it in front of his face, but not before Billy saw his grin.

Billy fought to control his own urge to grin. "Yeah, but you're busy, Mom. Plus, you'll have to bring Suze, since no one's around to watch her."

"Susan will have to sit quietly while your Mr. Brady and I have a little chat."

The letter in Tony's hand did not conceal his snort of amusement.

Billy turned away before his face betrayed him. "I'm going to eat. I'm starving." He walked into the kitchen, threw a fist into the air, and whispered, "Yes!"

He pushed his dinner into the bottom of the trashcan. Then he retrieved a sleeve of Ritz crackers and a jar of peanut butter from the pantry. With his hunger sated, he washed his dish and put everything away before pausing at the doorway to listen.

"Did you read it?" his mother asked Tony. "It practically admits he did nothing but watch the fight."

"True, but the letter is clear he wants to see you tomorrow. He must be concerned about something."

Billy's mom snorted. "You don't summon people for a meeting because you're concerned. You ask for an appointment convenient to both parties. He must think he's the Lord of Willowton or something."

Billy laughed. He walked into the front room, his face under control. "I'm going to my room. I've got some homework to finish for tomorrow."

"Good night, kid," Tony said.

"We'll talk about this after my meeting with Mr. Brady tomorrow. Check in on your sister, but *don't* wake her up," his mother added.

"Okay, Mom. Good night."

Billy looked in on Suze. Her right thumb firmly lodged in her mouth signaled she slept soundly. The door to the attic beckoned him. He needed the journal. Maybe it would be better to go up there in the morning. He thought about the previous night. *I'm not afraid of ghosts, am I? Can ghosts even hurt you? It hadn't done anything yet, except tell him to get some rest. Nothing scary about that. What will I say to Molly and Frank if I don't bring the journal? Molly's way scarier than some ghost.*

He kicked off his shoes and straightened his back before tiptoeing up the twisting staircase. He glanced at the desk. The journal awaited him, as usual, wrapped in the cloth and perfectly centered. The window showed no sign of frost. He released a long breath, grabbed the journal, and hurried down the stairs. He flopped onto his bed and began to read.

*November the Fourteenth, Nineteen Hundred Twenty-four*

*This afternoon, Mabel came to warn me of Father's plans to send me to a monastery.*

The entry went on to describe Thomas's day and the preparations for the spell that would free him from his cell. The next page appeared to be scribbled in haste, describing his returning to find his family dead. Billy read it over several times.

*My God! What happened here last night? My poor Mabel is dead. She lies in a heap in the bathtub, her white sleeping gown soaked red with blood. Father appears to be sleeping peacefully, apart from the bloody gash across his throat. Mother must have fought hard. She looks awful. Who would*

*commit such a heinous act? Oh Mabel! My little Mabel.*
*Who would hurt her? She would never have harmed a flea.*
*Someone approaches. I must go now, while it is still dark.*

*TZP*

Billy flipped through the rest of the journal. Blank. The last entry dated November 14, 1924. *Everyone thinks Thomas killed his family. It had to be someone else who committed this heinous act?*

---

He awoke to someone tugging on his foot.

Tony grinned at him through the fogginess clouding his brain. "I'm cooking."

Billy nodded and sat up. "I'll be right down."

Coming to, he looked for the journal. Not on the chair, where he had set it last night. He shook out the blankets and pushed his pillow to the floor in his search for it. *It didn't just get up and walk away. Maybe Tony picked it up?* Deep down, Billy knew exactly where to find it.

Back up the stairs he went, trying not to wake anyone. A shudder racked his body when his suspicion proved true. There it sat, in the middle of the desk, as though he had never touched it. With the journal under his arm, he made his way back downstairs and into the kitchen. The aroma of frying bacon assaulted his senses, and his mouth watered.

"Hey," Billy said, not wanting to frighten Tony again.

"Grab the bread and start some toast, will ya?" Tony grinned.

"What's so funny?" He pushed the slider on the toaster down.

"I'm thinking about taking the day off. It would be worth catching hell from the Weasel, to watch your mother take your principal apart."

"Yeah? You think she's still mad?"

"Still fuming when we went to bed. The longer she thought about it, the more pissed she got." Tony flipped the eggs into the air.

"You don't think she'll let it go after sleeping on it?"

"That has not been my experience." Tony winked at him.

Billy laughed. "Yeah, mine, either."

"So, tell me what happened yesterday."

Billy launched into the story, demonstrating the way Molly had landed her punches.

"Are these the same guys who roughed you up the other night?" Tony asked casually.

"Yeah, the same—"

"I could teach you to do what this chick did yesterday."

Billy paused, but said nothing.

"Of course, we'd have to figure out how to do it without your mother finding out. She'd rip my head off and kick it around the house if she found out."

Billy's mood picked up a little at the image Tony painted. "I'd like that, but Mom…"

Tony pulled on his coat and headed for the door. "I'll give it some thought. Got to go."

"See you tonight and—thanks." Billy looked around for his own coat and gathered up his books. His mother came scuffing into the kitchen behind him.

"Who are you, and what have you done with my son?" she asked.

"What did I do now?" Billy spun around.

"My real son never got out of bed earlier than he had to. So, who are you?"

He forced a laugh. "Very funny. You should take it on the road."

"You're leaving early again?"

"Yeah. I want to catch up with Frank and find out how Molly's doing."

"Are you in love with Molly? Maybe that's what's going on—your hormones are getting you up early."

Billy turned red. "I'm not in love with Molly. She's a friend."

"Maybe you're in love with Frank then."

"I'm not in love with anybody!" Billy said, sharper than he had intended.

"If you say so," his mother said.

*She looks a little too pleased with herself.*

"I guess I'll see you at nine," she said.

"You're still going to the school?"

"You bet I am." The color rose in her face.

Billy shuffled his feet and looked away for a moment. "Okay, I guess they'll send for me or something."

Billy's mother put an arm around his shoulder and kissed the top of his head. "Don't worry. I won't embarrass you *too* much." She pulled the collar of Billy's coat together and buttoned it under his chin.

A stiff wind accosted him when he stepped onto the porch. He started down the street and looked back at the house over his shoulder, muttering, "Who is that woman, and what has she done with my mother?"

---

Billy sat alone in the library, wondering what had kept Frank. He hoped Sal and Ernie hadn't ambushed him. *I should have walked to his house this morning.* Idly, he flipped through the pages of the journal, looking at Thomas's elegant script and the way it deteriorated in the last entry. He flipped the page, and his hands shook.

*November the Tenth, Nineteen Hundred Sixty-eight*

*I am so tired. I want to rest, but I cannot. Can you help?*

*TZP*

He flipped the page back and forth as sweat trickled down his face. *This is new. I'm sure of it. The handwriting's sloppy.* It looked more like the handwriting on the essay he found in his notebook. The script gradually smoothed out to resemble Thomas's characteristic hand. As he read it for the third time, the date finally registered. *November 10, 1968. Yesterday! But that's... impossible.*

The bell rang, startling Billy out of his trance. He gathered his books and hurried to class. No sign of Frank. Mrs. Albright raised one eyebrow when Billy walked in as the late bell sounded. Ernie and Sal sat together, their heads down in quiet conversation. *What did those dogs do to Frank?*

## Chapter Twenty-Two

Molly awoke feeling as though she hadn't slept at all. Quietly, she made her way to the bathroom and got ready for school before realizing she wouldn't be going today. In the kitchen, she brewed a pot of tea. With time to spare, she poked around in the pantry for something besides cereal for breakfast. She emerged with a box of Bisquick. Following the directions on the box, she mixed up batter for pancakes.

Heavy footsteps overhead preceded her father's appearance in the kitchen. The sizzling skillet didn't mask the sound of her father slumping into a chair with a groan. He looked awful.

"Is there any tea?" he mumbled.

"I'll get it."

Steam rose from the cup as she placed it on the table. "You want some pancakes?"

"No, thanks. I need a minute or two."

She placed a bottle of aspirin in front of him before she turned back to the stove. She wanted to talk to her dad about Derrick O'Riley and ask him what she should do about school and Mr. Brady, but fear constricted her throat and held her tongue prisoner. *How do I bring it up without starting a fight?*

She slid three pancakes onto a plate and set them in front of her dad. She had never in her life cooked for him. In truth, she wasn't a very good cook. Her greatest successes ended with tea and toast. Mamo did the cooking, but since she had gotten sick, the fare in their house had been grim except for the dinners Mrs. O'Brien delivered.

"There should be some maple syrup in the pantry. Check the top shelf." He eyed the plate.

"Here it is!" She tried to sound cheery. With two fingers, she lifted the sticky bottle and gingerly handed it to him before turning back to the stove.

"I'm sorry I got so mad last night," her father muttered.

"I'm sorry I hit that jerk, O'Riley."

"I don't think that's the honest truth, is it, lass?"

"Well, no. I'm glad I hit him. I'm sorry if it causes you trouble, though." She set down her own plate and sat across from him.

He smiled. Molly couldn't remember the last time she'd seen him smile.

"You sounded like your mother just then. She never took any sh—crap from anyone, either, you know."

"That's what Mamo said."

"Your Mamo… umm… seemed alert last night."

"Yeah. Maybe she's getting better," Molly said.

"I wouldn't count on it. The doctors said she'll have some lucid moments, but they will become fewer and shorter as time goes on."

Molly felt her lip quiver. She bit the inside of her cheek to keep from crying.

"You want to tell me what happened yesterday before I go to see Mr. Horse's Ass Brady?"

Molly smiled. "Is that his real name?"

"It should be." He mopped up syrup with the last of his pancakes. "So, let's have it. How did you come to be smacking O'Riley's kid?"

"Oh, I did more than smack him. I got him with a left to the gut and finished him off with a right on the chin. He never knew what hit him."

"I'm sure your brothers are proud." Her father shook his head.

Molly told the story from the beginning and explained how Billy and Frank were involved.

"Don't take this the wrong way, but why don't you have any girlfriends?"

Molly rolled her eyes and tried to keep the pain out of her voice. "I don't know, Dad. Girls don't like me." *My brothers were my friends, but they're gone.*

"I have to go to work. Will you check on Mamo and then meet me at the mill at twelve, sharp? I'll take a long lunch so you and I can go see Mr. Horse's Ass Brady together. How's that sound?"

"Okay, Dad. Thank you." Molly smiled.

Her father got up to leave, and Molly caught a glimpse of the man with whom her mother had fallen in love. *If only he wouldn't drink so much.* "Dad, I really am sorry if Mr. O'Riley gives you any trouble because of me."

His strong hand reached out and squeezed her shoulder. A real show of affection in her father's world. She craved a hug, but pride kept her from asking for it.

"It'll be fine. Don't you worry." He thumped out of the house in his heavy work boots, with his head hanging low and his shoulders slumped.

Molly prepared a cup of tea for Mamo. The alert and

perceptive grandmother who had been there last night was gone. In her place lay a fragile, senile collection of old bones that rattled when she moved. Back in the kitchen, Molly made watery oatmeal instead of toast. Mrs. O'Brien would be in soon to cook and help her grandmother, but Molly didn't mind helping out.

She sat and talked to Mamo while holding her hand, hoping she would come back from the place she hid inside her mind. She wanted to find out more about her mother, the mill, and their time on Congress Street. She had so many questions and wondered who else might know the truth.

The front door banged, startling her awake. She had a taunting recollection of an unpleasant dream, but it had dissipated too quickly. At first, she couldn't figure out why she was in Mamo's room, but it came flooding back to her when she looked into the unfocused eyes of her grandmother.

Mrs. O'Brien's voice echoed up the stairwell. "I'm coming Mary Margaret, the good Lord willing." Mrs. O'Brien poked her head in the door, breathing heavily. "Oh my!" her hands clutched her chest. "Molly, you scared the bejesus out of me."

"Sorry," Molly said.

"Oh, child, who'd expect to find you sitting there. What are you doing home?"

"I got in a fight at school yesterday. I'm suspended for a week." Molly gathered up the dishes from her grandmother's breakfast. "I can help for a while. I don't have much to do until I meet Dad at noon."

"That would be very nice. Fill the basin with hot water and bring it in here."

When she returned from the bathroom with the basin,

Molly asked, "Mrs. O'Brien, did you know Mamo used to live on Congress Street?"

"Oh heavens, yes. Your grandmother and I have been friends since we were wee." Mrs. O'Brien fussed with Mamo's hair while she talked. "Your granddad run me off when he found me visiting. Remember that, Mary? Too good for the rest of us after he bought the big house. I told you not to marry him, but would you listen to me? No!"

"Was he mean?"

"Aye, like a snake, and he got meaner as he got older." Mrs. O'Brien bent low to examine Mamo's face and hair. "You were the best thing ever happened to him, Mary, not that he appreciated you."

"Did he mistreat her?"

"No. He never showed his mean to your gran, mind you. Him and O'Riley, two of a kind they were. They did some terrible things." Mrs. O'Brien crossed herself. "Forgive me, Jesus, for speaking ill of the dead."

Molly couldn't imagine being friends with the O'Rileys. "Mamo told me we used to own the mill."

"'Twas before your mum passed, God rest her soul."

"Bought with blood money, she said. Whose blood did she mean?"

"Ancient history. It's water over the dam. Let it be, child. When, exactly, did your grandmother tell you these things anyway?" Mrs. O'Brien asked.

"Last night. She… woke up. I made her a cup of tea, and she told me about my mum, Seanair, and the mill."

"Mary, really! You shouldn't fill the child's head with the past or what might've been. She has her own problems."

Mamo smiled blankly as Mrs. O'Brien dressed her and moved her to the rocking chair. She maintained a running dialogue the whole time, sharing all the town gossip. "Mrs. Mullen caught Old Man Weiss with his finger on the scale when he weighed her roast last week. Of course, the old thief denies it. He's been doing it for years, and everyone knows it. What's a person to do? We can't all go driving fifteen miles to Masonville every time we want a soup bone."

Molly tried again to ask about the mill, but Mrs. O'Brien shook her head and pressed her lips together in a tight line. "Let it be, child. There is nothing to be gained digging up the past."

Frustrated, Molly excused herself to get ready to meet her dad and Mr. Horse's Ass Brady.

## Chapter Twenty-Three

Flanked by his parents, Frank walked through the school corridor. He prayed no one would see him. His parents hadn't taken him to school since the first grade, but his father had insisted they go as a family, so they could "get to the bottom of it."

"Good Morning, Francis," Mrs. Spencer said as Frank and his parents entered the office.

"Good Morning, Mrs. Spencer. These are my parents." Frank nodded toward them. "This is Mrs. Spencer."

"Yes, of course. I've met your mother many times." Mrs. Spencer stood and came over to shake hands. "And you must be the famous Mr. Bordeaux. It's very nice to meet you. Mr. Brady will be with you shortly."

"Famous. I didn't realize." Frank's father shook Mrs. Spencer's hand and blushed slightly.

"Your work at the NADC is widely known in some circles," Mrs. Spencer said.

"Not too widely known, I hope. It *is* mostly classified."

"Oh dear, of course not! I only know what I read in

*American Scientific Journal* about your work with advanced robotics."

Frank watched the bizarre exchange in amazement. Mrs. Spencer seemed giddy, fawning all over his father like he was Elvis or somebody. Frank took a seat next to his mother while Mrs. Spencer and his father continued to talk.

The main door to the office swung open with a bang, and a harried-looking woman with a scarf tied around her head shoved a stroller into the room.

"Mrs. Spencer, isn't it?" she asked.

"Yes, Mrs. Hashberger, please have a seat. Mr. Brady will be with you shortly."

"Mrs. Spencer, could you keep an eye on Susan for me while I meet with Mr. Brady? She'll be no trouble in her stroller."

"I-I guess she'll be all right," Mrs. Spencer looked doubtfully at the little girl in the stroller.

"Thank you, You're very kind. He's in here, then?" Mrs. Hashberger reached for the doorknob.

"You can't go in there!"

Billy's mother had already gone through the door, though, and Frank saw Mr. Brady lurch to his feet, the telephone still pressed to his ear.

"I know, Mr. O'Riley, but could you hold for one moment, please? Can I help you?" Mr. Brady growled.

"You must be Mr. Brady, I'm Maude Hashberger, Billy's mom. I'm pleased to meet you."

"I'm sure. Can you wait outside until I'm finished here, please?" He strained to look around her. "Mrs. Spencer!"

"Right here, Mr. Brady." Mrs. Spencer quickly came in and took Mrs. Hashberger by the elbow. "Please, Mrs. Hashberger, come with me. Mr. Brady will see you as soon as he can."

Mrs. Hashberger pulled away from Mrs. Spencer. "No, I will *not* wait outside. You summoned me to appear at nine o'clock." She pointed to the large clock on the wall. "As you can plainly see, the big hand is on the twelve, and the little hand is on the nine. *Right now.* Maybe you could put down the phone and explain to me why I'm here."

Frank's father's jaw hung open. His mother sat there as if everything were completely normal while she cooed at the little girl in the stroller.

"Mrs. Spencer, please close the door. I'll handle this," Mr. Brady boomed.

"No, you will leave the door open, Mrs. Spencer, so I can keep an eye on my daughter. Is the person on the phone staying on the line for our talk, as well, Mr. Brady?"

Mrs. Spencer backed out of the doorway and went to her desk with a bewildered look. Frank watched as Mr. Brady lifted the phone back to his ear.

"Mr. O'Riley? Sorry, I'll have to call you right back. Yes, I know, sir. We'll take care of it, I assure you. Of course. Yes, of course. All right, then. Goodbye, sir." Mr. Brady replaced the receiver with a bang. "Mrs. Hashberger, your behavior is unacceptable and unbecoming. Have a seat, please."

"I will not sit. Mr. O'Riley? Was that the same Mr. O'Riley who supposedly owns this town and everyone in it, including you?"

Frank couldn't believe his ears. *Did she really just say that?* He watched Mr. Brady's face turn a dark shade of crimson. His head looked like it might explode at any moment.

"I don't know where you heard such a ridiculous thing," Mr. Brady said. He seemed to be backpedaling as fast as he could. As far as Frank knew, no one had ever challenged Mr. Brady. Not ever.

"First, my behavior is not your concern, Mr. Brady.

Whether or not it is becoming, I can't say. It seems your behavior is the issue in this particular case. If I understood your letter correctly, you wanted me here promptly at nine o'clock to discuss my son's *non*-participation in a fight yesterday. Did you intend to summon me for a nine-o'clock meeting just to keep me waiting outside?"

"Mrs. Hashberger, as you may or may not realize, I'm a busy man—"

"I resent your implication that I'm not busy or my time is somehow less valuable than yours," Mrs. Hashberger cut in.

"That's not what I meant!" Mr. Brady bellowed.

"Then say what you mean, and refrain from raising your voice. I'm not one of your students. Why, exactly, am I here, if my son had nothing to do with the fight?"

"The point is, he did have something to do with it. He challenged Derrick O'Riley in the corridor yesterday, and when Derrick tried to walk away, Billy encouraged Molly to hit him."

"That's a lie!" Frank jumped up and walked to Brady's door. "And you know it."

"Son, don't interrupt. Come sit down. You'll get your day in court. Besides, she can handle herself." Frank's father had an amused look on his face.

"I want to make sure I understand what you're saying. You believe my son, who is new to your school, waltzed in here, staked out his turf, assembled a gang, and challenged the son of the richest man in town in just three days? Is that right?"

"Well, that's an oversimplification, but you have the gist of it," Mr. Brady said.

"That is completely absurd. Even if my son were the type to do such a thing, which he is not, you have to admit accomplishing this in a scant three days is inconceivable."

"I'm telling you the facts as I understand them. You may draw your own conclusions," Mr. Brady said.

"Facts, let's discuss the facts. Was anyone of authority present when my son encouraged a girl—a *girl*, mind you —to attack the biggest thug in the school? Who were your witnesses? Certainly not that young man sitting out there. While I know my son is no angel, neither is he the monster you described. Let's be clear, Mr. Brady, I'm nobody's fool. And self-important blowhards do not intimidate me. The next time you summon me to discuss Billy's behavior, you'd better make sure the situation warrants it, or we'll be meeting in the school board's offices to discuss *your* behavior. Good day."

Frank watched as Billy's mother turned on her heel, pushed open the door and wheeled the stroller out, all in one fluid motion. He couldn't stop grinning.

Mr. Brady followed her to the door, shaking his head. "If you'll give me one minute, I'll be right with you," Mr. Brady said, looking at Mr. and Mrs. Bordeaux. He backed into his office and closed the door.

"Too cool," Frank said to no one in particular.

## Chapter Twenty-Four

Relief flooded through Billy when Frank walked into class, with no visible signs of a beating. He produced a note for Mrs. Atkins and took his seat. Billy's relief proved to be short-lived, however, as the note was for him.

Mrs. Atkins cleared her throat. "William, Report to the office."

Billy looked to Frank for an explanation, but only received a shrug. The burden of his unknown fate weighed heavy on his shoulders and made him drag his feet, almost as though he were walking to the gallows.

"Good morning, Mrs. Spencer." Billy eased the door closed.

"Good morning, William. You've had an eventful start in Willowton."

"Yes, ma'am." *If you only knew.*

"Have a seat. Mr. Brady will be with you shortly."

He cleared his throat. "Mrs. Spencer?"

"Yes, William."

"Do you know much about the house I live in?"

"I've lived here all my life, so I can't help but know a few things. What's on your mind?"

"The kids say it's haunted."

"That's what kids do."

"Do you believe it's haunted?" Billy asked.

Mrs. Spencer stopped and peered at Billy over her glasses. "Those tales of ghosts and haunted houses are for the young."

"They say the son slaughtered the whole family and burned their bodies in the furnace."

"Honestly, I don't know how such things get perpetuated. That is definitely not true. A family did die in that house a very long time ago. I can assure you no one burned in the furnace," Mrs. Spencer said, looking away.

"When?"

"I don't remember the date. Look it up, if you're interested. The town library has books on the history of Willowton, and you can probably find old newspaper stories about the death of the Packard family."

"Yes, but do *you*—"

The door swung open, and Mr. Brady's large frame filled the doorway. He didn't look even remotely happy to see Billy again. "Mr. Hashberger, come in."

"Yes, sir." Billy forced a smile.

Mr. Brady stood at the edge of his desk. His eyes bored into Billy. "I had the distinct pleasure of meeting your mother this morning."

A groan escaped Billy before he could stop it. Mr. Brady stood close, towering over him. Billy had to tilt his head back to look up into the stern face. A knot of dread tightened in his stomach.

"I'm going to keep this short—stay away from Derrick O'Riley." Anger seethed beneath the calm voice. "Do I make myself clear?"

"Yes, sir, but—"

"No buts! Have I made myself clear?"

"Yes, very clear."

"Mrs. Spencer will give you a hall pass. Get out of my office."

Back in the classroom, Billy handed his pass to Miss Swanson and took his seat. "I have the journal," Billy whispered to Frank.

Frank's eyes grew wide behind his glasses. He mouthed "The library!" and nodded at the clock.

"What happened to you this morning?"

"My parents brought me to school. I saw your mother in Brady's office. My father said she handed him his head. You should've seen her. It's too bad you weren't there."

"Yeah, too bad."

The bell dismissed them, and Billy had to hurry to keep up with Frank.

Frank walked right to the check-out desk. "Good afternoon, Mrs. Esposito, just checking in. Billy and I are still working on that—um, thing from yesterday."

"Fine," she replied, never glancing up.

Frank let out a long breath as Billy led the way to the table. Before he sat down, Billy ceremoniously laid the journal on the table and unwrapped the cloth.

"Wow," Frank whispered in awe. "Can I read it?"

"That's why I brought it, isn't it? But let me show you something first." Billy sat and opened the book to the first entry. "See how he writes out the date instead of just using numbers? The handwriting is really old-fashioned and all."

Frank nodded, but he never took his eyes off the journal. He pointed to a place on the page with excitement. "He says right here how they locked him in the attic! See I told—"

"Yeah, but look what I found this morning." Billy flipped to the next-to-last entry. "Read this."

Frank's nose almost touched the page as he read the words. He flipped the page and read the last entry. "Is that it?"

"Read the date!" Billy hissed.

"Impossible."

"It wasn't there last night. I found it this morning. *He* must've written it last night."

"You're messing with me. You wrote this."

"Do I look like I'm messing around here? I wouldn't do that."

"You're saying the ghost wrote this?" Frank asked.

"Yeah, just like the message on the window the other night. What do you think it means?"

"It means Thomas didn't kill his family."

"I mean the last part, where he writes 'Can you help?'" Billy showed the line to Frank. "What do you think it means?" Billy tapped his finger on the page.

"Let me think. If he didn't kill his family, then who did? Maybe... um, let me read the whole thing first."

"Go ahead."

Billy patiently waited as Frank practically sped through the entries. I'll finish it in class."

"No!" Billy reached for the journal, but Frank slid it out of his reach.

"Why not?"

"Because what if you get caught with it? I don't want anyone to see it. Not until we figure this out."

"I'll be careful. Come on," Frank pleaded.

"Do you boys need your passes signed?" Mrs. Esposito asked.

"No, thank you, Mrs. Esposito." Billy looked at the clock.

"Who is your advisor?"

"Miss Albright," Billy said, looking around for the journal. He stared at it under Frank's arm.

She nodded thoughtfully as she looked at them.

The boys nodded and headed for the door. Billy turned around. "Mrs. Esposito, do you have old newspapers here?"

"Yes, we have the *Willowton Sentinel* back ten years."

"We need 1924."

"You'll have to go to the public library in town for anything dating back that far. They store them on microfilm these days," Mrs. Esposito said.

"Thank you. We'll check it out." Billy turned and followed Frank, and they walked into Social Studies just as the bell rang.

Billy kept an eye on Frank as he read the journal during class. O'Riley strolled in late, with the air of a recently crowned king and glared at Billy. They would have to give O'Riley a wide berth.

Near the end of English, Miss Albright approached Billy and Frank.

"Excuse me, gentlemen. Can you explain your absence from the cafeteria today?"

"We were in the library," Billy said quickly. "You can ask Mrs. Esposito."

"I will do just that. What were you doing in the library?"

"Billy moved into the old Packard house. He wanted to read about the murders," Frank piped in.

"I see, and how did your research go, William?" Miss Albright asked.

"Oh… um, not so good, actually. Mrs. Esposito doesn't have any papers dating back to 1924. She said we'd have to go to the town library."

"In the future, you will see me first before you decide to skip lunch and go to the library."

"Yes, ma'am," they said in unison.

## Chapter Twenty-Five

Molly sat in the office next to her father, waiting to see Mr. Brady. She fidgeted with the hem of her skirt. Her dad's leg bounced up and down. The main door to the office opened so quickly, the papers on Mrs. Spencer's desk fluttered. O'Riley and his father marched in. Molly admired her handiwork. His swollen lip made his sneer look lopsided and comical rather than sinister. Her father jumped from his seat and greeted Mr. O'Riley.

"Hey, Miles, good to see you." He held out his dye-stained hand.

"Patrick," Mr. O'Riley growled, ignoring his outstretched hand.

"These kids. What're we gonna do with them, huh?"

Mr. O'Riley looked Molly over as if she were a new car he was considering purchasing. His heavy stare made her lift her head. She held his gaze while the clock on the wall clicked the seconds off.

Mrs. Spencer cleared her throat. "He's waiting for you, Mr. O'Riley. You can go right in."

Mr. O'Riley didn't acknowledge Mrs. Spencer. He

turned and pushed his son into Mr. Brady's office ahead of him and slammed the door. Just before the door closed, Molly saw Mr. O'Riley's satisfied expression.

She watched her father clench and unclench his hands. Mrs. Spencer went back to her files, and Molly's dad became increasingly agitated. He will be late getting back to the mill. If Mr. O'Riley didn't know it before, he certainly knew it now.

Finally, the door was flung open, and Mr. O'Riley strode out. He stopped short and pointed a finger at Molly's dad. "I'll see *you* at the mill."

Mr. Brady leaned his oily face out the door. "Mrs. Spencer, give Derrick a pass to return to class, please."

"I hate that son of a butcher," Molly said under her breath after the principal had shut his door again.

"Molly!" her father said.

"Well, I do. He's making us wait, for nothing. He knows you should be at work."

"It's done now. Five minutes more or less won't make a difference." Her father paced the floor for ten full minutes before Mr. Brady opened the door again.

"Molly, Patrick, come in, please. Have a seat. Sorry to have kept you waiting so long," Mr. Brady said, shaking her father's hand. His principal mask was back in place. "We won't take up much of your time, Warren. Molly, you should start."

Molly's nails bit crescents into her palms. "I'm very sorry for hitting Derrick. I apologize for the trouble I caused you and Mr. O'Riley."

"So can she go back to her classes?" Molly's dad asked.

"I don't think that will be possible," Mr. Brady said.

"I just watched Derrick go back to class. Why is Molly being kept out of school when he's not?"

"Because, by her own admission, she hit Derrick first, and he didn't retaliate."

"Only because he couldn't hit me from the floor," Molly said.

"Enough, Molly!" Her dad turned to the principal. "Look, I see where you're coming from, but I'm sorry, you can't pretend Derrick O'Riley is not partially at fault here. You know him as well as anybody."

"The fact is, your daughter walked up to Derrick in the corridor and hit him more than once. I can only guess at what provoked her. I can't punish Derrick on a guess or hearsay."

"You're unbelievable. You can't punish Derrick on hearsay? Who do you think you're talking to? Some lawyer? I know better, and so do you!" Patrick stood up.

Mr. Brady gestured for him to sit back down. "Calm down. Here's what I'm willing to do: I'll reduce her suspension to two days. She can return to school tomorrow. I want a written apology, including alternate ways she plans to deal with her anger. She'll also do five days in detention after school."

"Fine," Molly said quickly. "I'll have my apology to you by tomorrow before school starts."

"Your detention will start tomorrow with Mr. Amato."

"Okay, fine. Can we go now? I have some creative writing to do," Molly said.

"Molly, you're not helping your cause," Mr. Brady said. "I feel the level of violence you demonstrated was excessive."

"You're right. I'm sorry. Thank you for allowing me back to school." Molly spoke through gritted teeth. "Let's go, Dad."

Molly and her father walked wordlessly across town to

the employee entrance at the mill. He paused with his hand on the door. "Are we okay?"

"I'm really sorry Mr. O'Riley is going to give you grief over something I did."

"Don't worry about it. If it wasn't you, he'd find something else to bust my shoes for."

Molly nodded.

"Is there something else?" he asked.

"Is it okay if I meet my friends after school? They promised to bring me any work I missed." She looked into her father's green eyes.

"Can you be home before Mrs. O'Brien has to leave?" he asked.

"Sure. I can call her from there too."

"You'll be okay with the boys there? I mean..."

"Mrs. Bordeaux will be home, and I think I've proven I can take care of myself."

"I should be home by five." He pulled open the gray steel door and disappeared into a noisy cloud of steam.

Molly watched the puff of steam rise along the wall. Lifeless ivy clung to the brick and grew over the windows. She wondered how her father could go to work there every day, knowing he had once owned the mill. To make things worse, he now worked for O'Riley. Of all the petty, mean-spirited people in the world, that man had to be the worst. A chill raced up her spine and sent a shiver through her. She pulled her collar up and started walking toward school.

## Chapter Twenty-Six

When the final bell rang, Frank watched as O'Riley and his entourage sauntered out of the classroom. He motioned Billy to wait. "I bet they're waiting for us out there."

They asked Miss Albright for a list of homework for Molly. Frank took the list, and he and Billy went to the door. Frank peered around the edge and saw O'Riley down the hall, leaning against the wall and talking with Sal and Ernie.

"So, now what?" Billy asked.

"Follow me." Frank calmly stepped into the hallway and went straight to his locker, three sets of eyes burning into his back. "Go get your stuff," he whispered to Billy. "I'll come when I hear you slam your locker closed." Frank stalled in the corridor. *I hope this works. If it doesn't, we're dead.*

The metallic clang of Billy's locker reverberated through the near-empty hall. Frank fast walked to meet Billy, confident he was being followed. As he rounded the corner, he broke into a run. "Go, they're coming." Billy fell in alongside him, and they darted around another corner. Frank led the way into the gymnasium then sprinted through the locker room and into another corridor. A quick turn at the metal shop brought them to the cafeteria. They burst into the cold air on the loading dock and started to laugh.

"You boys going somewhere in a hurry?"

Startled, Frank jumped at the sound of Shorty's voice. "Hello, Mr. Shorts."

"We just ditched O'Riley," Billy said.

"It's about time! I was beginning to wonder if you guys were going to hide in there until my suspension is over," Molly yelled.

"Molly! Man, I'm glad to see you," Billy said.

Frank jumped from the loading dock and ran over to her with his arms flailing in front of him.

"Bordeaux, if you try to hug me, I'll have to knock you out, right here, right now."

"What are you doing back here?" Frank asked, stopping short.

"I figured you would leave through the back when I saw O'Riley go back to class. Good thing, too, because they're hanging out by the gate, waiting for you."

"I can't believe it." Frank suddenly hugged her in spite of her threats.

"Tell us what happened to you. What did your dad say when you got home?" Billy interrupted.

"Excuse me, lady and gentlemen." Shorty looked down from the loading dock. "I suggest you kids take your discussion someplace else before our young gangster hears you all back here jabbering."

"That's the first sensible thing I've heard from a man all day," Molly said.

"Can you come over for hot chocolate?" Frank asked Molly.

"Why else do you think I'm here? I have to keep you

from eating too many cookies." Molly led them back to Frank's house in a roundabout way.

"That's if his mother lets us in," Billy said.

"After what your mom said to Brady today, you'll probably get the red-carpet treatment." Frank mimed rolling out the red carpet.

Billy looked at Frank warily. "What did she say?"

Frank told Molly and Billy what had happened in the principal's office that morning, including Mrs. Hashberger's threat to go to the school board.

Billy groaned. "She actually called him a self-important blowhard?"

Molly tapped Frank's temple with a finger. "Once something gets filed in that head, it's part of the permanent record."

"Great, my life just got *so* much easier. Now the principal hates my guts."

"Oh, stop whining." Molly shrugged impatiently. "Brady hates my guts too. Guess what? The feeling is mutual."

"I thought she was great. You should be happy," Frank said.

"Francis, do you have a thing for Mrs. Hashberger?" Molly teased.

"Don't kid around!" Billy said. "That's just not right. Besides, he's saving himself for Miss Albright."

Frank's face flushed crimson as his friends joked.

"So, you have a thing for strong women. Is that it?" Molly asked.

"That would put you." Billy pointed at Molly. "At the top of the list."

"Oh, please, that's not funny."

"Yeah, that's not even close to funny," Frank added quickly.

"What's that supposed to mean? You could do worse," Molly said. "A lot worse."

"I-I didn't mean anything. You know what I mean. R-Right?" Frank stuttered.

"I'll let it slide this time, but next time..." Molly curled up a fist and held it in front of Frank's face.

"I get the picture." Frank threw two wild punches into the air. "Pow, pow." Once again, his glasses went flying through the air.

Billy's hand shot out and caught them before they hit the ground.

"Hold it. Nobody move. I lost my glasses again."

Billy shook his head and held the glasses out to Frank. "They're right here."

"Nice catch, Hashberger." Molly cupped her hands and blew a breath into them.

"Thanks." Frank sounded disappointed.

"So, Molly, you never told us what happened to you. What did your father say?" Billy asked, while Frank settled his glasses in place.

"He was okay with it. I mean, he wasn't happy or anything, but he talked with Brady today, and I'm allowed back to school tomorrow."

"But last night, he—"

Billy elbowed Frank in the ribs.

"Ouch, what was that for?" Frank rubbed his side.

"You mean we got these assignments and books for nothing?" Billy asked, ignoring Frank.

"What was that about last night?" Molly looked directly into Frank's eyes.

"Nothing—"

"Can it, Hashberger. I'm talking to Frank. Go on."

"We kind of followed you home, and—uh—we sort of heard you and your dad talking."

"You mean yelling, don't you?"

"Well, yeah. I mean, we didn't mean to!" Frank tried to think of a way to justify eavesdropping, but couldn't.

"Shut up, Frank, before you make it worse. I'll see you two tomorrow." Molly angrily turned to leave.

Billy grabbed her arm. "Wait. It wasn't Frank's fault. I'm the one you should be mad at. I made him come with me."

Frank watched Molly's anger grow until she was seething. *Any minute now, she's going to deck Billy, and I'm going to have to help him home.*

"I'm really sorry," Billy said. "Thing is, I was worried about you. You said your old man might kill you. I didn't know what to do. Leaving you alone didn't seem right."

"Yeah, Molly, one for all and all for one, remember? You can't be mad at us for worrying about you," Frank declared, stepping closer to Billy. He watched Molly's eyes move from his face to Billy's and back again.

"I ought to beat the crap out of both of you, right now," she said.

"That's what friends do," Billy said. "If you need to hit someone, then hit me, but I'd do it again."

Frank saw the hint of a smile forming around Molly's mouth and knew they had penetrated her armor.

"You two are not the brightest bulbs in the lamp, are you?" she asked.

"Maybe not, but we're all you've got. Now, let's go see if Mrs. Bordeaux is polishing my crown." Billy put his arm around Frank's shoulder and started to walk. Frank looked back to see Molly smiling brightly for the first time since yesterday.

"I'm only coming because I want to read the stupid journal, you know!" she called out before running to catch up with them. Molly put her arm over Frank's other shoulder.

"One for all," Frank started.

"And all for one!" they finished together, laughing.

# Chapter Twenty-Seven

"Hi, Mrs. Bordeaux." Billy saw her first, waiting on the porch, arms crossed, shoulders hunched, her breath visible in the cold. The sight of her on the porch gave him pause until he saw her smile. It warmed him.

"Look at the three of you!" she called from the porch. "I would never have guessed you would all be laughing after this morning. Come on in. I was getting worried."

"Did you make chocolate chip?" Frank asked, holding the door for his friends.

"No cookies today."

"No cookies!" He looked at Molly and Billy. "Sorry, guys."

"You are such a dweeb," Molly said.

"Yeah." Billy smiled. "If we were only interested in the cookies, we wouldn't need to bring you along. Right, Mrs. Bordeaux?"

"I'll get the hot chocolate on," Mrs. Bordeaux said, leaving them in the front room.

Molly looked Billy in the eye and put out her hand. "So let me see. What does Willowton's most famous mass murderer have to say for himself?" She held out her hand for the journal.

Billy reluctantly handed it over and headed for the bathroom. He looked at his reflection in the mirror. *How did I manage to make such good friends?* When he returned, Molly was sitting on the floor with her back against the couch, engrossed in the journal.

"I think we've lost her." Frank shrugged.

"Frank, bring your friends into the kitchen!" Mrs. Bordeaux sang out.

"Come on, Molly," Billy said.

She stood up slowly, never taking her eyes from the journal, and walked toward the kitchen.

Billy stopped her at the door. "You can't read in front of Mrs. Bordeaux."

She glanced up. "I'll be discreet."

"No, you won't."

"All right, all right. Geez, Hashberger, you can be such a nag." Molly placed the journal under the pile of textbooks in the front room. "Happy now?"

"Are you guys coming? Mom made fudge brownies," Frank called.

Mrs. Bordeaux bustled around the kitchen.

"How far did you get?" Frank asked.

"I'm up to the spell," Molly said.

"Wow, these are really good," Billy said too loudly. He put a finger to his lips and nodded in Mrs. Bordeaux's direction.

"Thank you, Billy," Frank's mother said before disappearing through the door to the basement.

Molly stuffed a brownie in her mouth and washed it down with the hot chocolate. "Done. Now, if you'll excuse me, I've got some reading to finish." Without another word, she left the two boys sitting there.

"We might as well give her time to finish it," Frank said. Then he noisily slurped the marshmallow off the top of his cup.

"Is Molly all right?" Mrs. Bordeaux asked when she returned to the kitchen.

"She's trying to finish some important reading we brought home for her," Billy said.

"Yeah, because she wasn't in school today," Frank added.

"Are you staying for dinner?" she asked Billy.

"I, ahh, don't think I should."

Mrs. Bordeaux cleared their mugs from the table. "Ask Molly if she'd like to stay."

"Okay, Mother."

Frank and Billy wandered out to watch Molly turn pages.

Billy hovered over Molly until she looked up. "What is it, Hashberger?"

"Mrs. Bordeaux wants to know if you can stay for dinner."

"Can you?"

"Can't. I have to go home and find out what my mom thought of Mr. Brady."

"Oh, I forgot to call Mrs. O'Brien." She peered around Billy at Frank. "May I?"

Frank nodded.

"But I should probably go home for dinner too." Molly dialed her number. "Dad? Is everything all right?" Molly twirled the cord around her finger as she listened. "No. I'll be home soon. Okay, thanks, Dad."

Billy reached his hand out for the journal. "I'll bring it again tomorrow."

"Just wait. I have some time."

Billy glanced down and was astonished to see she was almost done. "Go on, you're almost finished."

He sat on the floor, watching Molly's expression as she read. Frank sat down next to him.

A few moments later, Molly closed the journal with such force, it popped. "Who do you think you're kidding with this?"

"I know what you're thinking, but I didn't write it," Billy said.

Molly looked at Frank. "Do you believe this guy?"

"Yes."

"You think the *ghost* wrote this, after all these years? All of a sudden, he puts his sheet on one day and decides to leave a message for Hashberger? Right out of the blue? Oh, please!"

"Well, at the risk of getting punched again, yes, I think it's authentic," Frank said.

"I'm trying to tell—"

"I'm not talking to you right now." Molly cut Billy off and turned back to Frank. "Give me one good reason why you believe it."

"Well, for one, have you seen his penmanship?" Frank motioned to Billy.

"This is called calligraphy, and there is a way to learn it." Molly pointed an accusing finger at Billy. "Maybe he wrote the whole journal. It's a hoax, like the Loch Ness Monster."

Billy stood up. "I'm going home. When you two figure out if I'm making this up or not, let me know. I'll see you tomorrow."

Frank ran after Billy and grabbed his shoulder. Billy shrugged him off. Carrying his coat outside, he shut the door in Frank's face. *That's just great. The first time I manage to make some friends, I tell them ghost stories I'm not sure I believe myself. What did I expect?* Billy pulled on his coat and walked toward home. His gloomy mood was not improved by the thought of facing his mother after her meeting with Mr. Brady. Regardless of what Frank had said, he was sure his mother was not done with him yet.

Billy turned the corner and stopped in his tracks. Three sets of teeth smiled at him from the darkness.

"Nice of you to join us, Hamburger," O'Riley sneered.

## Chapter Twenty-Eight

Frank came back to Molly.

"What got up his butt?" Molly asked.

"He's mad because you don't believe him." Frank shrugged.

"He'll have to be mad then, because I don't believe him!" Molly crossed her arms.

"Come on, Molly. Think about it. How would he know all that stuff? The dates and everything? I've lived here all my life, and I never knew when the murders took place. Did you?"

"No, but he could've looked them up. Or even made them up. How would we know?"

"We can look it up at the library tomorrow. Then we'll know."

"That won't prove he didn't write the journal. It'll prove he could've looked up the dates, just like we're going to." Molly walked toward the door. "I'd better get going too. I'll see you tomorrow."

Frank helped Molly with her coat and handed over her books.

"He'll get over it." She tied her scarf under her chin.

"I hope so." He opened the door for her, and she walked out onto the porch.

## Chapter Twenty-Nine

Billy stepped back and turned to run. His books fell from his hands as he accelerated into a sprint. Laughter pierced the night behind him. *I've got to get back to Frank's!* He was a block away. He heard footsteps slapping the cold sidewalk behind him. He was almost there when the door opened, projecting a rectangle of light that served as a homing beacon to Frank's house. He surged forward as Molly's silhouette appeared in the doorway. He lunged the last few feet and landed on the porch, startling Molly.

"What're you doing?" she yelled, jumping out of his way.

Billy leaned over, with one hand on each knee, until he caught his breath. He pointed behind him. "O'Riley... was waiting for me."

"You okay?" Frank asked, looking around.

Billy nodded then realized he had dropped his books. "The journal! I dropped it!"

"Let's go find it," Molly said flatly.

"I'll get my coat," Frank said.

He returned a minute later carrying a flashlight.

Billy led the group back the way he had just run, cautiously looking for any sign of O'Riley. "I wonder where they went."

"Who cares? I'll break his nose if he tries something," Molly said.

Billy heard the familiar sound of feathers on the cold night air. He stopped and looked up. "Did you hear that?"

"Hear what?" Molly asked.

A scuffle of feet silenced the three friends. Frank wheeled around and pointed the flashlight toward the sound.

"Well, well, well." O'Riley smiled, bathed in the anemic yellow light. "The gang's all here."

"If it isn't Fat Lip and the Cowards. Are you back for an encore?" Molly asked.

"There's nobody around to protect you this time, Houlahan," O'Riley spat.

"I think it was you who needed protecting," Frank said.

"You think so, Lardo? We'll see about that."

As O'Riley stepped forward, a dark shadow swooped between them and flew right at his head. He dropped to his knees and held his arms up in front of his face. Ernie hit the deck next to him. Sal screamed like a little girl as he ran down the street. The shadow swooped down again right over O'Riley's and Ernie's heads.

"It's Thomas," Frank said softly.

"Oh, please!" Molly slapped his shoulder hard.

Frank kept the flashlight trained on O'Riley. When he tried to stand, the owl attacked again. This time, it flashed its talons, cutting the backs of O'Riley's hands. He went down on his face, cursing.

"We should go," Billy said, sounding steadier than he felt. They backed away while the huge owl continued to circle and swoop, keeping O'Riley on his knees. The noise faded behind them as they rounded the corner.

"There's my notebook," Billy said, walking over to pick it up.

Frank waved the light around until it landed on a text-book. "Over here." He picked up the book and handed it to Billy.

"I don't see the journal," Molly said.

They widened their search, but the journal was nowhere to be found.

Billy began to experience the familiar sinking feeling in the pit of his stomach. He knew exactly where the journal would be.

"Maybe O'Riley picked it up?" Molly said.

"I don't think O'Riley has it," Billy said.

"Then where is it?" Frank asked.

"You won't believe me if I tell you." Billy remembered the hurt he had felt earlier.

"Try me," Molly challenged.

Billy shrugged. "It's home in the attic, sitting on the desk. That's where it always is when I can't find it."

"Let's go. I've got to see this," Molly said.

"No," Billy said. "I'll bring it with me tomorrow. You guys should go."

"I don't think we should separate right now," Frank said as the flashlight shook in his hand.

"Come on, Hashberger, you live with a ghost. What could possibly be so bad at your house you don't want us to see? You know my secret." Molly pulled Frank along as she walked in the direction of Billy's house. "Besides, our Boy Genius here is right. We should stick together." Billy looked at them, torn.

"Are you coming, or should we introduce ourselves to

your mother when we get to your house?" she called over her shoulder.

Billy had no doubt she would make good on her promise, so he hurried to catch up.

---

"Mom, I'm home. I brought my friends over to meet you," Billy yelled, motioning for Molly and Frank to wait by the door.

He started through the living room and noticed what a mess it was. His mother came out of the kitchen with Suze balanced on her hip.

"Here." She handed Suze off to Billy. "Come in. Throw your coats anywhere and sit down." She looked at Molly. "You must be the little lady who caused all the ruckus yesterday?" Billy's mom wiped her hand on her dress and held it out to Molly.

"That would be me. I'm Molly Houlahan. Pleased to meet you."

"I recognize *you* from this morning. You were in the principal's office," Billy's mom said to Frank.

"Yes, ma'am. I'm Frank Bordeaux. A pleasure to make your acquaintance."

"Let me go turn the stove off. I'll be right back," Billy's mom said.

"This is my little sister, Suze." Billy turned to the side so they could see Suze. "These are my friends, Molly and Frank. Can you say hi?" She burrowed her face into Billy's shoulder then peeked over at Frank.

"Hi, Frank."

Frank's face lit up. "Hi, Suze. Is this your big brother?"

"No," she nodded.

"Are you ticklish, Suze?" Frank asked.

She grinned.

"I bet you are." Frank poked her in the ribs gently, eliciting a giggle.

"Do you want to stay here with Frank for a minute, Suze?" She shook her head no, but reached out one arm toward Frank.

Billy passed her over to Frank.

"You have a real way with women," Molly teased.

"I'll be right back," Billy said.

"I'm coming," Molly said.

"I don't think that's a good idea. I'll only be a minute." Billy turned and ran up the steps, but Molly followed right on his heels.

"Molly, you shouldn't be up here."

"Keep going, Hashberger. I have to see this for myself."

At the very top of the attic steps, Billy paused and groped for the string to turn on the light. The room was suddenly filled with light, and Billy looked toward the desk. The journal was waiting for him, just as he had predicted. He directed Molly's gaze to the journal and shuddered involuntarily.

"I wouldn't have believed it if I hadn't seen it for myself," she whispered.

When they returned to the living room, Billy's mother was entertaining Frank. Billy steeled himself for the inevitable disaster.

"Found it," Molly said.

"I should get back to fixing dinner. You're sure you won't stay for something to eat?" Billy's mom asked.

"No, they have to get going," Billy said quickly.

"Thank you so much, Mrs. Hashberger, but Billy's right. The aroma from the kitchen is enticing, but we're already late. It was delightful meeting you," Frank said.

"Yes, same here," Molly agreed.

Once Billy's mom had left the room, Billy took a deep breath. "It was delightful meeting you," he mimicked Frank.

"You're such a suck-up, Frank Bordeaux," Molly accused.

"I was just being polite."

"Oh, please. And what was that about the aroma coming from the kitchen? No offense, Billy, but it smells like she's burning old shoes in there."

"Uh, yeah, now you know my secret. My mother can't boil water."

"So, was it there on the desk?" Frank asked as Suze started to fuss in his arms.

"Bad man. Bad man," she said, pointing her small finger at the journal.

Molly stared at Suze. "It's okay, Suze. I'll put it over here."

"Who is the bad man, Suze?" Frank asked.

Billy nodded to his sister. "She's afraid to go into the attic."

The journal suddenly fell from Molly's grasp. Her hands shook as she reached for it. "Look at this!" She handed it to Billy.

*November the Eleventh, Nineteen Hundred Sixty-eight.*

*I have helped you on more than one occasion. Will you not return the courtesy? I grow weary. I cannot rest. Will you help?*

*TZP*

Frank read over Billy's shoulder.
"Do you believe me now?" Billy asked.

Molly nodded, speechless. The three of them stood there for a moment, dumbstruck.

"Hey, kid, how you doing?" Tony bellowed from the kitchen doorway.

"Huh? Ahh... good. I'm good, Tony," Billy stammered. "How you doing?"

"I'm living the dream, kid. Living the dream."

"Tony, these are my friends, Molly and Frank. This is my mom's, ahh—"

"I'm the boyfriend," Tony finished for Billy. "Nice to meet you."

"Hey, Tony, do you think you could drive them home? There're late."

"Sure, I don't mind." Tony's held a hand to the side of his face in a conspiratorial gesture. " Looks like your mom isn't quite done burning dinner yet, but we'd better hurry. I'll tell her. Get in the car."

Frank looked relieved as they headed to the car. Molly took the front seat. "Okay, I believe you, but what do we do now?"

"We can't do anything tonight. We'll meet in the library before school," Frank said.

"What are we going to do about O'Riley?" Billy asked.

Molly twisted around in the seat so she could see them. "He won't catch us if we're at school early. After school, we'll stick together."

"How will sticking together change anything?" Frank asked.

"He's a bully. He won't come after us, three against three," she said.

"We'll be careful, plus we have... You know, the owl, or whatever that thing is."

"Shh, here comes your mom's boyfriend," Molly warned.

Tony started the car and backed out of the driveway. "Which way?"

Molly handled the directions. First they dropped off Frank then her. "Thank you very much, Tony. She pointed a finger at Billy. "I'll see you tomorrow."

Billy got out to move to the front seat.

"How about letting me have the journal tonight?" Molly asked.

Billy's grip tightened on the book. "What for?"

"Just an experiment: leave it with me, and we'll see who has it in the morning."

"I don't think so, but nice try."

"Fine, be that way." Molly walked up the steps to the porch. She paused and waved as Tony pulled away.

"She's cute and smart, I think." The green light from the dashboard illuminated Tony's grin.

"Yeah, I guess."

"There's no guessing about it. A blind man in an airplane could see she's cute."

"We're just friends, nothing else."

"Did I say anything? Besides, you probably shouldn't go out with a girl who can kick your butt."

"Good point," Billy agreed.

Billy looked out the car window as they drove through the streets of Willowton. How could he help Thomas? What could he do that a ghost couldn't do for himself? The whole thing seemed far-fetched, sitting in the quiet safety of Tony's car. Heat poured from the vents. Sleep wooed him.

Tony's words jarred Billy awake. "Do you know what she's cooking for dinner?"

"Nah, but I hope it tastes better than it smelled." Billy looked at Tony. "Did you know our house is supposed to be haunted?"

Tony laughed. "Maybe that's why I got such a good deal on the rent."

"No, really. Everyone in town talks about it."

"Every small town has a haunted house. People like to have a scary story to call their own. My grandmother believed in spirits, the evil eye, and all kinds of silly stuff. She would scare the daylights out of us when we were kids."

"So, you don't believe in ghosts."

"Kid, I've seen enough atrocities committed by man against his fellow man; I don't have to go around making up scary stories. The real thing is bad enough." Tony pulled into the driveway. "I don't think we can delay eating any longer."

Dinner was an exercise in pushing food around on their plates while very little of it was actually eaten. Billy wished he could get away with Suze's approach. She simply pushed her food right onto the floor without fanfare. After dinner, Billy headed up to his room to stare at the journal. He took out a sheet of notebook paper and wrote:

*Dear Thomas,*

*Thank you for your help tonight and for the other times too. I want to help you, but I don't know what to do. Can you tell me? My friends, Molly and Frank, will help too.*

*Yours Truly,*
*Billy*

He placed the folded sheet into the journal and returned it to the attic. Back in bed, his mind raced. He should have asked additional questions. Was Thomas really a ghost? Was he the owl too? Or was the owl a pet? Can you train an owl? How old was he? Billy considered retrieving the note and writing a new one, but his resolve soon faded. His limbs went limp, and his eyes closed as he surrendered to sleep.

---

Billy walked down the spiral steps, trailing one hand on the curved wall and listening for noises. The door was unlocked and standing open, so he tiptoed into the bathroom. Rage pulsed in his temples at the sight of the bloody body lying in the bathtub. Turning from the bathroom, he ran to the next room. A woman lay on the floor, blood leaking from her wounds into the floorboards. He tried to scream, but was unable to make a sound. Footsteps pounded up the stairs. Someone was coming, fast. He ran back to the third floor and lunged for the window. A sharp pain stabbed in his back as he leapt from the ledge into the dark night. The wind rushed up to meet his wings once again, and he struggled for control. He could feel something heavy lodged in his back; it caused him to spin left as he sped toward the ground.

Billy woke up, covered in sweat and breathing hard. Fear mixed with relief flooded through him at the realization it had only been a dream. Clutching his notebook, he dragged his blanket to the kitchen. He sat down at the table and wrote feverishly, trying to document his vivid dream.

---

Billy woke up again in response to a gentle nudge from Tony.

"Another nightmare?" he asked.

Billy nodded, wiping drool from his face. "Yeah."

"You have to tell your mother about this. This is bad." Tony motioned at Billy's notebook lying open on the table.

Glancing at what he had written last night, Billy replied, "You read it? What do you think she can do?"

"I'm no expert, but this is pretty graphic stuff. Maybe you should talk to a counselor, or something."

Billy moved to get up, but Tony grabbed his arm and gently pushed him back into the chair.

"Sit down. I'm going to tell you something I don't tell many people." Tony sat across from Billy and exhaled slowly. "For years after I came home from Korea, I had nightmares. They call them night terrors, actually. I relived the awful things I saw there. I still get them sometimes. When I wake up, I'm soaked with sweat, and I feel like I've been running for my life."

Billy nodded.

"The difference is, I actually saw those things," Tony said.

"So, you think I'm crazy?" Billy asked.

"No, but I do think you should talk to someone about it. And you should start with your mother."

"I'll think about it."

"Get cleaned up, I'll make us something to eat." Tony got up and went to the refrigerator.

Billy went upstairs to retrieve the journal first.

*November the Twelfth, Nineteen Hundred Sixty-eight.*

*I am glad to consider you as a friend. The spell must be reversed. This will allow me to move on in peace. You must go to Tearneach. She is the only one who can help you.*

*Yours in Gratitude,*
*TZP*

Billy stared at the journal for a long time. *How am I going to find some old witch? She probably died years ago.* Tony was setting two plates on the table when Billy returned to the kitchen. They didn't speak while they ate. Billy tapped his fingers then tried humming.

"You have to tell your mother about your nightmares."

"What if—"

Tony held up his hand. "I've given this a lot of thought. You should do it sooner rather than later. I don't want to be in the middle of this, but if you don't tell her, I will. It would be better if she heard it from you."

"You know what she's like. I mean, she's been pretty good the last few days, but if I tell her about this…"

"That's a risk you'll have to take."

"Yeah, easy for you to say," Billy muttered. He pushed away from the table and left the house, slamming the door on his way out.

## Chapter Thirty

Molly poured the tea when she heard her father's shoes clomping down the stairs. "Good morning, Dad."

"Not so loud." He walked into the kitchen, shielding his red eyes from the overhead light. He slowly did a three-sixty. "How long have you been up?"

"I couldn't sleep, so I cleaned up a little."

"Why is the door open? Are we heating the outside now?"

"Sorry." *I was airing out the stale beer smell.* "It was stuffy in here."

Her father pushed the door closed and slumped into a chair. "Is this for me?"

Molly banged the aspirin down on the table next to his tea harder than she had intended. Leaving her own tea untouched, she pulled on her coat. "I'm going in early to turn in my written apology."

He grunted something as she shut the door. Using her free hand to push her hair out of her face, she walked quickly across the broken sidewalks toward school. Eric Burden sang of getting out of this place in her head. When she got to Elm Street, she heard voices echoing off the houses. Her steps slowed. Listening intently, she could make out Frank's voice and hurried to the corner.

"Did you two have a sleepover last night or something?" she hollered across the street.

"Hey, Molly!" Billy yelled back.

"Wait until you see what Thomas wrote last night!" Frank handed her the journal when they reached her. They walked slowly through the gate as she read.

"If that's all he wants, why doesn't he just go find her himself?" Molly asked.

Billy gave her an exasperated look. "Why are you asking me?"

"I don't know. I thought you might know something. I forgot you're from Masonville," she said.

"Watch out; she's on a roll already." Frank pointed his finger at her.

"Don't encourage her."

"How come you're in such a pissy mood? Was dinner as bad as it smelled?" Molly asked.

"Gee." Billy put a finger to his temple thoughtfully. "What could be bothering me? Could it be I apparently have a ghost for a roommate? Or the nightmares I'm having when I go to sleep? Or that O'Riley would like to see my head mounted on the wall in his father's mansion? Wanna pick one?"

"Now that you've got that out of your system, can we talk about something besides you?" Molly asked.

"Hey, you guys, lighten up! 'All for one,' remember?" Frank said as he pushed between them. "Save this crap for our enemies."

"He's right. I think that's twice in two days." Molly held up her pinky finger. "Truce?"

Billy hesitated, leaving Molly's pinky in midair for a

long moment. Finally, he locked his pinky finger with Molly's. "Truce."

The front door to the school pushed open just as they approached, and Shorty's smiling face beamed at them. "If it isn't my three favorite students," he said as he held the door for them. "How are we doing this morning?"

"Great," Frank said. "Thanks, Mr. Shorts."

"Shorty, you've lived here a long time, right?" Billy asked.

"Most of my life. Why?"

"Do you know someone named Tearneach?"

Shorty's smile disappeared instantly, and his eyes moved from side to side, avoiding their gaze. "Where did you hear that name?"

Billy took a step back. "We're researching the Packard murders."

Shorty limped inside behind Billy. "My advice is to let a sleeping dog lie. That's old news, and nobody wants it dredged up again."

"Um, okay, sure. Thanks."

They dropped off Molly's apology and continued to the library in silence.

Finally, Billy asked his friends, "Man, did you catch that?"

"Yeah, I wonder what it was about?" Frank pulled out a chair for Molly.

"Thank you, Frank." Molly sat down. "If it's such old news, then what's the big deal?"

Frank grinned at her. "There must be more to it."

"If I didn't know any better, I would say he's afraid of Tearneach," Billy said.

Molly considered this. "How do you know he isn't?"

"I don't."

Molly pointed at Frank. "Okay, Brainiac. Make a list."

"How come I always have to do the writing?" Frank whined.

Molly glared across the table at Frank. "Because I said so."

"Good enough reason for me," Billy said.

Molly began, "First, what we know: One, Thomas's family was murdered on November 14, 1924. Two, he tried to do witchcraft."

"Tried?" Frank interrupted. "I think the journal proves he did it."

"Are we going to accept everything in the journal as fact?" Molly chewed on the end of her pen.

"That's a good question," Billy chimed in. "Do we believe everything in the journal? And, while we're on the subject of believing, do you guys believe me?"

Molly sat back and looked at Billy, pursing her lips. *Do I? After that freaky shit last night, how can I not? But still it's too weird.* "Finally, she leaned forward and folded her hands on the table. "Good point. Let's say I believe *you* believe what you've told us, and—"

"What does that mean?" Billy cut in, turning red.

"It means," she continued in a calm voice, "I believe you are telling the truth, but it's also possible someone is deceiving us. I don't think we should assume the new journal entries are real."

"That makes sense," Frank agreed. "Although, I don't have any other theories how the journal gets new entries or why it returns to the attic on its own."

"Do we agree Thomas didn't kill his family?" Billy asked.

Molly pointed to the list Frank had started. "That's a maybe."

Frank nodded, pushed his glasses up with a finger, and continued to write.

"So, where do we go from here?" Billy asked.

Frank raised his hand as if he was in class. "How do we go about finding Tearneach?"

"I think we start at the library. We'll look up everything we can find on the murders," Molly said.

"Are we going to try to find out who did it then?" Frank asked.

Molly blew out an exasperated breath. "I thought that was the whole idea."

"What about Tearneach?" Billy asked.

"Maybe you should ask Mr. Shorts again," Frank said.

Billy shook his head. "You ask him next time. We could check the phonebook for Tearneach. Maybe she's listed."

"Yeah, we'll let our fingers do the walking through the Yellow Pages." Frank walked his hand across the table. "She'll be listed under W for witches: Tearneach, specializing in spells and potions."

"Go ahead and make fun, but we have to find her if we're going to help Thomas." Billy leaned back and crossed his arms.

"The only thing we know for sure is the murders really happened. We'll start there." Molly stood, signaling the end of the discussion.

"Where are you going?" Frank asked. "It's too early to go to class."

"I have a question." Billy looked at Molly. "Who is the Houlahan that Thomas mentions in the journal?"

"My grandfather. Mamo told me he and old man O'Riley were friends."

"Your grandfather and O'Riley were friends?" Frank asked. "I thought the O'Rileys and the Houlahans were sworn enemies."

"We weren't always."

Molly went on to tell them what she had learned from

193

her grandmother and Mrs. O'Brien. When she was through, she felt drained.

Frank's jaw hung open. "I can't believe it. You owned the mill, *and* you're practically O'Riley's cousin," Frank said in astonishment.

"I didn't own it. My grandfather did. And I'm definitely not related to that creep," Molly shot back. "And the next time you suggest I am, I'll knock you clear into next week."

"Your dad owned it, though." Billy said.

"He sold his share to pay my mother's hospital bills. I was four years old when she died, so that would be around eleven years ago." Molly swallowed around the lump forming in her throat. "Mamo said my grandfather bought it with blood money, whatever that means."

Franks eyes grew large behind his glasses. "Blood money sounds pretty ominous."

"Maybe your grandmother knows about Tearneach," Billy suggested.

"She's not always with it these days. End of discussion."

Billy put his hands in the air, surrendering. "Okay, don't shoot me."

"Let's get going. I don't want to be in the halls when O'Riley comes in." Molly headed for the door. She stopped just inside the door to their homeroom. It was festooned with decorations for the season.

"Good morning, people. It's especially nice to have you back, Molly. Is your suspension over already?" Miss Albright asked. She was standing on a step stool pinning fake fall leaves to the wall.

"My dad came in yesterday and talked Mr. Brady into letting me return to school."

Billy cleared his throat. "Miss Albright, how would you

go about finding someone who lived in town, say, forty-four years ago?"

"Well, I would look in the phonebook first. It's the easiest place to start."

Billy swatted at Frank. "Told ya."

"If they weren't listed, I might see if the courthouse has any record of them owning property. You could also comb through the birth and death records for anyone with the same last name and ask them if they're related." Miss Albright gave them a shrewd look. "Are you two thinking of becoming reporters?"

"Not me. I'm going to MIT. I'm going to work for NASA," Frank said.

"William, do you want to become an investigative reporter? You could work for the *New York Times*, maybe?"

"I've never really thought much about it."

"Hand me that string of gourds, please." She pinned one end to the wall. "Is this related to the murders you're researching?"

"Yes. We thought it would be good to hear what someone remembered from the time, rather than just reading newspaper accounts," Frank said.

Miss Albright moved the step stool she'd been standing on. "It shouldn't be hard to find someone who remembers the murders from forty years ago."

"The people we've asked so far don't really want to talk about it," Billy said.

"I see. Well, remember, any information you get from a source like that will need to be corroborated. Keep notes on your research. You may find them useful during the Christmas break."

Frank and Billy looked at each other then back at Molly. Miss Albright fussed with the last of the decorations, stepped down, and looked at her handiwork.

"There. I think it looks rather festive," she said, dusting off her hands. "What do you think?"

Frank raised his arms and turned 360 degrees. "It brightens up the whole room."

"It's very, um, Thanksgiving-y," Billy said.

"Oh, yes. I feel like I'm back in elementary school," Molly said.

"I knew I could count on Molly for an honest answer," Miss Albright said. She took her usual place at the door when students started to drift in and greeted each one by name. Billy and Frank gathered around Molly's desk.

"What do you think she meant about keeping notes?" Frank asked.

"Who knows what she's thinking? At least the whole room is brightened up now," Molly imitated Frank. "And you! Thanksgiving-y? That's not even a word."

"So what? At least we didn't hurt her feelings," Billy said.

Frank rapped his knuckles on Molly's desk. "Don't look now, but here comes you-know-who."

They all turned to see O'Riley stride into the room, flanked by Sal and Ernie. Billy watched as he scanned the room until his gaze landed on them. He made a direct line for Molly's desk. She stood up as he approached.

"You think you're pretty smart, but we'll see who has the last laugh," O'Riley said.

"Mr. O'Riley. I believe your seat is on the other side of the room. Take it now, please." Miss Albright's voice cut through the classroom noise like a knife.

"We'll just see," O'Riley repeated.

Molly noticed several angry cuts on the back of O'Riley's balled-up fists as he walked away. "Did you see his hands?"

Frank nodded. "Thomas did it."

"You mean the owl, don't you?" Molly asked.

"They're one and the same," Frank said.

"Says you," she said.

"Seats, please!" The bell rang, and Miss Albright pulled the door closed.

Molly felt the day tick by at a snail's pace. She observed the teachers hovered a little more than usual any time O'Riley was in close proximity. *I wish we could just have it out and be done with it. This cat-and-mouse game is wearing me out.* She waited for Frank and Billy by the door at the end of the day.

"You got a plan?" Billy asked.

"I told you before. They're cowards. If it's three on three, they won't try anything. We just have to stick together."

Billy shrugged and turned to Frank. "You okay with that?"

Frank's eyes grew large behind his glasses, but he nodded and wedged himself between Molly and Billy. Three across, they walked down the now-empty corridors toward the front door.

"Why aren't we going out the back way?" Frank asked as they reached the door.

"Because we don't have to!" Molly spat. She pushed open the door and walked out first. Shorty's familiar limping gait at the end of the sidewalk was the only activity they noticed.

"Hey, Shorty. What're you doing?" Billy asked.

"He's spreading salt. What's it look like he's doing? Don't they have salt in Masonville?" Molly asked, feigning disbelief.

Shorty reached into a burlap bag and scattered a handful of rock salt across the walk. "They're calling for snow tonight. My knee says it's a big one."

"Mr. Shorts. I wanted to say thank you for letting us use the back way out yesterday," Frank stammered. "Billy showed us, and well, you know…"

"You are all very welcome. I notice you didn't think it was necessary today."

"Molly said they won't bother us when we're together, because they're cowards," Frank answered.

"Molly is probably right, but they're hanging around at the corner right now. You be careful, y'hear?"

"Yes, sir, we're sticking together," Billy said through chattering teeth.

"Mr. Shorts? We're doing a paper on the Packard murders for a school project. Would you answer some questions for us?" Molly asked in her best Perry Mason voice.

Shorty looked up sharply. "Who is this project for?"

"Miss Albright's class," Molly said, maintaining an air of authority.

"Hmm…" Shorty threw another handful of salt across the sidewalk. "I'm kind of busy right now. Maybe another time."

"Why won't you talk to us about it? You said yourself it's old news. What can it hurt?" Molly pressed.

Shorty spun on her, causing them all to step back. "The Packards were good people, except for that boy of theirs. It was a great tragedy, what happened to them, and a terrible loss to the whole town. That's why. And if I hear tell of you all creeping around that old wood, messing with that witch, I'll just have to pass it over to Principal Brady to take up with your folks, now, you hear? You stay clear. Now take my advice and find another subject to do your so-called school project on." Shorty dragged the burlap bag past them and limped away, throwing handfuls of rock salt onto the walk so hard, most of it bounced off into the dead grass.

"I've never seen Shorty lose his temper before," Frank said.

"That was helpful, don't you think?" Molly said brightly. "Let's get to the library before it closes."

Turning in the opposite direction of O'Riley and his friends, they walked up the hill as tree branches rattled like castanets in the November wind.

## Chapter Thirty-One

The musty smell of old paper, wood polish, and dust assaulted Frank's nose as he walked up to the tall checkout desk in the center of the library. He wiped the fog from his glasses on his shirttail before he looked into the tired blue eyes of the librarian. A soft wisp of gray hair defied gravity by standing up on the old man's otherwise-barren head.

"How may I help you, young man?" His voice croaked as though he were not accustomed to speaking.

Frank adjusted his glasses. "We want to look at the *Willowton Sentinel* from 1924."

"That material has been transferred to microfilm. Do any of you know how to use the microfilm readers?"

"N-n-no, sir," Frank stuttered.

Molly and Billy shook their heads.

The librarian sighed and rolled his eyes. "Very well, come with me."

The yellowness of the old man's eyes gave Frank pause.

"Are you coming?" he croaked, looking back.

Frank checked to make sure Molly and Billy were with

him. He had no intentions of going into the stacks alone with that guy. The skeletal figure led them through the stacks moving a lot faster than Frank would have thought possible for someone who looked about a hundred years old. "Here we are, young man. Is there any date in particular, or do you want the entire year?"

"November fourteenth and the week or so after," Molly spoke up.

The old man trained his eyes on her, as if seeing her for the first time, then asked in a monotone voice, "I see. Will all of you be wanting to use the readers?"

"Yes, sir, if it's possible? It will speed up our research," Molly said.

"Well, only two are working, but gather around, and I'll show you how to operate it." He quickly took them through the process. "Put everything back the way you found it," he said as he unfolded himself from the chair and slowly moved away.

"Yes, sir. Thank you for your help," Molly said.

He turned back to look at them and paused. "I have a book written about the Packard murders. Since we only have two readers, maybe one of you would be interested in it."

"Sure," Billy said, speaking up for the first time. "But how did you know we—"

"I'm old, not stupid, young man. Every few years, someone comes in here looking for information on the Packard massacre. Follow me."

Frank watched as Billy disappeared around the corner. "That guy gives me the creeps."

"Yeah" was all he got from Molly. Her eyes were locked on the viewer. Frank selected the roll labeled 11/15/24 and threaded it.

"Holy cow!" Molly said.

Frank jumped from his seat and came over to stand behind her. "What? What? Let me see."

## Chapter Thirty-Two

Billy heard the librarian's creaking bones as they moved through shelves of books towering over his head. The skeleton-like man pulled up short, and Billy almost walked into him.

Reaching for a high shelf without looking, he selected a book and handed it to Billy. "Do you have a library card, young man?"

"No, sir, I just moved here a few days ago."

After setting Billy up with a library card Mr. Glicken removed the card in the pocket attached to the back of the book, stamped it with the date, and replaced it with another card from a box on the desk. "It's due back in two weeks."

Billy sat down at a table and looked at the book. *Tragedy and Travesty in Willowton*, by Reginald Glicken. Billy glanced back at the desk where Mr. Glicken had stood a moment ago. *How many Glickens can there be?*

The introduction informed him that the author thought there was more to the murders than a teenage son gone mad. He leafed through the book slowly until he got to the center, which contained several pages of glossy black-and-white photos. The dead eyes of Mabel Packard stared up at him from the bathtub. His chest felt tight, and he couldn't breathe. His vision narrowed until he thought he was looking through an ever-shrinking tunnel. His last conscious thought was to breathe.

## Chapter Thirty-Three

Frank leaned in and pushed Molly to the left so he could look into the viewer. The picture was grainy, but the image was no less gruesome. "That picture, it's just—just like Billy described it in his dreams."

"Billy should see this." Molly elbowed Frank out of the way. "I'll get him."

Frank read the account of the murders and was amazed at the way the truth had morphed into fiction in the years after the event. The Packard family wasn't hacked to pieces with an axe. The headline claimed they were "brutally slain in their beds."

"Frank!" Molly's voice pierced the quiet, disrupting the dust bunnies that resided on the high shelves.

*Why is she yelling in a library?* Pushing out the chair, he fast-walked toward Molly's voice. When he reached the open area with the study tables, Frank saw Billy slumped over. "What happened to him?"

"Find the librarian." Molly tilted Billy's head back.

The librarian appeared out of nowhere with a paper cup of water in his shaking hand. He pushed Molly out of the way then pulled Billy upright by his shoulder before tossing the water into his face. Billy's eyes popped open, and he screamed, chilling Frank to the bone. Molly staggered back another step to give the old man more room.

He placed his bony hands on Billy's shoulders and knelt on the floor in front of him. "It's all right, son. Take a deep breath. You're all right."

Gooseflesh ran over Frank as he recognized the same photograph from the newspaper article in the opened book. He tugged at Molly's sleeve and pointed it out to her.

Billy's eyes were wild, but the old man kept talking to him in a low voice. After a while, he appeared to calm down. "Thanks, Mr. Glicken." Billy wiped the water from his face. "I'm all right."

"I'm afraid that book gave you quite a fright."

Molly had picked up the book leafed through it. She nudged Frank and mouthed the author's name, pointing at the librarian.

"Don't let him get up. I'll be right back." Glicken straightened himself up with considerable effort.

"Mr. Glicken, sir?" Frank asked. "Did you write that book?"

"A younger version of myself wrote it, yes. It seems like a lifetime ago," he said wistfully. Moving like a marionette, he went through a door behind the tall desk.

"Billy, are you okay?" Frank asked, pulling a chair up in front of him.

Molly flipped the book over to reveal a photo of a much younger Glicken. "Listen to this. Born in Willowton, New York, Mr. Glicken attended Brown University, where he received a degree in journalism. He currently resides in his hometown of Willowton, where he is a staff reporter for the *Willowton Sentinel*."

"I'll bet he wrote those articles too," Frank said suddenly.

Molly squatted in front of Billy. "How are you feeling?"

"Here we are." Glicken returned with an ornate silver tray supporting four mismatched mugs, a sugar bowl, and several teaspoons. He pulled a flask from his pocket, poured a small amount of something into a mug, and handed it to Billy. "A hot cup of Earl Grey tea with a touch of apricot brandy will make you feel better, young man." He handed Molly and Frank each a cup of tea and motioned for them to sit. Then he poured a generous amount of brandy into his own mug and sat down next to Billy, who was taking a sip of his tea.

"Do you have cream and lemon for the tea?" Molly asked.

"I should've guessed you would take your tea the Irish way," Glicken said, arching one bushy eyebrow at her. "Would you be so kind as to retrieve them? Straight through the door, the refrigerator is on the right. Thank you so much."

Molly made her way into Glicken's office. When she returned, she asked Billy what had happened.

"I think I fainted." Billy inclined his head toward the book lying between them. "There are pictures of..." He shuddered. "Of... our bathroom. It looks the same now as it did when the murders happened." He looked away. "Except for the body, of course, but I dreamt about that."

The library was completely silent. Frank stared out the windows and watched the snowflakes drift by. *Billy's afraid of the girl in the tub.*

"You've had dreams about the murders. Is that what sparked your interest in this matter?" Glicken asked.

"Billy lives in the old Packard house, so we thought we

would find out what really happened." Frank refocused his attention.

Glicken looked up sharply. "No one has lived in that house since the murders. Are you telling me you're living in there now?"

Billy nodded. "We're going to do a paper about the murders for a school project."

"What do you mean, you want to know what really happened?" Glicken asked.

"First, we want to dispel all the rumors about the murders. Then we want to figure out if Thomas really did it," Molly said.

"I see. Do you have some reason to believe he didn't commit the murders?" Glicken asked.

"Not exactly," Molly said. "But everyone we've approached about the murders refuses to talk to us about it. You were here when it happened. What do you think?"

Glicken arched his eyebrows, pushed his chair back from the table, and crossed one leg over the other. "What I think happened is in the book in front of you, for the most part, anyway. Maybe you should start there."

"Do you believe in ghosts?" Frank asked.

"As in the ghost of Thomas Packard haunting that old house?"

"Who else?" Molly asked.

"I don't believe in the supernatural, but I also don't believe all things are easily explained."

"You either do or don't," Molly said.

"I don't believe Thomas haunts the old house on State Street. I do believe the truth of what happened that night has never been told." The lights in the library flickered as though in response to the librarian's denial. He diluted his tea with another generous shot of brandy from his flask.

Frank looked out the window again. The snowflakes

were stacking up on the deep stone sills. "We should prob-ably get going." He pointed to the falling snow through the window.

Billy reached for the book, but Glicken beat him to it.

"I'm not sure you're ready to read this book."

Molly put out her hand. "You're right, Mr. Glicken. He's not. I'll take it."

He gave her an appraising look then handed the book to her. "Fine, come back when you've read it." He gath-ered up the tray and cups then retreated through the door into his office.

"He's a little spooky, isn't he?" Frank's eyes followed the disappearing Glicken.

"A *little?*" Molly asked. "He's one hundred percent spooky, if you ask me. I've got to put the microfilm away. Wait here with Billy."

Frank sat quietly observing his friend. "We should ask him if he knows Tearneach."

"I'm not asking him. You ask him," Billy replied.

Molly returned with their coats. "Now what?"

"Frank's going to ask Glicken if he knows Tearneach," Billy explained.

Frank threw his arms in the air. "That's not what I—"

Molly tossed their coats on the table. "Save it for another day. We need to get home right now. It's getting late. Besides, I want to read this book first, anyway."

"I'd like to read it too," Frank said.

"It's checked out to me, you know," Billy protested weakly.

Molly rolled her eyes at Frank. "Oh yeah, that's a good idea. You should read it so you can have even worse night-mares than you're having already."

Outside, Frank pulled on his hat and noticed the wind wasn't blowing for the first time in days. The snow fell straight down, and he heard a low hiss as thousands of flakes made contact with the ground. *How many snowflakes does it take to make a sound?*

"Man, there must be four inches already," Billy said, breaking Frank's awestruck moment. "Maybe they'll cancel school tomorrow."

Frank tugged at the earflaps of his hat. "I doubt it."

"What does it take to get school canceled around here?" Billy asked.

"An act of God, usually," Molly said. "If it keeps up like this, they might open late."

They walked in silence through the pristine snow, which reflected the streetlights in a dazzling display.

"What's next?" Billy asked, breaking the silence.

"I'll read Glicken's book tonight. Tomorrow, we'll meet early again and figure out what to do next." Molly stopped at the corner. "It's like a ghost town out here; not one car has been down the street yet."

"Yeah, it's too quiet." *It is a ghost town.* Frank shuddered at the thought. "I'm getting the willies."

"You always have the willies," Molly said, smirking. "I'll see you guys tomorrow. Keep your eyes open for O'Riley."

"Maybe we should walk you home," Billy offered.

"Yeah, and who's going to walk you home?"

"More importantly, who's going to walk me home?" Frank asked.

"Come on, I'll walk you home," Billy said to Frank. He waved to Molly. "See you tomorrow."

A snowball missed Frank's head by inches. He turned just in time to see the second one hit Billy squarely in the back.

"That's it, Houlahan! You're dead now!" Billy retaliated with several throws of his own.

"I'm so scared, I'm shaking in my boots," Molly yelled back, dodging the incoming snowballs.

Frank joined in, and snowballs and taunts flew in both directions across the street.

Molly continued her assault, somehow managing to avoid the double-barreled onslaught aimed at her. "You guys are pathetic," she cried. "I can't stand here all night and wait for one of you to get lucky. I'll see you tomor—"

A snowball in the face cut her off.

"You're in trouble now, buddy boy."

Frank saw the astonished look on Billy's face and took a step backward. Molly doubled over with laughter. She looked up and pointed but was unable to speak.

Billy and Frank glanced at each other dumbfounded. Molly continued to laugh. The boys joined in. When she caught her breath. "See you two doofuses later." She turned and walked toward home.

A snowball dropped from Billy's hand. "What just happened?"

"Darned if I know."

## Chapter Thirty-Four

Billy stared as Molly disappeared into the falling snow. "Let's go. My hands are freezing. What's with the goofy grin, Doofus One?"

"It's no goofier than yours, Doofus Two."

They walked in silence most of the way to Frank's house. Billy thought about Molly's laughter. He'd only known her a short time, but in that time, he'd seen sarcasm and anger, but never the joyous side of Molly. *Am I like that too? What do Frank and Molly see? That's easy—a pathetic loser.*

Frank interrupted his thoughts. "If school starts late tomorrow, why don't you come over to my house? We can hang out."

"What, oh sure. I'll come over at seven thirty either way, and we'll walk in together."

"Maybe we'll catch Molly again too." Relief echoed in Frank's voice.

"Yeah, maybe you can pelt her in the face with another snowball."

They stopped in front of Frank's house. "You want to come in?"

"Nah, I'm going home. I'm beat." Billy turned.

"Hey, Billy."

Billy turned back to see a serious expression on Frank's face. "Yeah?"

"Those pictures in Glicken's book, they were just like in your nightmares, weren't they?"

"Except my nightmares are in color." Billy shuddered at the memory.

"Are you going to be all right? I mean…" Frank's voice faltered.

"Dreams can't hurt you. Right?"

"I guess not."

"Okay. See ya."

"Wouldn't want to be ya." Frank forced a smile.

Billy turned away. *Nobody does.* A large dark shape perched in a tree drew his attention. He looked into yellow eyes piercing the night. "Let's go home. It's cold."

The owl's head twisted. Spreading its wings, it glided silently over Billy and flew ahead of him. He followed its flight path until it perched again, this time on a streetlight. It continued to make short flights, leading the way home. Billy hesitated when it flew past his street. The owl fluttered its wings impatiently. Shrugging, Billy followed. It left the street and took a path through a wooded area. Very little snow had accumulated under the boughs of the trees, which blocked most of the light. He slowed his steps as doubt and fear filled the pit of his stomach. It was dark. Too dark. Being alone made it feel that much darker. He wasn't sure what he was even following. An owl, a ghost, or some combination of both? The path stopped at a snow-covered road. The trees spread out, allowing the snow and moonlight to filter through.

Billy hesitated and looked back at the path. "I'm going

back." He started to retrace his steps. The owl flew so close, he felt the breeze on his face.

"All right, all right, but I'm not going much farther."

Shortly, he rounded a bend and saw a small house silhouetted against the night sky. A bare light bulb burning near the door was the only sign of life. The house looked old and more than a little crooked. Even in the dark, he could see it needed a paint job. A mailbox sat lopsided on a picket fence leaning drunkenly against an overgrown shrub. *It's been a long time since the mailman was here.*

The owl sat on what was left of a porch railing. Below the light, a hand-painted sign read "Readings By Appointment Only." The word *only* had been underlined several times to emphasize its importance. Painted on the side of the mailbox in the same scrawling hand was the name Tearny.

Billy's pulse thudded in his temples. He'd found Tearneach. The door opened. A figure stood in the opening, backlit by an eerie red light. He turned and ran as fast as he could in the snow, his thin-soled shoes slipping with every step, following his footsteps back the way he'd come.

## Chapter Thirty-Five

Tearneach stepped out onto the porch and adjusted the brightly colored turban resting on her head. She listened as the footsteps retreated up the road. "Don' worry, *mon ami*, he'll be back."

The owl's head twisted around to look at her. It fanned out its wings, revealing an impressive wingspan.

"I know, I know. Patience, *mon cher*. He mus' come to us."

The bird made several sharp hoots and jumped onto her outstretched hand.

"Trus' me, Thomas. We almos' done. Da boy—he will come back. Jus' da way you come back when you were young. Not'ing could keep you away."

She walked to the edge of the porch and lifted him into the air. "You know wha' mus' be done." She smiled as the owl flew away.

Back inside, she sat down at a small table and turned on a lamp. A scarf draped over the lampshade bathed the room in blood-red light, except for a small circle around the base of the lamp. A worn deck of Tarot cards sat near Tearneach. She turned them over one at a time and placed them in a precise pattern. Each card elicited a small "ooh" or "ahh" from her as she set it down.

"Oh, *cher*, no so good."

## Chapter Thirty-Six

Billy's heart beat a jungle rhythm in his chest as he opened the kitchen door and stepped into the warmth.

His mother approached him as he stepped inside. "Where have you been?"

"I went to the library to study with my friends."

"Well, I would appreciate a little notice when you plan to come home so late." She placed her hands on her hips. "It's common courtesy to let people know when you're going to be late."

"I'm sorry, Mom. We lost track of the time."

"Sorry doesn't cut it."

"I thought you were happy I made friends. I even brought them over to meet you last night."

"That's no excuse for being inconsiderate."

He knew this was going in the wrong direction. In spite of that, his frustration took charge. "I said I was sorry. What do you want from me?"

"I want a little respect and consideration. From now on, I want you to come straight home from school."

Billy raised his voice. "That's not fair. I didn't do anything wrong."

"Don't you raise your voice at me young man. You can go to bed without any dinner."

"That's no punishment." His own anger boiled to the surface. "Maybe if we had a phone, like normal people, I could call when I'm going to be late."

"Maybe, if your father sent some child support, we could afford a phone."

"Maybe, if you hadn't run him off, he'd still be here."

His mother raised her hand. Billy flinched.

Suddenly, Tony wrapped his arms gently around Billy's mother and kissed her neck. "It's all right, Maude. Breathe. Everything's all right."

Billy's mother relaxed into Tony's arms. He was shocked to see the hard edges of her face soften right before his eyes. Tony flicked his head quickly to the side, which Billy correctly interpreted as a signal to leave. On tiptoes, he backed out of the room in awe of what he'd just witnessed. *Is this guy some kind of hypnotist, or what?*

Walking up the steps, he thought about how close he'd come to being clobbered for the first time in memory. *I shouldn't have said that, even if it is true.* At the top of the stairs, he paused at the bathroom door. His mind went blank as a tremor rolled up his spine. Mabel's dead eyes looked up at him from the bloody tub. Squeezing his eyes closed, he grasped the doorframe to hold himself up.

"It's not real. It's not real." Keeping his eyes sealed, he felt his way across the hall and into his bedroom, holding his breath until safely inside. "Oh, man, I can't keep doing this." He collapsed onto the bed and slid the journal under his pillow for safekeeping. Sleep came for him fast and hard.

Screams shattered the nighttime silence, waking Billy. He sat up in bed and realized he was still wearing his school clothes. He was soaked through with sweat and shivering. When the lights came on, he blinked. His mother stood in the doorway of his room in her nightgown with a shocked look on her face.

Tony came in behind her, wearing only boxer shorts with red lips all over them. He pulled a blanket from the bed and wrapped it around Billy's shoulders. "You all right, kid?"

"I don't know…"

His mother moved in and hugged him. "You were screaming in your sleep."

"Oh," Billy said, as understanding dawned.

"Tell us about it," Tony prompted.

"I don't remember…" Billy shuddered. "Mabel. I saw Mabel. Her eyes—her eyes were…" Billy grew silent. "And something else." He shook his head to shake the memory loose.

"Who is Mabel?" his mother asked.

"She used to live here. She was murdered in the bathroom." There was a tremor in his voice. "I saw him. In the mirror… I saw him do it. I saw him stab her."

"You saw who stab who?" His mother took his face in her hands and looked into his eyes. "Are you doing drugs? Taking that LSD with your friends? Is that why you don't come home after school?"

"No, Mom, I just had a nightmare." Billy bit back his irritation.

"Is there a way to tell if he's using drugs?" she asked Tony.

"Of course." Tony knelt on the floor so he was at eye-level with Billy. "Maude, get me a flashlight."

When she left the room, Tony winked. "Take some deep breaths and let them out real slow. Follow my lead when she comes back." Tony looked straight into his eyes. "Was it the same dream as last night?"

Billy nodded. "Except I saw the man who did it this time. I don't know what to do. I'm afraid to go back to sleep."

"I know, kid. I know."

Billy's mother came back with a flashlight and handed it to Tony.

"Turn out the light, Maude."

Tony shone the beam into Billy's eyes one at a time. "Okay, follow the light with your eyes." Tony moved the light from side to side.

Looking up at Billy's mother, Tony flashed her a reassuring smile. "He's telling the truth, Maude. He just had a nightmare. Heat up a glass of warm milk for him. It'll help him get back to sleep."

"Mommy?" Suze called from her room.

"Great, you woke the baby up," his mother said.

"You go check on Suze." Tony stood up and placed an arm on Billy's shoulder. "Come on, kid. Let's heat up some milk."

"I'm coming, Susan." Billy's mother turned away.

Tony led Billy out of the room. He set a pan on the stove and poured milk into it. "You want to tell me about it?"

Billy thought about what he was willing to impart to Tony, who would almost certainly tell his mother everything. "It's hard to talk about serious stuff with a guy wearing boxers with big red lips all over them."

"Do the best you can."

Billy swallowed hard. "Three people were murdered in this house forty-four years ago." He thought for a moment. "On this very night, as a matter of fact. On my birthday."

"Is this part of the ghost story you were telling me about before?"

"Yeah, but it's true. I looked it up in the library today, I mean, yesterday."

Tony turned back to the stove and stirred the milk. "That's where you were last night?"

"Yeah. Me, Molly, and Frank went to the library to look up the newspapers from back then." Billy paused, remembering the events of the previous evening.

"Go on, I'm listening."

"The father, mother, and daughter were murdered, and the son disappeared. Everyone thinks Thomas, the son, murdered his family."

Tony poured warm milk into a glass and set it on the table before he sat down across from Billy.

"The girl was stabbed in the bathroom. I saw pictures of her. The bathroom looks the same. The mother and father were found in the room you and Mom use."

"You read this in the newspaper? Accounts of the murders?" Tony's tone was serious.

"Yes."

"Then it's no wonder you had a nightmare about the murders."

"I saw the man who stabbed Mabel in my dream. His back was toward me, but I saw his reflection in the mirror."

"You *dreamed* you saw who stabbed Mabel; you didn't actually see anyone." Tony put his hand on Billy's shoulder as he spoke. "I know it may have seemed real to you, but it was just a dream."

Billy looked down at his big toe, which was sticking out

of his sock. "Okay, I only dreamed it. It's just it seemed so—"

"I get that. Drink this before it gets cold." Tony slid the glass of milk closer to Billy.

"Put this on before you get sick." Billy's mother threw her robe at Tony. "Suze went right back to sleep, thank heaven."

Billy watched as Tony shrugged into his mother's nubby white robe.

"Thanks, babe."

The image of the man in the mirror flashed through Billy's head like a comet, leaving a contrail of emotional debris in its wake.

"Could you stoke the fire a little before we go back to bed? Maybe it won't be so cold in the morning."

"Sure, babe. I'll be right up."

She gave Tony a peck on the cheek before heading upstairs.

"You want to give me a hand for a minute, kid? I'm not exactly dressed for shoveling coal." Tony made a clumsy attempt at a pirouette, pretending to show off the robe as though it were an evening gown.

"Sure." Billy followed Tony into the basement, where the coal furnace hulked in the center of the room. It looked like an ancient metallic tree rooted to the concrete floor with metal branches reaching over Billy's head. Tony approached the furnace in the same way he did the kitchen stove. With a few quick, efficient moves, he had the coals glowing in the firebox.

"Grab the shovel over there and load it up from the bin." Tony motioned toward the coal bin with his free hand.

As directed, Billy sent a scoop of coal into the behemoth.

"Two more." Tony said.

With their mission complete, Tony led the way back upstairs. He pulled his car keys off a nail by the kitchen door and handed them to Billy. "Run out to my car. There's a bag in the trunk. Bring it in for me, will you?"

"My shoes are upstairs." Billy held one foot in the air and wiggled the big toe poking through the end of his sock.

"Yeah, mine too, and so are my pants. It's only a little snow."

"I could catch my death out there without shoes," Billy quipped, impersonating his mother.

"So what? You want to live forever?"

Billy took the keys and let himself out. He looked around, astonished at the amount of snow that had fallen since he'd come home. There had to be more than two feet on the ground. Without hesitation, he leapt from the porch and ran to Tony's car. He grabbed the bag and was back in the kitchen in no time.

"The snow is up to my knees, and it's still coming down."

"Well, you be sure to let me know when it starts going up." Tony hung his keys back on the nail and took the bag from Billy. He slid a gift-wrapped package out of the bag and handed it to him. "Happy Birthday, kid."

"Thanks, Tony. I don't know what to say."

"Thanks pretty much covers it." Tony grinned. "Open it, already."

Billy tore off the wrapping paper and opened the box. Inside, he found a pair of red leather boxing gloves. "Now I really don't know what to say."

"My feelings won't be hurt if you don't want them. Just say so, and I'll return them. Your mother will never have to know."

"Are you kidding? I want them! But only if you're going to show me how to use them?"

"If you're sure, we can spar in the basement when I get home from work."

Billy slid the gloves on and took a couple of practice punches. "This'll be cool."

"Let's get to bed. I'm going to have to leave extra early tomorrow because of the snow on the roads. You want me to wake you for breakfast?"

"Yeah, I'm starving." He put the gloves back in the box, took an awkward step toward Tony, and extended his hand. "Thank you, Tony."

Tony grabbed his hand and pulled him into a hug. "You're welcome, kid. Now, off you go, and no more dreaming."

When Tony released him, he noticed the shine in Tony's eyes.

"Yeah, I'll try." He picked up the gloves on his way.

In his room, he put on the gloves again. The smell of new leather flooded his nose when he held them up to his face. He switched off the light, feeling safer than he had in a long time.

---

Billy felt a tugging on his foot. When he opened his eyes, he saw Tony's grinning face.

"Hey, Tony," he croaked.

"Come on, kid, get cleaned up. Breakfast is already started. You might find it easier to eat without the gloves on, though," Tony said.

"Huh? Uh yeah, I must have…"

Tony closed the door, chuckling.

Billy stood in the hallway outside the bathroom door,

praying he wouldn't find any sign of Mabel or her killer. His stomach rumbled as the smell of bacon swept up the stairs. He grabbed a washcloth, towel, and a bar of soap and went downstairs. He walked into the kitchen with his arms full and hoped Tony would understand.

"Good morning."

Tony turned around from the stove, took one look at Billy, and walked over to the kitchen sink. "Let me get these things out of the sink for you."

"Thanks, I don't want to seem like a baby, but—"

"No sweat." Tony cleared the sink and went back to the stove, where the bacon sputtered in the pan.

Billy stripped down to his briefs and did his best to wash up in the kitchen sink. "I can't remember ever being up this early."

"Did you get any sleep?" Tony asked.

"I must have dropped right off." Billy felt his face flush when he remembered Tony had seen him with the gloves still on his hands earlier. He pulled on a pair of clean pants and slipped the belt through the loops.

"Me too. It didn't hurt that the house was warmer. I didn't have to fight your mom for the covers."

Billy tucked in his shirt and smoothed it down the front. "Good as new."

"Get the toast. Everything else is almost ready." Tony turned back to the stove and dished out eggs, bacon, and home fries.

Billy buttered and stacked the toast on a plate. "I'm starving."

"Let's eat." Tony poured coffee for himself and sat down.

They ate in silence until Billy's stomach was pleasantly full. "So, what're you going to tell Mom about the boxing gloves?"

"I'm not sure. It depends on how she reacts when she sees them, I guess."

Billy snorted and almost passed a piece of bacon through his nose.

"It's not *that* funny."

"Oh, yes it is."

Tony looked thoughtful for a moment. "Okay, here's what we do. Leave the box on the table as though you unwrapped them this morning. I'm going to work. If she asks you before you head out, tell her I gave them to you and left."

"No offense, but that seems kinda cowardly."

"It's not *kind of* cowardly. It's completely cowardly, but I'm good with it. She'll have all day to stew or"—Tony held up his hand with fingers crossed—"or to come around."

"Yeah. Are you taking any bets on which way that'll go?"

"No gambling. I'll teach you how to gamble next year." Tony winked. "I've got to get going. It looks pretty deep out there, and I want to get to work before the idiots get on the road." Tony pulled on his leather coat.

Billy followed him out into the dark and started to clear the snow from Tony's car. The Impala started with a roar then settled into a soft rumble.

Tony brandished a long-handled snow scraper. "I hope they plowed the main roads," he muttered softly. "This'll be a good test for the new snow tires."

"I hope they pass, for your sake." Billy brushed snow from the front of his coat.

Tony paused at the door to the car. "Hey kid, happy birthday."

"Thanks. Good luck." Billy waved as Tony eased the

car down the driveway, only spinning the tires a couple of times.

The taillights disappeared in a red cloud of exhaust. Billy was left to his thoughts again. The face in the mirror came back to him. The grim face of determination framed with unruly red hair disturbed him. It seemed too familiar somehow.

The hoot of an owl pulled him back into the present. Looking up, he saw the silhouette perched in the tree.

"You're up late," Billy said, his mind flashing back to Tearneach's shack. "The sun'll be up soon. You'd better get to wherever you go during the day." Billy turned and went inside.

The box holding his birthday gift lay on the table where he had left it. The breakfast dishes were clean and drying in the rack next to the sink. *Only one more thing to do before I head over to Frank's.*

Although the house was warmer this morning, the attic remained frigid. Standing at the desk, Billy flipped the journal open and searched for a new entry.

*November the Fourteenth, Nineteen Hundred Sixty-eight*

*You must go to Tearneach. She is the only one who can help me. She awaits your visit, even now. If you truly want to help, you must go to her alone. She will tell you what must be done to free me from bondage. My only hope for peace rests with you.*

*Yours in Friendship,*
*TZP*

# Chapter Thirty-Seven

Tearneach busied herself inside the dark house, sorting through dried herbs. A puff of breath sent a cloud of dust from the top of the jar into the air. Holding it to the light, she squinted at the object floating in the briny liquid. She fished it out and placed it next to the others on a massive wood slab table standing in the middle of the room. A large python wrapped itself around the stone mortar and the large copper bowl in the center of the table, making it look like a macabre holiday centerpiece. The snake's tongue sampled the air every now and again, while Tearneach worked and hummed a melodic tune.

"Now, where did I put da chicken-bone meal?"

The owl sat on a perch in the corner, tilted its head, and blinked in response.

"Oh, here t'is. We are ready, except for da last ting, of course." She threw back her head and cackled loudly. The owl shook out its impressive wings and hooted.

"I know, *mon ami*. Patience." She cackled again. "We will call on Legba dis very night and open da conduit to da spirits." She moved the mortar and pestle near her and stroked the snake as she did. "Is fine, Li Grand Zombi, keep your slumber for now." Then she measured some jimson weed into the mortar. Her soft humming accompanied her preparations.

## Chapter Thirty-Eight

Billy slid the journal under his arm and thought about how Molly and Frank would react to being excluded. *Molly's gonna freak, of course. And Frank? He'll freak too, in his own way.* Billy wrote a quick note to his mother.

*Mom,*
*Left early to walk to school with Frank. I'll come straight home.*
*Billy*

He placed it on the boxing gloves and set out for Frank's house. The snow was deep, but at least it had stopped falling for the moment. He walked through the streets in the tracks left by Tony's car until he turned onto Maple Street. There, he forged a new trail through the knee-deep snow. His Masonville shoes were not cut out for such weather. The smooth soles slipped and slid, and snow fell into his shoes around his ankles. By the time Frank's house was in sight, Billy's feet were blocks of ice, and he was mad at himself for going out in this crappy weather.

Mr. Bordeaux stood on the narrow path he had shoveled from the porch to his car. He had on the same silly hat Frank wore, complete with earflaps and chinstrap, and his face was as red as Tony's car. He gave Billy a quick wave, then went to the door and yelled for Frank.

"You're up early," he said, a little out of breath.

"Yes, sir. I promised Frank I'd come over early so we could walk to school together."

"He'll be right out, but there is no school today. They just announced it on the radio."

"Frank said they never cancel school around here."

"It's very unusual because the students all walk to school. Maybe the staff couldn't get in today." Mr. Bordeaux moved the snow shovel he was holding from one hand to the other. "Where is that boy?"

The door opened as if on cue, and Frank stepped out. "Billy, I didn't expect to see you today."

Mr. Bordeaux headed toward the snowdrift concealing his car. "You boys have all day to talk. Help me excavate the car."

Billy handed Frank the journal and his notebook. "Can you put them inside?"

"Sure." Frank whirled around and tossed them into the house.

Billy winced.

Frank leaned close to Billy. "Is there anything new?"

Billy nodded.

Frank took a sudden leap off the porch and slipped on the packed snow. His feet went up and his butt came down, earflaps flying.

Billy laughed and offered a hand up. They helped Mr. Bordeaux clear off the car by using their hands to send small avalanches of snow off the roof, hood, and trunk. Frank's dad opened the door, slid inside, and started the engine. Billy and Frank continued to move snow away from the front of the car to give Mr. Bordeaux a clear path.

After another half hour, Mr. Bordeaux finally pulled away from the curb and drove down the street. Billy stared down at his frozen feet. "I can't feel my toes."

Frank looked at his friend's feet. "Don't you have galoshes?"

"You mean boots? No, I don't. Because in Masonville, they cancel school for this kind of weather, like any normal, civilized, red-blooded American community should. That way, nobody unnecessarily dies of frostbite or snow blindness."

"Come on, Captain Cranky. My mother will fix you up."

In the foyer, Frank started to strip down. Billy watched in amazement as his gloves, hat, coat, scarf, boots, snow pants, sweater, and finally, flannel shirt all came off. Frank stood waist-deep in a pile of discarded clothes, sweating and smiling.

"What?" Frank asked.

"It's a miracle you could even move under all those clothes."

Mrs. Bordeaux entered, took a quick look at Billy, and smiled. "Your feet must be soaked through. Take off those shoes. Frank, get him a pair of dry socks." She got a towel from the bathroom, handed it to Billy, then began to pick up Frank's discarded clothes.

Billy stuffed his socks into his wet shoes. When he wasn't looking, Mrs. Bordeaux scooped them up with Frank's wet clothes and whisked them away.

"Here you go," Frank tossed a pair of warm socks and sheepskin slippers to Billy.

"Thanks."

"Come on. There's hot chocolate in the kitchen." Frank picked up the journal and flipped to the newest entry.

Billy pulled on the socks, and his feet felt better immediately. He stood up in the soft pile of the slippers and felt warm all over. "These are nice."

"So what's with this? Why does he want you alone? We're a team."

"That's nothing. Wait until I tell you what happened last night." Billy sat down at what had become his usual spot in Frank's kitchen and took a long drink from his mug.

"What happened?"

"Can you call Molly first? I only want to say this once."

Frank dialed and handed Billy the receiver. The line crackled and hummed in Billy's ear, and he almost hung up on the third ring. He released the breath he'd been holding when he heard Molly's voice.

"Hello."

"Molly? It's, uh, Billy."

"I know who it is, doofus."

"I—that is, we were wondering if you could come over to Frank's?"

"I have to make sure Mrs. O'Brien is coming first. I don't want to leave Mamo alone."

"I think I found Tearneach last night," Billy blurted out.

"I'll call Mrs. O'Brien right now. I'll be there as soon as I can."

Molly hung up, and Billy stood there with the receiver pressed to his ear until the dial tone came on.

"Well?" Frank asked.

"She said she'd be here as soon as she could."

"You found Tearneach last night?"

"I think so."

Frank led the way back into the kitchen. "So tell me! Where is she?"

"Wait. There's something else I want to know before Molly gets here."

Frank waited for Billy to continue.

"What's the story with Molly's brother?"

Frank took off his glasses and cleaned them on his shirttail. "Three of Molly's brothers and Derrick O'Riley's older brother were coming down Quarry Road in O'Riley's GTO. They were drunk. The car careened off the road and crashed. Two of Molly's brothers and O'Riley's brother died, but Patrick, he's the one in jail, was thrown from the car and survived. The sheriff said Patrick was driving, so that's why he went to jail. Molly thinks he got railroaded."

Billy wiped away chocolate clinging to his upper lip. "What so you think?"

"I think they're all guilty. The older kids hang out up at the quarry, where they drink and make out and stuff. That wasn't the first wreck they had up there. Someone was bound to get killed sooner or later. The fact that it was O'Riley's oldest made it worse."

Billy shook his head slowly. "Man, it's no wonder they don't like each other."

"That was the coolest car in town: a 1964 silver GTO with a 389, a four-barrel Holley carburetor, and a four speed Hurst shifter on the floor. We called it the Gray Ghost because nothing around here could touch it. They used to race it up at the quarry. Not so much now. Since the accident, I mean."

"I didn't know you were a car guy?"

Frank stared wistfully into the distance. "You should

have seen it fly. Three hundred and forty-eight horsepower, over one hundred and twenty miles an hour."

Billy nodded thoughtfully.

"So are you going to tell me where Tearneach is?"

There was a loud banging on the door. "That's got to be Molly."

## Chapter Thirty-Nine

Molly made a fist and rapped on the door. "Come on, Bordeaux. I'm freezing out here," Molly hollered.

"Well, come in, then." Frank swung the door open.

Molly stomped her feet on the porch and hustled inside. "Shit, it's cold." She slammed the door behind her, handed Frank the book she was carrying, and rubbed her hands together vigorously. Then she made the sign of the cross and mumbled a fast prayer. "Amen."

Molly looked down at Billy's feet and started to laugh. "What's with the slippers? Did you two have another sleepover? People are going to talk."

"No, my feet were wet when I got here. Does everyone in Willowton have galoshes?" Billy countered, pointing at Molly's feet.

"The smart ones do. Right, Frank?"

Frank was staring at the book Molly had put in his hand. "Huh? Yeah, right."

Molly stuffed her mittens into her pockets and slipped out of her coat, hat, and scarf. Then she shook out her hair.

"Hold still, Hashberger." Molly steadied herself with one hand on Billy's shoulder and kicked off her boots. "Whew, that feels better. Did you save me any hot chocolate?"

"No, but Mother will make some more."

"Are you really so helpless, you can't heat up a little milk on the stove? Never mind, don't answer that."

Mrs. Bordeaux was already at the stove when the three friends trooped into the kitchen.

"Good morning, Mrs. Bordeaux." Molly took a seat at the table.

"Hello, Molly. Isn't this just splendid! You have the day off, and you're spending it together," Mrs. Bordeaux gushed.

"It'd be nicer if it weren't so cold." Molly turned her attention to Frank and Billy, who were sitting across from her. "What's up with you two? By the look on your faces, you'd think you just trudged a half mile in knee-deep snow." Molly lifted her hair off her neck with both hands. "Oh, I forgot, that was me."

"Here you are, Molly." Mrs. Bordeaux set a hot mug in front of her. "This will warm you up."

Frank and Billy held their mugs out for refills.

"Thank you, Mrs. Bordeaux," Molly said. The hot chocolate traveled down her throat and into her empty stomach, radiating heat.

Mrs. Bordeaux left the room but immediately returned with Molly's wet coat and boots, which she carried through the kitchen and down into the cellar.

"So, tell me everything."

Billy sighed and told them everything he'd seen last night after dropping Frank off.

"So, the owl led to you to the house?" Molly asked.

Billy nodded over the rim of his mug.

Molly looked at Frank. "Do you know where he's talking about? I can't place it."

"It sounds like the old Dark Hollow Road, before they straightened out the bend and put the new bridge in over the creek."

"You're right. I forgot the old road was back there. Can you even drive there anymore? Nah, the bridge is in bad shape."

Frank shrugged and slurped Marshmallow Fluff off the top of his mug.

"So is the house," Billy added.

Molly imagined the abandoned stretch of road. "We should go check it out."

Billy frowned. "Maybe you should read this first." He opened the journal so she could read the entry.

"What a load of crap," Molly raged.

Billy set down his mug. "What now?"

"This bit about you coming alone." Molly pointed at the journal. "We need to check this place out."

"Wait, I have one more thing to tell you." Billy paused for a long moment then continued. "I had another dream last night. I saw Thomas's sister, Mabel, getting stabbed."

Frank leaned in as Billy lowered his voice.

"I saw the man who stabbed her." Billy's voice trembled. "It was like I was there, watching from the doorway. I saw his face in the mirror."

Molly recognized the nervous energy coming from Billy. *He's afraid.*

Billy ran a hand through his hair. "He had curly red hair."

"Take a deep breath. It's just a dream." Frank's voice was soothing. "You didn't actually witness a murder. And redheads are a dime a dozen around here, in case you haven't noticed."

"I know." Billy scratched his head in frustration. "If we could get a picture of Thomas, we would know for sure he didn't do it."

"Again, only a dream," Frank said.

Molly looked at Frank. "Where's Glicken's book?"

Frank retrieved it from the foyer. When he returned, he handed it to Molly.

She opened to the photos and flipped pages.

"What does it say?" Billy asked.

"Glicken lays out this whole case about how Mr. Packard and Reverend Pane were trying to shut down the bootleg business in Willowton. Guess who the bootleggers were?"

"Just tell me," Billy said.

"O'Riley and Houlahan," Molly scanned the photos. "Glicken's theory is they either killed the Packards or conspired to have them killed, to keep from being exposed. The cops were already on O'Riley's payroll way back then, so they blamed the crazy son. That's must be what Mamo meant when she said the mill was bought with blood money."

Billy and Frank were speechless.

"Billy, come look at this picture."

Billy moved to her side and peered over her shoulder. "That's him. The one from my dream." He pointed to the man standing on the left. "I saw him stab Mabel."

Molly read the caption aloud. "'Pictured from left to right: Noel Houlahan, Miles O'Riley, and Sheriff Michael Baine, in front of the newly completed textile mill. Unlikely partners?'"

"Sorry." Billy placed a hand on her shoulder.

"Yeah, really sorry," Frank added softly as he reached out to touch her hand.

"Don't get all weepy on me now. This is old news,

right?" Molly shook the boys off. Her throat constricted. *My grandfather was a murderer!* "Is there anything we can we do about it?"

"Like you said, this isn't exactly news. Glicken wrote this book forty years ago. If he couldn't prove Thomas didn't do it back then, what chance do we have now?" Billy shrugged helplessly and returned to his seat. "I'm pretty sure dreams are not considered evidence in court."

"Well… he didn't have Thomas," Frank said. "Or Billy, for that matter."

"You're putting a lot of stock in a ghost who doesn't want us around and in Billy's dreams. Which brings me back to the journal. There's something going on here we're not seeing." Molly picked up the journal.

"You've been suspicious of Thomas and the journal from the start. Why don't you believe him?" Billy asked.

"Because he obviously doesn't trust us, or he wouldn't try to separate us."

"That's a good point. Three heads are better than one. Why is he pitting us against each other? We just want to help," Frank said.

"Well, maybe it's because…" Billy's voice trailed off.

"Because what?" Molly demanded.

Billy avoided her gaze. "Because you're Molly Houlahan. Why should he trust you?"

"Do you trust me?" she asked.

"Of course I trust you!" Billy nearly shouted.

Frank stood up so quickly, his chair fell over. "We're the Three Musketeers. We don't have anything if we can't trust each other. We've been over this before!" Frank gesticulated wildly.

"It's the Three Misfiteers. Now, sit down before you break something. We get it, one for all and all that stuff." Molly stood and moved their cups to the sink. "Billy's right.

I don't trust Thomas, but I trust you guys, so I'll do whatever it takes to clear Thomas, whether he likes it or not."

"What now?" Billy asked.

"Let's start by drying these mugs and putting them away." Molly placed a clean mug in the dish drainer and threw a towel at Billy.

Billy dried the mugs and handed them to Frank, who put them away while Molly wiped down the sink.

"Well, this is perfect," Mrs. Bordeaux said from behind them. "Real teamwork. Thank you for the help. Now you have to clear out of the kitchen so I can get lunch started."

"Can we help with anything?" Molly asked.

"Yes, dear. Why don't you get these two boys out of my way and keep them out of trouble?"

"I can get them out of your way. I'm not sure I can keep them out of trouble, though." Molly herded the two boys out of the kitchen.

Frank dropped into an overstuffed chair with a sigh, as though the work of putting away three mugs had exhausted him. Billy sat on one end of the couch, and Molly sat on the other. She placed the journal and Glicken's book on the coffee table.

"I think we should go check out the house you found last night," Molly whispered.

"But Thomas said I——"

"This is what we'll do." Molly leaned forward. "After lunch, we'll go look at the house. You know, just check it out and get the lay of the land. If it looks safe, we'll send Frank to the door."

Frank's jaw dropped, and Molly laughed.

"Relax. Billy will be right behind you." She looked pleased with her plan. "What should we do until lunch?"

Frank went to the dining room and returned with a game. "Parcheesi, anyone?"

They played on the floor until Frank's mother announced lunch. Then they filed into the dining room and sat down to steaming bowls of tomato soup. Mrs. Bordeaux returned from the kitchen with three grilled cheese sandwiches and a bottle of milk.

"We're going back outside after lunch. Is our stuff dry yet?" Frank asked his mother as she poured the milk.

"I'll check."

Mrs. Bordeaux returned with an armload of coats, scarves, gloves, and boots. "All of your things are in the foyer. I found an old pair of Francis's galoshes for you to try on, Billy."

When the trio trooped into the foyer, they found all of their things separated into three piles. They helped each other with their boots. Billy leaned on Frank, while Molly helped Billy cram his foot into Frank's old boots, which were stiff from disuse.

Mrs. Bordeaux came to the door to inspect them before they left. She carried a knit cap and matching scarf and handed them to Billy. Then she buttoned the top button of Frank's coat and snugged his hat. "Very good." She turned her attention to Molly. "Should I find you a hat for you, dear?"

"No need, Mrs. B. Nothing penetrates all this hair."

"Thank you for the boots and everything," Billy said as Mrs. Bordeaux adjusted the scarf so it would keep him warm.

"You are very welcome." She moved to the door and ushered them out. "Have fun." Once outside, they walked in single file, with Billy forging a trail through the snow in his borrowed boots. Molly stayed right behind him as he led them down the path and through the woods. He stopped when he reached the snow-covered road.

Molly looked left and right. The leafless trees that lined

the old two-lane road encroached overhead. They rattled like castanets when the wind shook them. She heard Frank's labored breathing and decided they could take a short break. "You're right, Frank. This is the old Dark Hollow Road. I bet no one ever comes back here anymore."

Frank merely nodded his agreement. Billy was unusually quiet. *Maybe the snow dampened their voices the way it muffles the rest of the world.* Molly felt the world closing in around her. The need to get moving suddenly overtook her. "Which way to the witch's cottage?"

Billy didn't speak. He lifted his arm and pointed to the left. Taking the lead, Molly pushed through the snow until she saw a thin curl of smoke drifting from the chimney of a ramshackle house. "You guys wait here. I'll be right back."

"Where are you going?" Frank asked.

She spun around and placed a finger over her lips. "Sh! Just wait here." Molly walked straight to the house, examined the name on the mailbox, and read the sign next to the door. *It's exactly like Billy had described it.* She raised her hand to knock and hesitated. The door swung open before she worked up the nerve to rap. Molly took a step back in surprise. A small-framed woman with smooth, coffee-colored skin stood in the doorway. A red scarf was wrapped around her head. Her dark eyes glittered as if lit from within.

"Come in, *ma chère. Rapide, rapide, s'il te plaît.*" Taking Molly firmly by the wrist, the woman pulled her into the house. "So, *chérie,* what brings you to my door on such a day as dis one?"

"Well, school was canceled, so I took a walk to get out of the house." Molly paused as she tried to organize her thoughts. She had not expected to get inside the house. An owl in the corner hooted then shook out its wings. "Holy shit! You have an owl in here." She crossed herself and murmured a quick prayer.

"*Oui*, pay him no mind. We are old friends." Tearneach smiled, and her lyrical voice soothed Molly's fears slightly.

"I've lived in Willowton all my life and never knew this house was here. Have you lived here long?"

"Oh, yes, a very long time it has been dat I live here. Not many visitors come. Did you, perhaps, come for a reading?"

"I saw the sign, but I don't know what a reading is." Molly loosened her scarf as the heat from the fireplace began to warm her. The smell of burning wood mingled with a sweet smell Molly couldn't identify.

"Oh, child, I'm a seer. I can tell you tings about your-self even you don' know yet. I know many ways. Tarot, tea leaves, or trowing da chicken bones—all will see da future."

"I-I don't have any money."

Tearneach threw her head back and cackled. "Firs' time is free." She motioned to a straight back chair at a small table. "Sit."

"Thank you, but I should be going." Molly began to back up in the direction of the door. "Maybe some other time."

"Give me your hand before you go, *ma chère*."

Molly hesitantly pulled off her mitten and extended her hand. Tearneach gently turned it over so the palm faced up. She examined Molly's hand closely while lightly tracing a very long yellow fingernail over it. Tearneach hummed a melody Molly had never heard; she began to feel a little drowsy.

"You have had much pain for one so young. Many losses you have experienced already. You are strong and have a long life line, but with much pain yet to come." Tearneach shook her head slowly.

Molly suddenly pulled her hand away and backed away toward the door. "Thank you, Miss, uh…"

"Tearny, jus' Tearny to my friends."

Molly pulled the door. Billy and Frank were standing right there, blocking her way. "Get out of my way." She separated the boys and jumped from the step. "Let's get out of here!"

"Come back soon, *ma chère!*" Tearneach yelled from the shack and let out a long cackle, raising the hairs on the back of Molly's neck.

## Chapter Forty

As Billy turned to leave, the woman reached out and plucked a few hairs from behind his ear. "Ouch!" He absently brushed away her hand and pushed Frank down the steps. "Go, go, go." They chased after Molly.

"Molly, wait," Frank called.

She didn't stop. Billy urged Frank to run faster, but Molly continued to widen the distance between them, even disappearing for a time on the path. When Billy and Frank caught up with her, she was standing on the edge of the freshly plowed street, with her hands on her knees, panting.

"What happened?" Billy asked, breathing hard.

Molly shook her head as she tugged off her mittens. "I... I need... a minute." She pulled a small gold cross out from under her coat. Clasping it in her left hand, she crossed herself and whispered a soft prayer that lasted longer than usual.

Billy watched her closely. Her prayer sounded familiar, but he couldn't remember the last time he'd been to church, let alone the words to a prayer. The rumble of an approaching snowplow drowned the rhythm of Molly's words. The racket increased as it rounded a corner widening the road as it passed. The snow angled off the blade and created a wall of snow between them and the plowed street. Billy noticed that, among the three of them, Frank seemed to be suffering most. Giving Molly the time she'd requested, he turned to Frank. "You okay?"

"Too... many... cookies." Frank pointed at the freshly plowed street.

Molly climbed over the snowbank. The boys followed, and they walked down the street together in the gray gloom.

The suspense was killing Billy. He finally stopped and turned Molly to face him. "So what happened back there?"

"First of all, that can't be Tearneach. That lady is too young to be the Tearneach Thomas writes about in the journal. She's weird enough to be a witch, though—that's for sure—and the owl was in her house too."

"It has to be her," Billy argued.

Molly held up her hand to stop him. "I'm telling you. That lady can't be over thirty-five. Maybe she's her daughter or something."

"What did you say to her?" Frank asked.

"I didn't say anything. I wasn't planning to talk to her. I just wanted to see who lived there."

"So what took so long? You were in there five minutes." Billy pulled of his knit cap and ran a hand through his sweaty hair lingering over the spot the woman pulled his hair.

"She read my palm," Molly said dreamily. "She said she could see my future."

"And?" Frank asked.

Molly told them what Tearneach had said before she had run out the door. She stabbed a finger at Billy's chest and looked into his eyes. "Don't you go over there alone. As a matter of fact, you shouldn't go over there at all."

Billy saw what he could only describe as an expression of fear in Molly's eyes. There and gone again in an instant. "Why not? You did," Billy said.

"I wasn't exactly alone. You were coming to get me." She paused. "*Weren't* you?"

"Well, yeah, but—"

"But nothing." Molly poked him with a finger. "She's weird. I'm telling you now—stay away from there."

"What about Thomas?" Billy asked.

"We'll have to wait and see if we can help him."

The trio stood in a tight circle in the middle of the road. The gray sky pressed down on Billy. He saw something moving out of the corner of his eye, but it was too late. Snowballs rained down on them from behind the bank at the edge of the road.

"Take cover!" Molly shouted and ran for the opposite side of the road.

"My glasses!" Frank yelled and dropped to his knees, feeling around in the snow.

Billy stopped and turned just in time to catch a snowball in the face. He dropped to the ground, turned his back to the onslaught, and scanned the area for Frank's glasses. "Got 'em! Stay low and *run*." Billy slapped Frank's back.

Snowballs continued to pelt his back and shoulders. He looked up and saw Molly returning fire in an attempt to keep their attackers at bay. Once he had slipped Frank's glasses into his pocket, he ran for cover while trying to keep Frank in front of him. When they reached the snowbank, Frank started to climb over it but Billy grabbed his feet and tipped him over the bank to safety. Then Billy dove head first, almost landing on top of him.

"Are you two all right?" Molly asked.

Frank squinted up at Billy. "Glasses?"

"Right here." Billy reached into his pocket and handed them over.

"I could use a little help here." Molly leapt up and threw two snowballs in rapid succession.

"It's always the second one that takes them by surprise," she said with pride as her throw made contact with someone across the street.

Billy scooped up some snow and packed it together until he had four snowballs ready.

Molly put a hand on Billy's arm. "Shh. I think they're moving. Watch over there. Frank, you watch across the street. I've got this side. Keep making snowballs."

Billy watched the street as the snow started to fall again. In spite of the cold seeping into his hands, he continued to make snowballs.

"I just saw them cross the street at the corner," Molly said, slightly breathless. "We can make a run for it now."

"I can't run anymore," Frank said. "I say we ambush them right here. We can spread out over there." He motioned to the houses at their backs. "We'll take cover around the porches. When they show up looking for us, we'll have a stockpile of snowballs and the perfect ambush."

"I like how you think," Molly said.

Frank drew his plan out in the snow. "Molly, you take the center, since you have the best arm. Billy can cover down there, and I'll hit their flank."

Billy saw Molly smiling broadly.

"I'm in," Billy said and lifted three lids off the trash-cans lined up next to one of the houses behind them. "Pile your snowballs in one of these, then you can use it as a shield when we open fire."

"We go on your signal," Molly said to Frank.

Frank nodded. "All for one."

"And one for all," they all said softly before moving into position.

Billy watched three shadows slither through the gray afternoon toward them. He hoped Frank was well-hidden; they would have to pass him first. As they came closer, the knot in Billy's stomach contracted. *What's he waiting for?*

At Frank's bloodcurdling yell, O'Riley, Ernie, and Sal looked like deer caught in the headlight of a speeding train. Billy watched O'Riley turn to see who or what was making all the racket just as Molly's first shot exploded on his forehead, causing his head to snap back. They were close, and it wasn't easy to miss, but Billy's first throw sailed wide of Sal's head. The next one was right on, and Ernie caught it in his open mouth. Time seemed to stand still as the snowballs flew, until Sal scrambled over the bank and into the road for cover. O'Riley and Ernie followed suit.

Billy advanced to the snowbank and kept up the onslaught while he watched them run for the second time in as many days. Molly and Frank joined him and threw what snowballs they had left at the retreating bullies.

Billy grinned at Frank. "You're just full of surprises."

"Battlefield tactics aren't exactly new, you know. Napoleon developed attacks and counter attacks in his head constantly."

Molly cuffed Frank on the back of the head. "Good work, Brainiac. Maybe they'll think twice about coming after us again."

"Can we stop at my house? I should check in since there's no school, and my mom was in one of her moods last night."

"Yeah, while you're there, you can ask her if you can come over for dinner," Frank said.

"I don't think that's happening today. She was all

pissy about me coming home late last night. Plus, it's my birthday. She'll probably try to make a cake or something."

"It's your birthday? Today?" Frank's eyes grew larger.

"Yeah, I'm fifteen today."

"You're the biggest doofus I've ever met!" This time, Molly cuffed Billy on the back of the head hard enough to knock his wool cap off.

"Hey, what was that for?"

"For not telling us it's your birthday."

"Yeah," Frank added and swatted Billy on the shoulder.

Billy turned and stared at Frank. "Watch it. You're not a girl. I'll hit you back."

Molly stopped in her tracks and balled her hands into fists. "I know what to give you for your birthday now."

"What?"

"A pair of matching black eyes, unless you take back your crack about not hitting girls."

"Why? I don't think of *you* as a girl."

Molly threw a lightning-fast right jab to the center of Billy's chest. "Take that back too."

"Ouch! Crap, Molly."

"Take it back, Hashberger." Molly shifted her stance.

"Man, oh man, can't you two get along for more than five minutes at a time?" Frank stepped between them again and held up his hands like a traffic cop. He pushed Billy back a few steps. "Take it back, Billy, before she really loses her temper."

"Fine, I take it back, but I still don't hit girls."

"And you," Frank said, turning to Molly and pointing a gloved finger in her face. "You need to apologize for hitting him, because he's right. We're not bullies, and we were taught not to hit girls, unlike some people."

When a smile spread across Molly's face, he breathed a sigh of relief.

"I'm sorry. Sometimes my temper gets ahead of me."

"Sometimes?" Billy muttered.

Frank narrowed his eyes at Billy as a warning. "Let's go. I'm getting cold."

"I don't know how you can feel anything under all the clothes you have on."

"He's sensitive," Molly said as they climbed the snow-bank to walk in the street.

They clomped up the steps to Billy's house and took turns brushing each other off before going in.

"Mom, I'm home," Billy yelled as he pushed open the front door. He saw his mother coming down the hall, boxing gloves in hand, and turned back to Molly and Frank. "Crap, I forgot about those."

His mother hesitated mid-stride when she saw his friends. "Hello again. Why don't you take off your things and have a seat?" she said pleasantly. She nodded toward the gloves. "I need to speak with you, young man. Come in the kitchen *now*."

"I'll be right back." Billy left his friends in the living room and followed his mother into the kitchen.

"Where did these come from?"

"Tony gave them to me this morning before he left for work. It's a birthday present."

"Why would Tony give you these? Did you ask him for them?"

"No! He said he would teach me how to defend myself."

"Where did he get the idea you need to learn how to fight?"

His mother's calm demeanor surprised Billy after the

previous night. "I don't know. I mean I told him how cool Molly was when punched O'Riley out the other day."

"Fine, I'll take this up with Tony when he gets home."

"Mom, this was really nice of him."

"I guess it was, but you know how I feel about fighting."

Billy nodded.

"Now go."

In the living room, he found Frank holding Suze. She had his glasses on and giggled when he threatened to tickle her. A twinge of jealousy shot through him.

## Chapter Forty-One

Frank played with Suze but kept an eye on the kitchen door, worrying about Billy. What little Billy had shared about his home life informed Frank that it wasn't anything like his own.

Billy rejoined them. "I hope Tony gets home soon."

"What's going on, and what's with the boxing gloves?" Molly asked.

"Tony gave them to me for my birthday. He's going to teach me how to fight."

"Cool." Frank retrieved his glasses and set Suze down. He breathed on the lenses and wiped them with his shirttail.

"My mom doesn't think it's cool at all, but that's Tony's problem now. She wants to know if you guys want to stay for dinner, cake and ice cream for dessert."

Molly looked over her shoulder surreptitiously and whispered, "No offense, Billy, but last night it didn't, you know, smell too good."

"Besides, we'll have to check with our parents first. Right?" Frank added, looking to Molly for confirmation.

"Right. My dad will be looking for me when he gets home."

Billy's mom swept out of the kitchen with a smile. "So, can you stay? We're having baked ziti and garlic bread for dinner."

Billy looked up in surprise. "Baked ziti?"

"Tony's stopping at his mother's for her 'famous' baked ziti. You know how he is about his mother's cooking." Billy's mother rolled her eyes. "I swear, he'll never cut those apron strings."

"It's so nice of you to ask us, Mrs. Hashberger, but Molly and I will have to ask our parents first," Frank answered politely. "Can we let you know later?"

"Sure. You have plenty of time."

"Mom, can I go with them? Tony won't be home until five thirty or later, depending on the roads. Especially if he's stopping at his mother's house. I'll be home before then. Okay?"

"Go ahead." She grabbed Billy's face in both her hands and kissed him on the forehead. "Happy birthday."

When they filed out of Billy's house, Frank began to skip down the street and sing tunelessly. "We're having a birthday party."

"What is baked Wheaties?"

"It's not Wheaties; it's ziti. Tony's mother must be an angel or something, because everything he brings home tastes like heaven. I can't vouch for the cake, though. My mother is making something in the kitchen. No telling what it'll turn out to be."

"Everything tastes great with ice cream." Frank spun around in the street with his arms stretched out. His birthdays were usually spent quietly at home with his parents. He hadn't been invited to anyone's birthday since the first grade. *This is what it's like to have friends!*

"Hey, doofus. You want to stop spinning around in the middle of the street? You're going to get dizzy, fall down, and break something," Molly yelled over the noise of a delivery truck trundling by.

Frank pushed between his friends and threw an arm over each of their shoulders. "Oh, I think I'm dizzy."

"Hey look—the lights are on at the library. You think stick man is there?" Billy asked.

"You mean Mr. Glicken?" Frank asked.

"Who else? He looks like a bag of bones."

"Let's go see," Molly said. "I've got some questions for him."

Frank followed Molly as she made a beeline for the library through an open field. The library shone like a beacon in the late afternoon gloom. The sidewalk and steps had been cleared, but new snow continued to fall. They stomped their feet to knock the snow off before they tried to enter the old building.

Glicken met them at the door and unlocked it. Frank saw from his dour expression that they weren't welcome.

"Officially, we aren't open today due to inclement weather."

"We saw the lights and thought we would stop by to say hi," Billy tried.

"As I said—"

Molly cut him off. "Are you going to stand there jabbering all day, or are you going to let us in? It's cold out here."

Glicken frowned. "I might let you in if you remember your manners, young lady."

"Why, good day to you, kind sir. May we come in and join you for a cup tea?" Molly attempted a Southern drawl and batted her eyelashes.

"That's more like it." Glicken bent at the waist and

extended one arm. "Please, come in. I'll put the kettle on." Glicken locked the door behind them. They hung up their coats, followed him into the library, and sat down at a table.

"I have some questions about your book," Molly ventured.

"Shall I get the tea first?" Glicken looked at the three friends. They nodded eagerly, then his skeletal form ambled in the direction of his office.

"What are you going to ask him?" Billy asked.

"Watch, listen, and learn," Molly whispered.

Frank had two questions of his own. *What else does Glicken know? And will he share it?*

"Earth to Frank," Molly said, waving a hand in front of his face. "Are you with us, Brainiac?"

"Huh? Yeah. What?"

"We were just saying it's a little weird for a former newspaper reporter and writer to be working as a librarian," Molly said.

"I hadn't thought of that. I was wondering what he—" Frank stopped as Glicken set the tray on the table between them.

"Continue, young man. Exactly what were you wondering?" Glicken asked as he poured tea for everyone.

Frank looked at Molly, hoping she would take over and rescue him. She didn't.

"Well, you clearly think Thomas was framed for the murders. You imply the sheriff, O'Riley, and..." Frank shifted in his seat. "And Molly's grandfather had the most to gain. I didn't get a chance to read the whole book, but I was wondering, was there something you left out when you wrote it?"

Molly rolled her eyes as she added cream and lemon to her tea. "Could you be less specific?"

"Easy, Miss Houlahan. It's a very good question, actually. As a young reporter, I was very careful to separate fact from conjecture. If I had known then what I know now, I would have written a different book."

"So, what's changed?" Billy asked.

"For one thing, I was afraid of what might happen to me if I accused them of something I couldn't prove."

"Were you afraid you'd be next?" Frank sipped his tea then decided to add more milk.

Glicken laughed. "I wasn't afraid of that exactly, although I probably should have been. I was afraid they would get me fired from the newspaper, which they did. I didn't know how long O'Riley's reach was in those days, but I learned the hard way." Glicken pulled out his silver flask and gave himself a generous pour. Billy pushed his mug toward Glicken's. "Not tonight, young William. Once was quite enough."

"Where was I? Oh yes, I not only lost my job with the *Sentinel*, but every reporting job I got after. Somehow O'Riley had me blackballed right out of journalism. Everywhere I applied along the East Coast, I was rejected."

"How do you know it was O'Riley?" Molly asked.

"I was an out-of-work journalist. My job was finding out what people don't want you to know." Glicken paused and slowly shook his head. "Not that O'Riley was very subtle about it, mind you. I knew he was a bootlegger, but I thought he was strictly small potatoes when I wrote the articles in the paper and, of course, the book."

Glicken leaned back in his chair, balancing on two legs. "I learned later on that the mill was a large distillery and that he and his partners were shipping booze all over the East Coast and the Midwest. They weren't making bathtub gin. They were producing high-quality bourbon, and it was in great demand."

"Where were Elliot Ness and the Untouchables?" Billy asked.

"Don't confuse bad television drama with fact, young man. This was Prohibition. It wasn't popular with the general public. People wanted their booze, and they turned a blind eye as long as they got it."

"And that's why they got away with murdering the Packard family? Because people wanted to drink?" Frank shook his head in amazement.

Glicken shrugged his bony shoulders. "That's at least part of the reason."

Molly set down her chipped cup. "Who's Tearneach?"

Glicken's chair came down on all four legs with a bang. "Where on earth did you dig that name up?"

"We can't reveal our sources at this time," Molly said coolly.

"Spoken like a true investigative reporter." Glicken lifted his cup in salute. Regaining his composure, he tilted his chair back again.

"Who is she?" Billy prodded.

"She was a crazy old bat who lived out on old Dark Hollow Road. She was supposedly a voodoo priestess. Why are you asking about her?"

Molly ignored the question. "How old was she?"

"I don't know, exactly, but she was no spring chicken."

"Did she have any kids?"

"Not that I know of. I hope not. Do you think she had something to do with the Packard murders?"

"Do you?" Billy asked.

"She was in Old Man Packard's crosshairs too. He and Reverend—what was his name?" Glicken rubbed his chin.

"Paine," Molly interjected.

"That's right, Reverend Paine. They were trying to run her out of town because she was practicing whatever it is voodoo priestesses practice. I always thought she was pretty harmless. She looked scary, though, if you met her on the street. Not that she left her cottage very often."

"You don't know where we can find her, do you?" Frank asked.

"She was old forty years ago. She must be dead by now."

"I told you she couldn't be Tearneach!" Molly blurted.

Glicken narrowed his eyes, and Frank understood Glicken knew more than he was saying. "What do you know of Tearneach?"

Molly stood up. "We should be going now. It's Billy's birthday. We're having cake and ice cream."

Frank hesitated, but followed Molly's lead when she gave him and Billy both the look.

## Chapter Forty-Two

Billy's confusion over their sudden departure had him bursting with questions. He wished he'd had an opportunity to read Glicken's book. He felt left behind. Molly and Frank had shared what they considered the relevant parts of the book, but he suddenly felt in the dark.

Molly turned on Billy. "Do you believe me now? Whoever lives in that house can't be Tearneach."

"I believe you. But she must be able to help. Why else did Thomas lead me there last night if she's not?"

"There's a lot going on here I can't explain." Molly started to walk away without them.

"Hey, Molly, wait up," Frank whined. "Where're we going?"

"I have to leave a note for my dad if I'm going to eat baked Wheaties with the birthday boy."

"Baked ziti." Billy looked at Molly. "Who do you think the lady living out on Dark Hollow Road is, if it's not Tearneach?"

"Tearneach's daughter or her niece." Molly paused. "I mean, there are too many coincidences for her not to be related in some way. I don't see how the old woman's daughter can help us clear Thomas's name. Do you?"

"I think we're missing Thomas's message," Frank said. "He didn't say anything about clearing his name. He said she could free him from his bondage. In addition, the earlier message said the spell must be reversed so he could go to his grave in peace. The first message mentioned he was tired and wanted to rest."

"I read them too," Molly said. "What's your point?"

"He's saying Thomas doesn't care if his name is cleared. He wants to be freed of this world," Billy said. "Right?"

"Exactly. We're going about this the wrong way. We don't have to know who killed the Packards to help Thomas pass to the other side," Frank said, getting excited.

"Do you hear yourself talking? You sound as if you believe in witches and spells. Give me a break. There has to be another explanation," Molly argued.

"You saw the message in the journal the night O'Riley jumped me," Billy said. "You said you believed. What changed?"

"This gets more unbelievable every day. What's next? Little green men from Mars?"

Frank laughed. "Everyone knows the little green men are from Saturn. Martians are tall and silver."

Molly cuffed Frank. "Let's stick to one unbelievable thing at a time, okay?"

They turned a corner, and Billy recognized Molly's house in the middle of the block. He and Frank followed her along the side of the house. The walk and steps had been shoveled and salted. They entered through the back door into the kitchen.

"Have a seat. I'm going to check on Mamo." Molly hurried out of the kitchen.

Billy looked around the kitchen while Frank balanced a dime on its edge.

Molly came back into the kitchen and put her finger to her lips as she joined them at the table. Mrs. O'Brien bustled in right behind her. "I have to wait for Mrs. O'Brien to come back. You guys can go if you want to. I'll catch up."

Molly made the introductions as Mrs. O'Brien shrugged into her coat. "I won't be long, lads."

Billy rocked back on two legs of the chair, and Mrs. O'Brien gave him a stern look. "The chair has four legs for a reason, young man."

"Yes, ma'am." Billy brought the chair down while his face grew hot. "Sorry."

Mrs. O'Brien backed out of the door and kept a watchful eye on Billy, while muttering something under her breath.

Molly tuned in her radio station. "Summertime Blues" gave way to "Piece of My Heart." "So, what did I miss?"

Frank lifted his finger from the dime he tried to balance on its edge, and it promptly fell. "We should go to Tearneach and ask her how we can help free Thomas."

"Are you nuts?" Molly asked. "You weren't listening to a word I said earlier."

Billy hesitated knowing they wouldn't like his answer. "The message said I should go alone."

"I've been thinking about that. Let's say I believe Thomas, the ghost, and the owl are one and the same. Assuming the crazy lady living on Dark Hollow Road is related to Tearneach and she knows how to reverse the spell. What does she need *you* for?" Molly poked Billy in the arm for emphasis.

"Another excellent question. If she's a voodoo priestess, why *does* she need you?" Frank repeated.

"I don't know. Thomas said he needs my help, and I promised to do what I can."

"So you're going to do it, even if it doesn't make sense?" Molly asked.

"Why not?"

"*Because* it doesn't make sense." Molly threw her arms in the air. "Frank's right. We should go together."

"All for one and one for all." Frank said.

"All right, already. But if she pushes us all into a cage to fatten us up for the oven, just remember, I tried to save you." He turned his attention to the dime that Frank had finally balanced while The Beatles asked how Lady Madonna managed to make ends meet.

The door burst open, and Mrs. O'Brien rushed in, slamming it behind her. "Shite, I nearly froze me arse off out there!"

Billy burst out laughing at Mrs. O'Brien's cussing; Frank and Molly joined in.

"Mrs. O'Brien! Such language," Molly said.

"Aye, forgive me, Father." Mrs. O'Brien crossed herself.

"You won't forget to tell Dad I'm eating dinner at Billy's, will you?"

"I won't forget. Now off with you."

They piled out of Molly's house and walked to Frank's, keeping to the streets even though many of the walks had been shoveled and salted. Mrs. Bordeaux met them at the door.

"Hello, children. How was your day?" she asked cheerfully.

"It was good," Frank said. "Can I eat at Billy's tonight, Mother? It's his birthday."

"Happy birthday!"

"Thank you," Billy said.

Mrs. Bordeaux put an arm around Frank. "Come straight home after dinner. It is a school night, after all."

"Yes, Mother. I'll come straight home." Frank rolled his eyes.

"I need the journal," Billy said.

"Where is it?"

"I left it on the coffee table with the library book."

"Okay." Frank left them in the foyer.

Billy felt Molly's gaze weighing on him. When he looked up he saw her intense green eyes and furrowed brow. "What?"

"There are things going on around here that I can't explain. And I'm not comfortable with that." Molly paused. "We don't know each other that well, but I'm telling you that lady, Tearneach or whoever, she's not right."

"I don't understand what's going on, either, but I'm ready for it to stop." *And I'm going to do whatever it takes to that end.*

"What is taking that boy so long?" Molly asked, loosening her scarf. "I'll go check."

Billy looked out the window as the last of the gray light evaporated from the sky. He dreaded the thought of his new friends seeing his mother in action. He hoped she would still be in a good mood when they returned to the house. Her ever-shifting moods created the obstacle course of his daily life. Molly returned with Frank, who had a dismal look on his face.

"What?" Billy asked.

"It's not there."

Billy nodded wearily. "Well, I guess it can only be one place then."

Molly shook her head slowly as they filed out and the darkness swallowed up what little light remained of the day. Billy stopped at the sound of an owl. He looked at the tree limbs hanging in the sky like so many skeletons. "Did you hear that?"

"Over there." Frank pointed across the street.

Silhouetted against a cloud-filled sky, Thomas perched on a branch watching over the trio.

"That's getting to be kind of creepy," Molly said. "Does he have the journal up there with him? Maybe he's leaving a message for the birthday boy."

"Oh, you're so funny." Billy watched the shadow closely.

As they passed by, the owl left the tree. He spread his wings and glided straight toward them. At the last possible moment, the owl pulled out of the dive and passed right over their heads with a loud screech.

When they reached the next corner, the owl flew past them again. He led them to Billy's house as he expected, and they marched into Billy's house for the second time that day while the owl perched in a tree out front. Billy's mother was stretched out on the couch, reading. Suze was on the floor, surrounded by wooden blocks.

"Hi, Mom. We're back."

She looked at them over the top of her book. "You don't say."

"Hi, Mrs. Hashberger," Molly said.

"Hello, Moll—"

Suze cut off her mother's greeting. "Fraannnk!" she yelled across the room.

"Susan! Inside voice, please." Turning to Frank, Billy's mother said, "You've made quite an impression on my daughter, young man."

"Yes, ma'am. I guess I made a new friend."

"Make yourselves comfortable until Tony gets home."

"Mom, can I show them the room in the attic?"

She turned a page in her book. "Sure."

Molly and Frank followed Billy up the steps. At the bathroom door, he paused.

"Look familiar?" Billy asked.

Molly gave the room a hard look. Frank kept his distance but seemed unable to move from his spot when Billy and Molly continued down the hall.

"Frank, let's go," Billy called.

Frank stood there, staring into the bathroom.

"Frank," Molly hissed.

Billy quickly walked back to Frank, with Molly right behind him. Billy grabbed his arm to urge him along. Frank still didn't respond.

"He's as cold as ice. Help me," Billy said, putting Frank's arm over his shoulder. Molly did the same, and together, they pulled him away from the door. In Billy's bedroom, they sat him on the edge of the bed. His whole body started to shake as though he had the chills. Molly grabbed Billy's blanket and wrapped it around Frank's shoulders.

"Frank, can you hear me?" Molly asked.

Frank stopped shaking as suddenly as he had started. He looked at them as though they were nuts. "What are you doing?"

"You were in a trance or something," Molly said.

"Was not. I was looking at Mabel..." Frank's eyes blinked behind his glasses.

Billy watched as the realization hit Frank. "You saw her?"

He nodded.

"For real? You saw something besides an empty bathroom?" Molly asked.

"She was hiding inside the tub," Frank said in a hoarse whisper.

Molly knelt in front of Frank, looked straight into his eyes, and gave him a piercing stare. "I've known you since the first grade, Frank Bordeaux. You tell me the truth. What did you see in there?"

"I saw a girl dressed in white, crouching down in the tub. It was her, Molly. I swear it."

"Did you see anything?" Molly asked, looking up at Billy.

"No. I don't really look if I can help it."

"Are you okay?" Molly asked Frank.

"I don't know." Frank stood up, still a little wobbly on his feet.

"Sit down. Take a few minutes. Maybe you should wait here while Billy and I go check on the journal."

"No way! I'm going too. You're not leaving me alone with that." He pointed across the hall at the open bathroom door.

"Okay, okay. We won't leave you." Molly patted Frank's shoulder. "Let us know when you feel like going upstairs."

Frank took a few deep, noisy breaths and stood up again. He seemed steadier this time. "I'm ready. Let's get the journal and get out of here."

Billy led them up the twisting staircase of the attic and turned on the light when he reached the top. Frank followed him while Molly brought up the rear. Billy pulled open the door to the other room. Billy leaned in far enough to turn on the light then motioned toward the desk. Frank gasped at the sight of the journal. Molly stepped into the room and flipped it open. She quickly turned the pages until she came to the entry they had read earlier.

Billy held his breath as she turned one more page.

"Holy crap!" Molly crossed herself and murmured a prayer.

## Chapter Forty-Three

*November the Fourteenth, Nineteen Hundred Sixty-eight*

*It is imperative you meet with Tearneach before the next full moon. She will provide you with the power to combat the villainous persons who pursue you. I have continued to show my good faith in this regard. However, I grow weary. Tearneach waits patiently for your arrival. I cannot overemphasize the importance of your participation in this process. She requires your assistance. Do not disappoint me in this matter, I beg of you. The moon will soon be full.*

*TZP*

Molly's spine stiffened, and she turned to look at her companions. "I don't know what to say."

"You can say you believe, for starters," Billy said.

"I'm cold." Frank rubbed his hands up and down his upper arms. "Can we go?"

"In a minute!" Molly's hands shook. *I'm not afraid of*

*ghosts.* She clenched her fists. "Is this the window where you saw the message?"

Billy nodded.

Molly moved around the room, touching everything as she went. "Can you feel it now?"

Billy nodded again and let out a slow breath.

Molly watched it travel a short distance before it dissipated in the chilly air.

"Frank's right. It's too cold. We should probably go."

"I feel the cold, that's all." Molly put a hand on Frank's shoulder. He was turning gray. "How do you feel?"

"Claustrophobic," Frank said softly. "He's here."

"Can you speak?" Molly asked loudly as she looked around the room.

No one spoke for a long minute.

"Are you Thomas Packard?"

Again, there was no response.

She let out a long breath. "Can you give us a sign you're here?" Still nothing.

Slowly, she turned a circle. "Come on, show me something!"

"Billy? Are you up there?" Tony bellowed up the stairs.

"Yeah, we're right here," Billy yelled back.

Tony's voice got louder as he came up the stairs. "The coast is clear, and dinner's warming up in the oven."

"What'd she say about the gloves?"

"She said she wouldn't kill us until after your guests leave. Ask them if they want to stay over—indefinitely." Tony smiled. "Get a move on. I'm starving."

"We'll be right down." Billy turned back to Molly and Frank. "Come on, dinner's waiting."

"What should I do with this?" She held out the journal as though bugs were crawling across the pages.

"Might as well leave it." Billy pointed to the desk. "This is where it will end up anyway."

Molly led the way, with Frank on her heels. Billy turned off the lights and followed them. When Billy emerged from the stairway, Molly noticed how dark the stairs were. They were darker than one would expect—and much colder.

"You can wash up in there if you want." Billy motioned toward the bathroom.

"I think I'll pass," Frank said quickly.

"Francis Bordeaux, what would your mother say?" Molly asked.

"She won't say anything, because she'll never know."

"Fine." Molly pushed past the two boys into the bathroom and closed the door. In a soft voice, she said, "Come out, come out, wherever you are."

She glanced into the mirror. The face of her grinning grandfather stared back. His eyes were as vacant as the windows of an abandoned house. She put a hand over her mouth to stifle the scream threatening to escape from her throat. Crossing herself, she turned the faucet on and closed her eyes. Goose flesh marched up her arms as she repeatedly whispered, "I'm not afraid. You're not real. I'm not afraid. You're not real."

Slowly, she opened her eyes again and saw only her own somewhat-shaken reflection in the mirror. Forcing a smile, she emerged from the bathroom, still reeling from her vision, but determined not to share it with her friends. *Not yet. I need time to think. Frank is spooked enough, and I can't figure out what Billy's thinking now.*

"Let's eat." She sounded steadier than she felt. She looked past the clutter of Billy's family possessions for the first time and saw that the stained wallpaper was peeling and curling at the edges. Paint flaked off the cast-iron radiators, and the hardwood floors were warped. A family had been brutally murdered here, and a ghost resided in the attic. *What other secrets does this old house contain? And how many of them is it willing to give up?* Molly shuddered involuntarily.

"Ground control to Molly. Come in, Molly. Do you read?" Frank waved his hand in front of her face.

"What?" she snapped.

"Are you okay?" Billy asked.

"I'm fine."

"You were kind of out of it for a minute," Frank said.

"I was thinking." She glared. "You should try it some time. Of course, thinking requires a brain."

Billy shook his head and looked at Frank. "I don't know where she was, but she's back."

"Shut up, birthday boy, and lead the way to dinner before I do something you'll regret."

"Oh yeah," Frank said. "She's back."

Molly pushed Frank toward the kitchen door. "You first."

"Frank," Suze yelled, raising her spoon and flinging ziti across the room. Only a small portion of her face was free of tomato sauce.

"Sit anywhere, kids. Tony's serving," Billy's mother said from her seat at the end of the table.

As soon as Molly sat down, Tony set a plate in front of her. The red sauce and cheese mingled with the pasta and gave off an aroma that caused Molly to salivate. A platter of garlic bread and a large bowl of salad occupied the center of the table. Billy passed the salad to Frank and helped himself to a big piece of the bread.

"What smells so good?" Molly asked.

"Garlic, my dear. Garlic. It keeps the vampires away, you know." Tony set his own plate down last.

"Yeah, it keeps everyone else away too," Billy's mom said.

"Nothing can keep me away from you, babe." Tony smiled at Billy's mother and passed the garlic bread. "Maude said school was canceled. So, what've you kids been up to all day?"

"We hung out at Frank's house, then we stopped at the library on the way to Molly's," Billy answered.

"What's with your sudden interest in the library?" Billy's mother asked. "You never set foot in the one in Masonville."

Frank looked up with surprise on his face. "We've been researching the murders that took place here."

Molly saw the terror land on Billy's face.

"Murders in Willowton?" Billy's mom asked.

"Right here in this house," Frank added. "Of course it was a long time ago."

"When exactly?"

Molly noticed Frank tensing up. He tore off a piece of bread and chewed a long time. She decided to grant Frank a reprieve.

"Actually, it was today, November fourteenth, 1944."

"Our house is supposed to be haunted." Billy took a large forkful of pasta.

Molly assumed that was to avoid the follow-up question.

"I see." Billy's mom zeroed in on him. "Is this why you've been acting so mysterious lately?"

Tony cleared his throat. "I don't believe this is a good topic for a celebration dinner."

Billy's mom shifted her gaze to Tony. "And how much of this story do you know?"

"Just what the kids shared with me the other night."

"Is this the thing you were on about the other night when you woke the whole house?" Billy's mom directed her attention back to her own dinner. "Perhaps you're right about it not being a topic for conversation. But I want to hear all about it later."

Plates gradually began to clear, and Tony was on his feet. "Seconds, anyone? We've got plenty."

Frank lifted his empty plate immediately. "Sure, this is great."

"Don't fill up on dinner. We have Billy's favorite cake, fudge marble, and ice cream for dessert," Billy's mom said.

"I scream," Suze yelled through her mask of red sauce.

Tony served Frank more ziti and started clearing the dishes. Molly offered to help.

"I've got this, thanks," Tony insisted.

"You're Billy's guest," his mom said, waving Molly back into her seat.

Tony lit the candles and set the cake down in front of Billy. The requisite song was sung, the candles were blown out, and Tony whisked the cake away.

"Maude, would you do the honors, please?" Tony asked.

"Excuse me, it seems I'm needed."

When the cake was served, Molly was surprised to find it tasted good in spite of its appearance. "The cake is very good, Mrs. Hashberger. Thank you so much for inviting Frank and me for dinner."

"You're welcome. It's nice to see Billy has made friends so quickly here in Willowton."

"How about I run you two home before it gets too late?" Tony offered.

"That would be great," Frank said. "I should be getting home anyway. It is a school night."

"I'll be right back, babe," Tony said.

"I guess I'm left with the dishes," Maude snapped.

"Luck of the draw." Tony chuckled.

"Yeah, I'm lucky." She lifted Suze from her highchair. "Come along, beautiful. You need a bath."

Molly shuddered at the mention of a bath. *Nothing would ever get me to take a bath in this house. Not ever.*

Tony already had the car running and warming up when Molly led Billy and Frank out of the house. She jumped into the front seat again.

"I'll come to your house in the morning, Frank," Billy said.

"What about you, Molly?" Frank asked. "After the beating we handed the evil triumvirate today, I don't think it would be good to get caught out alone."

"I don't think we have to worry about them if we meet at school early enough."

"If it's all the same to you, I think Frank and I should come by your house so we can walk in together," Billy said.

"I've told you before, I can take care of myself."

"Yeah, but who's going to take care of us?" Frank asked.

Tony looked over at Molly. He was laughing so hard, he had to wipe tears from his eyes.

"It wasn't that funny," Molly said.

"I know. It wasn't meant to be. That's what makes it so funny." He steered the car around the corner onto Frank's street.

"Okay, I'll wait for you in the morning, but you'd better not be late." Molly glared at them.

"So, I'd like to hear more about this beating you handed out today," Tony said.

"They threw some snowballs at us, so Frank suggested we ambush them. We nailed them good when they tried to sneak up on us," Molly explained.

Tony pulled up in front of Frank's house. "My advice

to you is not to escalate this feud. You have to give them a graceful way to let it die, or it'll never stop."

"You don't know O'Riley. He won't stop," Billy said.

"I beg your pardon, but he didn't invent bullying. I know him better than you think. If you stand up to him long enough for him to understand you won't go running home to mama every time he says boo, he'll look for an easier mark. But you have to give him a way to let it go without making him look bad."

"How do you suggest we do that?" Molly asked.

"Stay out of his crosshairs until he finds someone else. You'll just fade away."

"But what about the next guy he picks on?" Frank asked.

"It's noble of you to want to teach him a lesson, but a tiger can't change his stripes. He's a predator, and he'll always be one. He only changes his prey."

"Yeah, but if you're the baddest thing in the jungle, you don't have to worry about being the prey," Frank said as he opened the door. "I'll see you early tomorrow, and then we'll pick up Molly."

"Wait, I still have the boots your mother gave me," Billy said.

"Keep them. You'll need them tomorrow. They were old ones anyway."

"Thank you for the ride and for dinner. Everything was great," Frank said.

"You're welcome there, Mr. Badass," Tony chuckled.

Molly and Billy burst out laughing.

"It wasn't that funny," Frank said, mimicking Molly's earlier comment before he closed the car door.

Billy rolled the window down and yelled, "Actually, it *was*."

"You should think about what I said." Tony looked

directly at Molly. "Tony's Survival Guide, rule number one: When attacked by a bear, you only have to run faster than one other person."

"Cute. Do you have more than one rule?" she asked.

"I have a dozen or so, but only one per customer."

"What a shame," Molly said.

The rest of the trip to Molly's house was quiet, and her thoughts returned to the image of her grandfather grinning out of the bathroom mirror. She shivered. He'd looked different than in the old photographs. The face in the mirror had looked possessed, even demonic. He had looked almost gleeful at the prospect of committing a multiple murder. Was that possible, or had she just imagined it?

Tony pulled over to the curb. "Here we are."

"Huh? Yeah, sorry. I was daydreaming." Molly got out of the car and waited for Billy. "Walk me to the door."

At the front door, Molly turned around and looked Billy in the eye. "I believe you. I believe all of it." She paused. "I... I saw something in the bathroom mirror."

"What?"

"My grandfather. It was disturbing. You shouldn't go in there. I think he murdered those people." She turned to go.

"Wait."

She went inside, leaving a bewildered Billy standing on the doorstep.

## Chapter Forty-Four

When Tony and Billy arrived back home, Billy was excused so his mother and Tony could discuss the boxing gloves. The day had been long, and Billy slipped into an uneasy sleep against his will. Visions of snakes and owls filled his head and were accompanied by the grating laughter of a woman.

---

He sat up in bed breathing hard and drenched in sweat. The house was dark and cold. Thomas peered into his room from the window with those spooky eyes.

"What do you want now?" he asked softly.

It blinked and hooted in response.

"Fine, I'll get it." Billy looked at the owl, slack-jawed, with the realization he'd just understood the owl. "This is too weird."

He slid out from under the covers and went to the door, where he listened for sounds of life. Tony's snoring offered all the reassurance he needed to venture upstairs. The always-present chill in the attic was more intense than usual, so he snatched the journal and retreated to his room to read it.

*November the Fourteenth, Nineteen Hundred Sixty-eight*

*Come at once. Your destiny awaits. Tearneach will show you the way. She will allay your fears tonight. Untold knowledge and power will be at your command. You will not regret your actions.*

*TZP*

*This is a bad idea. Besides it's way too cold to go stomping around in the snow tonight.* He pulled the blankets over his head and tried to warm up after the trip to the attic. Molly's warning reverberated in his head. "Don't you go over there alone. As a matter of fact you shouldn't go over there at all."

Billy found himself sitting on the edge of his bed, fully dressed except for his shoes. He stood up with the journal under his arm and his shoes in his hand and made his way downstairs. Fumbling around in the dark kitchen, he pulled on his coat, hat, and boots then slipped out the door.

Perched on a low limb, the owl waited for him. Snow was falling through the night sky, and Billy felt colder than he could ever remember being in his life, despite the additional clothes Mrs. Bordeaux had given him. He walked in a daze until he reached the path.

*What am I doing out here? I need to turn around right now.* Even as he thought it, his feet continued to carry him toward Tearneach. Where the path opened up onto the old Dark Hollow Road, his steps slowed. The snow came down with more ferocity. *I must be dreaming this. Like the night I dreamt I was flying.* The phrase *your destiny* repeated in his head like a mantra.

As he rounded the bend, he saw the porch light burning brightly. The owl sat on the railing, looking like a feathered doorman. Sweat trickled down Billy's face in spite of the cold. His growing fear engaged the more rational part of his brain. *I shouldn't have come. Molly didn't scare easily, and even she was frightened by Tearneach.* Still, his feet carried him closer, one step at a time.

The owl watched him approach. Billy felt its cold stare. He stopped at the mailbox. *I can't do this.* The owl hooted loudly and threw its huge wings apart. The door to the shack opened, and Billy stumbled backward. He regained his balance, turned, and ran.

"Stop, *mon petit,*" Tearneach called.

Billy stopped in his tracks. *What am I doing here?* Her presence seemed to engulf him. When he turned back toward the house, she stood only inches away. Eventually, he found his voice and whispered, "How did you...?"

"'Tis okay, child. Come in where 'tis warm." Tearneach laid a soft hand on his cheek and smiled.

Calm spread through Billy and made him somewhat giddy. "Yeah, it's cold out here."

"*Oui,* very cold. Come. Tearneach will take good care of you." She turned and led Billy into the shack, picking up the owl with one outstretched arm as she passed it.

"Sit by da fire." She lifted the bird onto the back of a wicker chair. "You have chosen well, Thomas. He has da heart of a lion to come on a night when da Beaver Moon hides behind da snow clouds."

"You know who I am?" Billy asked, coming out of his haze.

"Of course. I'm a seer. I know many tings, child."

Two candles—one white and one black—burned on

either side of a bowl within a near perfect pentagram on the slab-like table. Smoke drifted into the air from a brass cup, giving the room a sweet smell Billy couldn't identify. Nearby, but outside the pentagram, sat several saucers and a snake.

"You have a *snake*?"

"*Oui*, 'tis Li Grand Zombi, da spirit of healing and knowledge."

Billy shook his head. "How do you know who I am?"

She threw her head back and laughed. It raised the hair on the back of his neck. He'd heard that laugh before. He'd heard it in his dream.

"Oh, child. I have gathered strands of de hair from your head. You can have no secrets from Tearneach. I know you better dan you know yourself." She bustled about the room and set two tin cups on the table. Opening a jar, she shook some of the contents into each cup.

"You have my hair?" Billy watched her with fascination, remembering how she had reached for him that afternoon. He started feeling a little sleepy.

"Some hot tea will take da chill away. *Oui*?" She reached for something next to his head and retrieved a kettle from a hook over the fire. She filled both cups.

"None for me, thanks. I'm not much of a tea drinker." *I can make a run for it any time I want. She's not very big, and there's no lock on the door.*

"You must taste it, at least. 'Tis my own herbal mixture." She handed him a cup.

"That's what I'm afraid of." It smelled good. "There's no eye of newt or anything weird in here, is there?"

She laughed again.

He took a small sip. The tea was sweet and spicy.

"Is good, no?" she asked, taking a drink from her own cup.

"Mmm, very good." He drank some more. He set the cup down and shrugged off his coat. "So, what's his deal anyway? Is he a ghost or an owl?"

"'Tis not so very simple as dat. He was wounded while changing from man to owl. When he came to me, he was dying. I conjured his essence from de animal totem. He only flies by night. He is without form by day."

"You're not old enough to have been here in 1924."

She laughed. "Tearneach is older dan she look."

Billy held out the journal. "Did you write this?"

She took the journal from him and opened it. Then she laughed again, even louder. "I cannot write so good."

"It says you and I can help free him of his bondage."

"True dat."

"It says you will provide me with the power to beat my enemies and untold knowledge will be at my command. What about that?"

"You, my child, have many questions. Is dat what you want? To defeat your enemies?"

"I want them off my back, sure."

"You must be careful what you wish for. Thomas learned dat lesson de hard way."

"What does that mean?"

"Thomas wished for his family to be out of his life. He did not expect de conjure to end de way it did."

"You killed his family?"

"No, child. I conjured Thomas into de spirit world. He made request to Legba his own self."

"I don't get it. He asked what's-his-name to kill his family?"

"You cannot understand all dere is to know in one night. It takes years, but Thomas, he was good student. He learn fast. Give me da cup."

Billy handed over his cup. Tearneach gazed into it then

turned it this way and that. "You have very powerful mojo."

Billy laughed. "Yeah, I got my mojo working."

"Is no ting to laugh about, dis. Very serious. You like Thomas. You could be powerful conjurer of hoodoo."

He shuddered and realized her voice alternately calmed and chilled him. He wanted his coat back but found his thoughts to be sluggish again.

*What will Frank and Molly think? I can't wait to tell them.* It no longer seemed strange to be sitting there, listening to Tearneach's lilting voice. He loved her accent and the rhythm of her speech. It was soothing. He thought he could listen to her all night.

"You must be tired, child. Come, sit here." Tearneach took Billy by the hand and led him to the big wicker chair upon which the owl was perched.

"I am kind of tired, but I should go soon."

"Yes, you will go very soon. Sit. Rest."

Billy slouched into the chair and let his eyes close. His brain felt fuzzy. He heard Tearneach move around the room, but he didn't feel like opening his eyes to watch. Then he heard her chant.

"Oh, Spirits, as I offer up dis incense for your blessing, please cleanse and remove all unwanted influences from dem. Oh, Spirits, please also imbue dese items with magical power. Oh, Spirits, as I sprinkle dis holy water, please banish all negativity from dese magical tools and instill dem with spiritual power."

Summoning every ounce of will in his body, Billy cracked one eye open. Tearneach held the snake over her head as she danced around in the small space near the table and sang.

"Papa Legba, open da gate for me, Ago-e

Ativon Legba, open da gate for me;

Da gate for me, Papa, so dat I may enter da temple
On my way back, I shall tank you for dis favor."

Billy tried to move, but his arms and legs felt too heavy
to lift. The fog in his brain shifted around. *I should get out of
here, but I'm so tired. A little nap won't hurt, and then I can go home.*
He suddenly realized he couldn't move, and he felt too
weak to struggle.

# Chapter Forty-Five

Molly awoke in the middle of night from a fitful nightmare. She remembered only that Billy was a part of it and that it scared her badly. She took her sketchbook and retreated to the kitchen to make a cup of tea to still her shaking hands. With the tea cooling in her cup, her pencil scratched away. The image she had seen in the mirror at Billy's house revealed itself on the page. The eyes of a madman looked up at her from the paper.

She glanced at the clock in surprise; it was almost four in the morning. It was pointless to try to sleep now. Instead, she poured more tea, turned on the radio, and tuned it to WABC FM out of New York City. It only came in clear late at night. Her father didn't like the station because it played "hippy music."

She sipped her tea at the table and watched the snow fall. The phone jangled next to her head, causing her to spill her tea. The receiver was in her hand before it rang a second time.

"Hello?" she asked, wondering who in the world would be calling at this hour.

"Molly! I'm so glad I reached you," Frank said in a rush.

"Frank?" Molly asked.

"Yes."

"What's wrong? Are you okay?"

"Yes, uh, no. I mean, it's Billy. I think he's in trouble."

"What's happened?" Molly asked, twisting the phone cord around her finger.

"I think he might've gone to see Tearneach by himself."

Molly stretched the phone cord and wiped up her tea. "Is he crazy or just plain stupid? Wait, how do you know this?"

"I don't know for sure, but I had a dream, and I didn't know what else to do."

Molly's own nightmare tried to return to her, but she couldn't quite bring it in to focus. "You're not making any sense. Start from the beginning."

"I saw Tearneach dancing around with a snake, and Billy was in trouble."

"Yeah, we've already established that. Why do you think he's in trouble?"

"There's no time. We've got to go!"

"Calm down, Frank. You had a bad dream. Drink a glass of warm milk and go back to bed. I'll see you in the morning."

"No. I have to do something. Billy's in trouble. I can feel it. I wouldn't have called if I wasn't sure. I can't call Billy."

"And if you did, his mother would kill you for calling this early. Go back to bed, Francis Bordeaux, before I come over there and tuck you in myself."

"I can't. I'm going over there."

Molly lifted her gaze to the ceiling. "Good Lord, save

me from idiots and friends, which are one and the same in this case,"

"Molly," Frank paused. "I'm scared."

She didn't like where her thoughts were taking her. "You know, you take this whole 'all for one' stuff too far sometimes. Go back to bed."

"I'm already dressed. I'm going. With or without you, I'm going. It's up to you."

Despite her annoyance, Molly smiled at this new Frank, this risk taker. Before she knew it, he would be running with scissors. Molly looked at the tangled mess she'd made of the phone cord. The remnant of her own dream drifted back to her again.

"He'd do it for you, you know."

He would too, and so would Frank. She'd seen it in both their faces. They would show up for her if she needed them, no matter how stupid it sounded.

"Molly? Are you there?"

"Yes, I'm here. I have to get dressed. Don't do anything stupid. Wait for me."

Frank let out a long sigh of relief. "Yeah, okay."

"Promise," Molly pushed.

"Of course. I promise. I'm crossing my heart right now."

"Don't call me back. I'm on my way." She didn't wait for a response. *Have I lost my mind?* She pushed the thought aside. After she dressed, she scratched a quick note for her father.

*Dad,*
*I left early for school. See you tonight.*
*Molly*

Molly hurried through the quiet streets of the only

place she'd ever lived. Her thoughts played over what might happen next. Never would she have predicted how her life had changed in the last week. She hardly believed it herself. What strange events lay ahead? *Life used to be so... so what?*

"Predictable." That had changed when Billy moved into the old Packard house. She rounded a corner in time to see Frank emerge from his house. She waved from the street.

"Thanks, Molly."

"Just for the record, this is all your idea." Molly pointed a gloved hand at him.

"Duly noted."

"Where to?"

"Tearneach's shack." Frank pursed his lips.

"Don't you think we should see if Billy's home first?"

"No, he is at Tearneach's. I know it."

"So you said. Do you want to tell me about this dream?"

"I've already told you. I can't explain it, but I know he needs us. And he needs us now."

Frank started off at a brisk pace. Near the trail leading into the woods, Molly paused.

"Look." Molly pointed to a set of footprints entering the path. "They're fresh. It has to be him."

Frank nodded. They started running. Frank's labored breathing put him right on her heels.

"How're you doing?"

"I'm fine," he panted.

At Old Dark Hollow Road, she waited for Frank to catch his breath. "Do you have a plan?"

Frank grinned and pulled a bulky black object from his coat pocket. "My father brought it home from the lab to look over the circuitry."

"What is it?"

"I'm not sure. It's supposed to stun a person."

"Uh-huh."

"If you touch someone with this end and push this button, they'll get an electrical shock."

Molly tilted her head back and looked into the falling snow. "God, are you listening to this? I recall asking you to save me from idiots and friends. This would be a good time. Amen."

"What?" Frank asked.

"Just keep it in your pocket." The snow started falling savagely now, and the wind kicked up blowing right into their faces. "Let's go."

They stopped in front of Tearneach's shack, panting. Molly saw the resolve in Frank's eyes and stopped trembling.

## Chapter Forty-Six

Billy blinked as sweat dripped into his eyes. He willed his hands to move. No dice. A sweet, sickening smell drifted over to him from the table, where the candles flickered. An impression Tearneach had buried him up to his neck in perfumed sand suddenly formed in his mind. *This must be what it's like to be paralyzed.*

He panted, ragged, shallow breaths, and his head pounded with every beat of his heart. *I can't move. I should've listened to Molly, but it's too late now.* His mother always said, "You can wish in one hand and shit in the other, and see which one fills up first." He knew which hand had filled, and it didn't smell good.

If he got the chance to run, he was going for it. First, he needed his arms and legs to cooperate. He watched Tearneach extract a feather from the owl. Next, she yanked more hair out of his head and placed it with the feather between the candles inside the pentagram. His stomach clenched when she approached with a large knife.

"Don' worry, chile. I won' hurt you too much." She

cackled, and the sound reverberated inside Billy's head long after she stopped. She placed a shallow dish under his hand and cut into Billy's thumb, squeezing several drops of blood onto the dish. This, too, took its place within the pentagram.

"'Tis almos' time, Thomas." She draped the snake over her shoulders and spun around in circles.

"Papa Legba, open da gate for me, Ago-e

Ativon Legba, open da gate for me;

Da gate for me, papa, so dat I may enter da temple

On my way back, I shall tank you for dis favor."

Billy thought he heard someone knocking at the door. He strained to listen over Tearneach's singing. A tiny ray of hope rose within him.

Tearneach grew quiet and moved over to the pentagram with purpose. *Bang, bang, bang!* No mistaking it this time. Someone banged on the door hard enough to shake dust from the ceiling.

"Who dat?" Tearneach screeched.

In response, she received three more loud bangs. Muttering under her breath, Tearneach picked up her knife, went to the door, and opened it just enough to peek out. "*Ma chère?* Wha' you wan'?"

"We want to talk to Billy," Molly demanded. "We know he's in there."

Billy had never heard anything so sweet as Molly's bossy tone.

"Go home, girl. Dis no place to be on such a nigh'."

"We aren't leaving until we talk to Billy."

The door opened a little more. He wanted to warn Molly about the knife, but nothing came out except a guttural moan.

"You make mistake. Billy is no here. Now, chile, you mus' go."

"Okay, sorry to have bothered you. We thought he came here to see you."

"Only Tearneach here."

"Sorry to bother you."

The door closed with finality. Billy emitted a throaty, rasping groan. Despair set in, adding weight to whatever evil magic held him down. Until now, he hadn't considered what the outcome of his predicament might be. He began to wonder if he might die tonight.

Tearneach went back to the table and threw something into the flame of the white candle, making it flare into a bright flash. She put Billy's hair and the feather into the dish with his blood then held it over the black candle.

"In da name of da powerful spirits

I ask you, do my bidding

Let Thomas walk da graveyard dirt

Past damnation and misery 'til no more pain."

Billy's field of vision began to narrow like a shrinking porthole, getting smaller with each passing second. The owl's wings opened fully, and it emitted a loud screech that filled the room.

Tearneach smiled broadly. "Yes, Thomas, now! Fly to your new home."

Suddenly, Frank burst through the door and spun into the room. Billy heard Tearneach scream as a snowball hit the side of her head and sent her turban flying into the center of the pentagram against the black candle. Billy struggled to focus his eyes on the scene in front of him. His brain raced as he tried to interpret the dream-like images crashing around in his skull.

"Nooo," Tearneach screamed as she reached for her flaming turban.

Images unfamiliar to Billy flashed through his brain like a deck of playing cards in a strong wind. A second snowball hit Tearneach in the throat and cut off her scream. The owl screeched and launched itself off the chair at Frank. Another snowball knocked it out of the air and sent it headfirst into the floor. Frank scattered everything on the table, knocking over the candles and spilling the contents of the various bowls in the process.

## Chapter Forty-Seven

Molly ran into the shack as Tearneach grabbed Frank from behind and wrapped an arm around his throat. Her grip tightened around his neck as she waved the knife, keeping Molly at arm's length.

"It cannot be dis way!" Tearneach shrieked.

Franks eyes fluttered until he sagged. Before Molly could react, Tearneach stabbed at Frank then dropped him in time to lunge toward Molly. The electrical device fell out of Frank's pocket and rolled across the room to Molly's feet. The crazed look on Tearneach's face gave Molly pause. Smoke filled the room and blurred her vision. As she took a step back, Molly stumbled over the carcass of the owl and landed on her rear end. Tearneach raised the knife over her head and lunged for Molly.

Molly rolled to one side to avoid the arc of the knife as it descended. Her hand came down on the device, and she fumbled for the button. She pushed it against Tearneach's bare arm, saying a prayer. Her hand vibrated, and a buzz crackled over the din.

Tearneach stiffened and collapsed onto the floor, face

first. Molly looked at her in disbelief and slowly got to her feet. She coughed violently as her lungs filled with hot smoke. She pulled her scarf over her mouth, tied it at the back of her neck, and went to Frank.

Tears burned her eyes and rolled down her face. "This is no time to take a nap. We've got to get out of here." Molly lifted Frank's shoulders off the floor.

*Please God, let this be a bad dream.* She wrapped her arms under his armpits, clasped her hands together, and walked backward while dragging his limp body. *No more cookies for you.* She kicked the dead owl out of her way and struggled out the door and off the porch, where she dropped Frank in the snow. Fresh air filled her lungs, and she coughed uncontrollably while leaning her hands on her knees. After one final deep breath, she ran back into the burning shack.

She expected the smoke, but the loud roar of the flames took her by surprise and disoriented her. She heard glass jars explode over the blistering noise of the fire. Dropping to her knees, she crawled across the floor, looking for Billy, while keeping a sharp eye out for the snake. *If I see the snake, Billy's on his own. A girl's got to draw the line somewhere.*

Struggling to breathe, she lowered her head to the floor and sucked in the searing air. Another violent coughing fit wracked her body. The hot floor seeped through her gloves. Molly pulled her sleeves over her hands and continued her search. *If I get out of here alive, I'm going to kill these two.*

Crawling deeper into the smoke, she suddenly saw Billy lying in a heap on the floor. "Billy, can you hear me?"

She stood up, grabbed his ankles, and headed toward the door. Flames licked at her exposed skin. His body caught on something just as she reached the doorway. His ankles slipped through her grip, and she fell onto the porch, coughing.

A hand helped her to her feet. She looked up into Frank's blurry face, shocked to see him standing.

"Take a leg, we've got to get him away from here," Frank said.

Molly nodded as another coughing fit overcame her. They pulled together, and Billy's body came free. His head bounced down the three steps from Tearneach's porch. Snow collected between his legs as his body slid down the walk to the old Dark Hollow Road. They took shelter behind the fence and collapsed next to the mailbox. Molly's lungs heaved as she struggled to breathe.

Frank leaned over Billy. His eyes were open, but Molly could only see the whites. Frank pressed his ear against Billy's chest, and when he finally looked up, he shook his head grimly.

The little wood frame house burned like a roman candle, illuminating the forest and heating up her face. Her vision blurred, but she didn't want to take her eyes off the fire. She didn't want anyone else to come off the porch. In the distance, she heard the sound of the siren that alerted the volunteer fire company into action.

"Molly!" Frank was up and hovering over Billy. "I think he's breathing."

Tearing her gaze away from the burning shack, she looked down. Sure enough, he appeared to be coming around. Suddenly, he coughed, gasped, and coughed some more.

"Billy, can you hear me?" Frank yelled into his face.

Billy leaned over and retched into the new-fallen snow.

"Can you stand up?" Molly recognized for the first time that he was not dressed for the weather. She helped him up out of the snow. They hurriedly brushed snow from his back.

Billy's only response was more coughing, but he managed to get his feet under him.

She pulled off her scarf and wrapped it around Billy's neck, then she pulled Frank's hat off his head and slid it down over his ears. Frank recognized the issue and took off his coat. Molly noticed the slash in Frank's coat where Tearneach had stabbed him.

"Are you hurt?" she poked her fingers through the slit.

"It's just a scratch. To many layers, I think."

Once they had Billy covered up, they guided him away from the fire. They were struggling to keep Billy on his feet. He wasn't quite lucid, but he seemed to be getting better. They turned onto the path where the snow wasn't as deep.

"What now?" Frank asked.

"I don't know. We need a place where we can get warm and figure out what to do." Molly said.

"Billy's is closest."

"Yeah, my house. We'll be safe there."

Suddenly a pair of headlights illuminated the street. Molly froze and stared at the approaching car. "Shit!"

Her and Frank once again ran with Billy supported between them. They stayed low behind the snow-bank and crept away from the street. She had to stifle a coughing fit for fear the driver might hear her. A half block away they saw the driver get out of the car and start up the path toward Old Dark Hollow Road.

"Glicken. What's he doing here? Frank murmured.

Billy started to speak instead he coughed something up he then spat in to the snow. "Who was that?"

Molly wiped tears from her eyes. "Yeah, I' pretty sure it was Glicken."

Frank nodded. "Come on we've got to get him out of the cold."

The sound of their boots crunching on the snow was the only sound until they reached Billy's house.

Billy pointed. "The kitchen door."

## Chapter Forty-Eight

Billy led them into the kitchen and motioned for them to have a seat at the table, where only a few hours ago, they were singing "Happy Birthday."

Frank had his arms wrapped around himself, and his teeth were chattering. "We can't stay."

"Thanks." Billy slipped off Frank's coat and hat. Molly helped him get it over his damaged arm. Billy took in the state of his two friends. Both of them looked as if they were rolling around in an ash pit. Frank had a wound in his arm, and Molly constantly muffled her coughed.

Frank eased himself into a chair across from Molly. "What are we going to tell people?"

"We aren't going tell people anything." Molly pointed her finger at Frank. "No one has to know anything."

"But that lady died."

Billy looked up sharply. "You mean Tearneach? She died?"

Molly nodded. "We have a lot to discuss, but we don't have time to do it now. I've got to get home before my dad wakes up.

"Me too," Frank agreed.

Billy gave Molly her scarf back and walked them to the door. "Do you want me to wake up Tony so he can drive you home?"

"And tell him what, exactly?" Molly frowned. "Let's go, Frank."

"Hey, guys." Billy paused with his hand on the door. "Thanks. Seriously thanks for coming to save me."

Frank gave him a week grin. "One for all and all for one."

"Can it, Francis." She poked a stiff finger into Billy's chest. "As for you, you haven't heard the end of this, Hashberger."

He watched them walk up the street until they disappeared. Then he washed up in the kitchen sink. At last, he stretched out on the couch and listened to the house noises. His eyes closed.

*"You need your rest too, friend."*

Suddenly alert, Billy sat up and looked around. There was no one there. He had heard this new voice as clearly as if it were whispering into his ear. "Who's there?"

*"It's me. Billy."* The words echoed in his head. *"Thomas."*

## Who is this guy?

Dave spent his formative years, front and center, watching horror movies on Saturday afternoons, and reading Edgar Allen Poe nightly before nodding off to sleep. He prefers mysteries about the dark nature of a world beyond what the naked eye can see.

When Dave is not traveling, he resides in Sunny Arizona with his wife and three furry companions.

amazon.com/DaveBenneman

goodreads.com/dbenneman

facebook.com/DaveBennemanAuthor

twitter.com/DaveBenneman